New York Times & USA Today Bestselling Author

KELLY ELLIOTT

Copyright © 2015 by Kelly Elliott
Published by K. Elliott Enterprises

Cover design by Lisa Jay
Photography by Shannon Cain with http://photographybyshannoncain.com/
Editing by Tiffany Hamburger and Erin Noelle
Interior design and formatting by JT Formatting

First Edition: December 2015
Library of Congress Cataloging-in-Publication Data
Who We Were – 1st ed
ISBN-13: 978-1-943633-05-0

www.kellyelliottauthor.com

For exclusive releases and giveaways signup for Kelly's newsletter at
http://eepurl.com/JoKyL

This book is **DEDICATED** to my sister,

Mary.

You fought like a girl
and beat that **bitch** head on.

I *love* you!

#MinnieStrong

I'd like to give a **SHOUT** out to my
dear friend,

Trish Kuper.

Keep kicking cancer's **ass** girl!

Brynlee

"You never do anything, Brynlee!"

I rolled my eyes, grabbed a book, and collapsed onto the couch. "I'm exhausted, Crystal. Just go without me."

"Ugh! Why do you have to be a Debbie Downer all the time?"

I exhaled loudly, trying to get my frustration across to my best friend, who was also my roommate. "It could have something to do with the fact that I also work, unlike some people." I motioned over to Crystal with my eyes. She shook her head and laughed.

My body jumped up slightly when she plopped down next to me on the couch. "Why do you work? Your parents are filthy rich with their huge-ass vineyard in Napa Valley."

I'd never had the urge to punch Crystal before this very moment. She didn't understand my need to excel at school. The pressure from my father alone was what propelled me to dive headfirst

into school and strive to do my best. I let out an exasperated sigh. "I'm all stinky from my workout class."

Crystal rolled her eyes as she frowned. "Jesus, Brynlee, go shower and clean up. I don't want to go to this thing without someone I know."

"Travis will be there!" I said as I got up and headed to the shower. Unfortunately, Crystal was on my heels following me.

"It's a group thing. I can't show up alone."

I moaned as I rolled my neck. My patience was wearing thin. "Why not? If there is going to be a group of people there, who gives a flying fuck?"

Crystal groaned as she fell face first onto my bed while I turned and walked into the bathroom. As I reached into the shower, I turned the knob all the way to hot and then looked at myself in the mirror. Leaning in closer, I couldn't help but stare at my reflection as I constricted my eyebrows and face into a frown and sighed. My brown hair was pulled up into a ponytail and my hazel eyes were slightly bloodshot from lack of sleep. My small but full lips formed a pout as I shook my head.

I quickly stripped out of my clothes and jumped into the shower and stood under the steamy hot water.

"Don't wash your hair! We don't have time for that!"

It was wrong of me, but I smiled as I yelled out, "Too late!"

"Damn it, Brynlee!"

I couldn't help but giggle as I quickly shampooed my hair. In a way, I wouldn't have mind getting out and spending some time with people. My life revolved around school and the gym I worked at. I taught three different aerobic classes at Life Time Fitness and I loved it. Crystal constantly made comments about my body.

You work out almost every single day, where do you get that ass and those hips?

My response was always the same. *Genetics.*

I wasn't overweight by any means, but I also wasn't a stick fig-

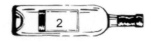

ure. I was five-two and weighed a healthy one hundred and twenty-five pounds. Lynn, our other roommate, liked to say Crystal was jealous of my curvy figure. I wasn't lacking in the boobs or ass area, and I liked it that way. All those damn squats paid off.

When I turned off the forceful spray, I could hear Crystal talking to someone on the phone. "Yes, I won't be late. I'll probably be early if I can get her to hurry up."

A banging on the bathroom door caused me to jump. "Crystal! You scared the piss out of me!" I shouted as I wrapped a towel around myself.

"Good. That saves us more time with there being no need for you to go before we leave."

Throwing the door open, I glared at her as she smiled while still on the phone. She was holding up one of my black dresses and a pair of red fuck-me shoes. *No*, I mouthed as I made my way over to my closet.

"You finally get to meet Brynlee!" she exclaimed into the phone. "Yes, she's coming with me. No, Lynn can't make it. Okay, see you soon, baby."

I chewed on the inside of my cheek, and looked around my closet. "I have no clothes."

"Hence the reason why you have to wear this. Brynlee, you have a fabulous body— show it off."

My eyes widened in shock. "I thought you thought I was fat?"

Crystal jerked her head back and gave me a funny look. "Why in the hell would you think that I thought you were fat?"

"Because you're always making comments about my ass!" I said, grabbing the black dress and stalking back into the bathroom.

"Hell, I only talk about your ass because I have ass-envy."

Peeking my head out the door, I laughed. "Ass-envy?"

"Yeah, ass-envy. Do you know how many guys would love to grab onto an ass like yours and fuck the hell out of you?"

Frowning, I snarled my lip up at her while I grabbed the dress

3

from her hands. "Nice."

"I speaketh the truth." Crystal shrugged her shoulders as if what she said was perfectly fine. "I can't help it if you're still a virgin."

Anger boiled up as I slipped the dress over my head. Thank goodness it had a built in bra, because I wasn't in the mood to wear a strapless one.

I walked out of the bathroom and narrowed my eyes at my roommate. "I'm not a virgin, Crystal, so stop saying that!"

Crystal held up her hands in defense. "Fine. You've screwed a few guys, but I bet you've never actually let a guy *fuck* you."

I reached down and grabbed the shoes as I sat on my bed and blew out a deep frustrated breath. "Remind me again why we're friends?"

"Tell me I'm not talking truth here."

"Define *fuck*."

Crystal leaned over to look at her teeth in the mirror. "If you need me to define the word, you've already answered my question."

"You never asked a question. You said you bet I've never been fucked." Standing, I smoothed the dress down as Crystal turned and looked at me.

"Hot damn girl. What about your wet hair?"

I winked as I replied, "I'll throw it up in a French twist."

"Nice! Okay, back to if you've been fucked before. Have you had sex in a shower?"

Sighing, I muttered, "I wish."

"It's not that great. You're not missing anything."

I shook my head as I sat down and began putting makeup on. Out of all my friends, I wore the least amount of makeup. A little bit of natural-colored eye shadow, understated eyeliner, mascara and blush. Lipstick when I was feeling flirty.

"Note to self, shower sex sucks."

Crystal began brushing my hair while I applied makeup. "I didn't say it sucked, I said you weren't missing anything," she cor-

rected me. "Okay, let's move on."

Looking up, I watched her concentrating on whether she should ask her next question or fix my hair.

"Have you ever had sex from behind?"

"Nope."

Crystal's mouth dropped open. "Who the hell have you been having sex with, a corpse?"

I couldn't help but laugh. "Well the first guy I had sex with was my high school boyfriend. It was in the back seat of his car, and it was not pleasant."

"No one's first time is."

Nodding, I agreed, "Truth. Let's see, Nate was just a boring-kind-of-sex guy. He either wanted to be on top or for me to be on top. We never did anything else. As soon as I came, he'd flipped me over and pump a few more times before grunting in my ear."

"High school boyfriends suck ass. What about the guys you've dated here at UT?"

Lifting my gaze up to the ceiling in thought, I said, "They weren't that much better. Jake only liked for him to be on top."

"Have you had sex against a wall?"

"No."

"Oh God girl, that is one thing you have to do. It's fucking amazing."

I knew why I had a love/hate relationship with Crystal. She reminded me so much of my older sister Melanie. Both had dirty mouths and liked sex. A lot of sex. But Melanie was now raising a son as a single parent back in Napa Valley because she liked sex so much.

"Anal sex?"

I dropped my hand down onto the dressing table and stared at Crystal. I was sure my mouth was on the floor.

"I'll take that as a no. Hurts like hell at first, but let me tell you... it's amazing."

"Gross."

"Don't knock it until you try it, Brynlee."

I shook my head quickly and began putting my eyeliner back on. "I'll pass, thank you."

Crystal snickered and said, "Just let a guy put his finger in you while he fucks you hard. You'll have an orgasm so amazing you'll want to track me down and kiss me."

Rolling my eyes, I asked, "Can we move on please?"

Crystal looked up as she tapped her chin. "Hmm... it's like when you go crazy for each other. Like you want to crawl into his skin, and he can't seem to go fast enough or hard enough. He has a desire to get deeper inside of you. It's raw, Brynlee. But it's not enjoyable if you're not with the right guy. There is fucking and then there is *fucking.*"

I applied light pink gloss on my lips, then rubbed them together and made a popping sound. Crystal stuck the last pin into my hair and smiled. "Looks beautiful."

I spun around and peered up at her. "How do you know the difference?"

With a quick smile and shrug, Crystal replied, "You just do. Listen, you can have sex with any guy, but when you meet the one who totally rocks your world, he'll make your stomach dip with just his smile. Oh God, you know sex with him is going to be out of this world."

"Travis?" I asked, wiggling my eyebrows.

A blush moved across her cheeks. "Oh my God, you're in love with him, aren't you?"

Crystal looked down and let out a soft laugh. "Maybe, I don't know."

I stood and reached for her hands, "Oh I'm so happy for you."

Crystal hugged me back as she began talking again. "He's amazing, Brynlee. He makes me feel so loved. I've never experienced this before, and the sex with him is fucking freaktastic. I'm

just taking it slow."

My heart pinged with jealousy, but I quickly pushed it away. "I'm happy for you, sweetie. Well, let's go. I need to meet this man who has won your heart so I can give him my stamp of approval."

Sitting at the table, I aimlessly tapped my fingers as I looked around. Leave it to Crystal to pick an expensive restaurant like Jeffrey's.

While my roommate was busy talking to someone next to her, I attempted to ignore the guy sitting on the opposite side of me. He must have given me at least ten bad pick-up lines since I sat down.

"There he is!" Crystal squealed as she jumped up. I glanced over and watched her walk up to a handsome blond who immediately wrapped her up in his arms. *Go Crystal. Mr. Hotty Pants.*

As I lifted my wine glass to my lips, my breath hitched as I caught sight of Travis' friend standing next to him. He was looking directly at me as I felt my entire body warm just from his stare.

Then he smiled.

And I died.

Holy hell. He has a dimple, my weakness. Perfect white teeth. Oh crap... there are two dimples.

Taking a sip, I slowly put the glass down on the table as I tried to smile back and not give the appearance that he was causing my entire body to tremble with how incredibly good looking he was. Not to mention the intense stare he was giving me was causing my lady bits to throb.

Travis leaned over and said something to his friend. Dimples then snapped his focus over to Travis as he pushed a hand through his messy, yet sexy, brown hair and shook his head.

Swallowing hard, I glanced over at Crystal, who appeared to be just as taken by Travis' friend as I was. My eyes moved slowly back

to him and I couldn't help but bite down on my lower lip while taking in his lean body. He was dressed in tan slacks and a light-blue button down shirt that showed off his broad chest.

Yum.

He definitely worked out; you could tell just by the way his clothes fit him in that oh-so-perfect way that gave you a hint of what was underneath.

Crystal clapped her hands as she got everyone's attention around us. "Okay, so we need people to shift down please." Pointing at the guy sitting next to me, she asked, "Lewis, will you move down two seats?"

Thank goodness we were in a private room with the way Crystal was raising her voice. Poor Lewis looked at me and said, "She's making me move, I'm so sorry. Maybe we can chat later."

I tried like hell to look sad as I replied, "Oh yeah, sure."

Standing, I moved to the seat where Crystal had been sitting, thinking she was going to have Travis next to her, and then Travis' hot friend next to him. She gave me a slight push as she said, "Babe, you're right there, I'm here," Crystal corrected as she pointed to what was my chair. "Brynlee is here, and Brody, you're on the other side of Brynlee."

Brody. What a sexy name.

My eyes met his as he smiled and nodded his head while making his way over to the chair Crystal had directed him to. I grabbed Crystal's arm and whispered, "What are you doing?"

Turning and giving me a mischievous smile, she whispered back, "Trying to get you fucked."

My mouth dropped to the ground.

"Hi. The name is Brody."

Oh God. His voice is sexy too. My stomach clenched as my heart dropped.

Inhaling a deep breath, I found my voice. "Hi, Brynlee."

Brody pulled the chair out for me and smiled as I nodded my

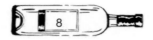

head. "Thank you."

He pushed the chair in and softly ran his hand down my shoulder, causing my entire body to shudder, then break out in goose bumps.

My cheeks heated and my body felt as if it were on fire as I pushed my legs together.

"Are you hot, Brynlee?"

My head jerked up as I stared at Lewis, who was now positioned across from me. *Oh great.* "W-what?"

"Your face. It's all red."

"Yeah, you're breathing fast, Brynlee. You okay?" Crystal teased knowingly. Slowly, I twisted and shot her a go-to-hell look.

"I'm perfectly fine. It's a bit warm in here with all of the bodies, that's all."

As I reached for my wine, I caught a quick glimpse at Brody and noticed he was smirking.

Ah hell. This is gonna be one hell of a long dinner.

Two

Brody

My mother always said, "You only feel true love once in a lifetime, so don't ignore it."

I never really got what she meant by that, but she told me when it happened, I'd know.

After years of waiting, it finally happened the moment I walked into the room and saw Brynlee. Her eyes met mine, and I swear I'd never felt my stomach twist and turn like that. She was gorgeous. Dark brown hair pulled up neatly on her head, green eyes that danced with excitement, and skin that looked like it had been kissed by the sun. When I accidentally brushed my hand across her shoulder, my entire body caught fire.

It only took me a few minutes to get myself back under control so I could speak to her, but the jerk sitting across from her started talking to her.

"So, Brynlee, what are you getting your degree in?" he asked.

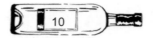

Brynlee smiled politely, but I got the feeling she didn't want to talk to him. "Business management."

Bingo. My cue.

"Really? Same here," I cut in as I turned to Brynlee. "Well, chemical engineering with a minor in business."

Brynlee turned and looked at me with the sweetest smile. I actually had to concentrate on breathing while I looked at those beautiful bee-stung lips. "Wow, that's impressive. I wonder if we've had any classes together?"

Hell no. I'd remember seeing this beautiful creature.

"Must not have."

Keeping the grin on her face, she shrugged. "Well, some of those classes were huge. You could have been in the back or something."

I lifted my beer and took a drink as Brynlee's eyes fell to my lips. Setting my beer back on the table, I gave her a panty-melting smile, ensuring to show my dimples. She seemed to like them. Her breath caught every time she looked at them. "I'm pretty damn sure I'd have noticed you if you were in any of my classes, Brynlee."

Her mouth parted slightly open and her cheeks flushed instantly.

Ahh ... nice. She blushes easily. I wonder what else I could do to her to make blush. If I reached over right now and touched her leg and ran my fingers up to ...

Adjusting in my seat, I cleared my throat and looked back across the table to the dick. Clearly pissed off, he shot me a dirty look as if to warn me he had eyes on her first. We'll see about that.

"What about you, Dick?" I asked.

Brynlee choked on her water as I reached over and lightly rubbed her back, causing my body to go haywire again and my dick to start having a mind of its own. "You okay there?"

Her body shuddered and that made my heart sink. *Jesus, does my touch affect her that much?*

"Lewis, my name is Lewis."

Keeping my hand on Brynlee's back, I made a smug expression and said, "Oh sorry dude, for some reason I thought your name was Dick."

Her body jerked again, but she recovered quickly.

"No, it's not."

"Anyway, I'm okay, I just swallowed wrong," Brynlee said as she looked at me. In that moment, I wanted to know everything about her.

"Where are you from originally?"

Brynlee picked up her napkin and started fiddling with it. She must not have minded my hand on her because she made no move for me to drop it. "Um, Napa Valley."

My eyebrows lifted as I slowly nodded my head. "California girl."

Smiling that sweet-ass smile again, Brynlee began chewing on her lip. "Yep," she said, popping the *p*.

"What made you pick Texas?" I asked, dropping my hand to the back of her chair and left it there. If she sat back, I'd get to feel her soft skin again.

With a quick shrug, she said, "I don't know. I guess I just wanted to get away. My parents are pretty ... controlling, I guess you could say."

"How so?" I probed further as I took another drink of my beer and motioned for another one as the waiter walked by.

"Well, um, my older sister, Melanie, kind of gave my parents hell. By the time I got to my senior year of high school, they were trying to plan out my life for me. The only way to prove I wasn't my sister was to leave. So I did."

"Wow. That had to be hard, leaving your family. Did you know anyone here?"

Brynlee turned and gazed into my eyes. She seemed appreciative of my words. "No, I didn't know anyone. I met Crystal the first day, and we've been best friends since."

I flashed her a smile as her eyes darted from one dimple to the other. Then she sucked her lower lip in between her damn teeth again.

She was a dimples girl.

Reaching up, I pulled her lip from her teeth. "Ouch. You must be hungry with the way you're chewing on that lip of yours."

A flush stained her cheeks as she let out a nervous chuckle. "Bad habit when I'm nervous."

Moving my body closer to her, I whispered, "What are you nervous about?"

I swear my fucking heart plunged into my stomach and then somehow landed back in my throat. The look of desire that spread across her beautiful face was breathtaking. Her green eyes burned with fire as she leaned closer to me. Our lips were inches away from each other when she winked and whispered, "I'm worried that Dick here is going to ask me for my number. I'm not very good at saying no."

Jesus. Does she have any idea how sexy she is? I don't think she does, and fuck if that doesn't make her even sexier.

"I'll remember that little piece of information."

I moved back before I allowed the urge to pull her lips to mine. Brynlee followed and sat back in her seat. Her chest rose slightly faster, and I got the feeling she wasn't one to flirt mindlessly. Clearly, our exchange did something to her as much as it did to me.

The waitress set Brynlee's plate down first and then mine. Right as she put the fork in her mouth, I looked at her and asked, "So, Brynlee, how about we exchange numbers now, before we forget?"

Her head turned to look at me as her eyes widened in surprise. Motioning toward Dick, she realized what I was doing. Or at least, what I wanted her to think I was doing.

"Oh right." As she set the fork down and reached into her clutch, I stole a peek at Lewis. He practically had steam coming from his ears. Brynlee handed me her phone and I punched my num-

ber in, and then quickly sent myself a text so I would have her number.

I winked at her as I handed her back her phone. She laughed and shook her head before placing her phone back into her purse.

"Keep next Monday open," I said before I took a bite of fish.

She wiped her mouth softly and swallowed. "Why?"

I glanced at her and gave her a look like she was crazy. "We're going on our first date."

Brynlee moved about in her seat as her mouth fell open and then shut again. I had a feeling she was the type of girl who cared more about studying and making her parents proud of her, rather than screwing around with guys. Her innocence poured off her and turned me on in more ways than I cared to think about. My heart pounded so loud in my chest at the idea of finding out just how innocent my sweet girl was.

Three Weeks Later…

Brynlee smiled as she walked up and stopped just in front of me. "Fancy meeting you here."

My eyes traveled over her body as they finally made it back to her beautiful face. Her hazel eyes sparkled as she grinned bigger. "You're beautiful."

Brynlee reddened as she looked away. I placed my finger on her chin as I lifted her eyes back to mine. "Why do you look away when I say that?"

Swallowing hard, she closed her eyes and whispered, "I feel like I'm dreaming when I'm with you."

I leaned down and gently kissed her lips. She let a small moan escape from her lips as my pulse quickened.

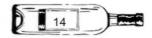

Pulling my lips from hers, I slid my hand down her arm and linked our fingers together. "Tell me why you feel like you're dreaming, sweetheart."

Her eyes softened while she let out a sigh. "I've never met anyone like you, Brody. You're insanely good looking, romantic as hell, you treat me like I'm a princess, your kisses are magical, your touch does crazy things to my body, and you didn't try to get into my pants on our first date. Or second. Or third, and so on. Even though I'm really starting to wish you would at least try."

I lifted my hand and pushed a strand of her brown hair behind her ear. "Someone as special as you, Brynlee, you're worth the wait. But, now that you mention it, I kind of had this whole special evening planned for us."

Brynlee's eyebrows lifted as she gave me a questioning gaze. Her lips parted open just enough for me to hear the whimper.

I kissed her forehead as she placed her hands on my chest. "Brody, I have to be honest with you about something."

My fingers laced tighter with hers as I guided her over to the bench and we sat. "I always want you to be honest with me, and I swear to you I'll do the same. I'll never hide or keep anything from you, Brynlee."

With a giggle, she asked, "Even if the dress I'm wearing is so hideous and I love it so much, you'll tell me it's hideous and not let me embarrass myself by wearing it out?"

Pulling my head back with a look of shock, I frowned and said, "As if you could make anything hideous, but yes, I would be honest and tell you the dress was awful."

Brynlee looked down and began wringing her hands together as she cleared her throat. "My sister Melanie got pregnant five years ago. It was during my senior year of high school. I'd never seen my father or mother look at either one of us with such disappointment as they did when my sister when she told them she was pregnant. He quickly wiped it from his face, but we both saw it. I vowed I'd never

15

let my father look at me like that."

"Is that why you bust your ass so hard with your classes?"

"That's one reason. The other is I want to take over my family's vineyard one day and run it."

I pulled my head back and stared at her. "You never told me they owned a vineyard."

Brynlee shrugged and said, "I don't really tell anyone."

I wasn't sure why she never told anyone and I didn't really care. She had to have had her reasons.

"Anyway, I need to be honest with you before we take it to the next step."

My heart jumped to my throat and I barely got the words out of my mouth. "Tell me."

Brynlee's eyes met mine and I wasn't sure how to read them. She looked nervous and unsure of something. I was hoping she wasn't about to tell me she was a virgin. That would make *me* nervous as hell. We'd messed around a lot over the last three weeks, and a few nights ago, we started getting carried away. Before I knew it, we were rubbing against each other completely clothed and the moment Brynlee came, my life changed. I knew this was the girl I wanted to make me feel like that for the rest of our lives.

"I'm not sure how to say this without being embarrassed."

With a reassuring squeeze of my hands, Brynlee took a deep breath in and slowly blew it out. "I'm not that experienced when it comes to … sex."

My eyes widened in panic.

She shook her head and said, "Oh no, that's not what I mean. I'm not a virgin."

Okay. I can breathe again.

"Not that I wouldn't mind being the first person to make love to you, it's just been a really long time since I was with a virgin."

Brynlee chuckled. "No, what I meant was, the few guys I've dated—we never really did anything but normal sex."

I wanted to understand what she meant by that and I needed to know what she expected from me. "What's *normal* sex? Missionary?"

With a nod of her head, she replied, "Pretty much."

I let it soak in and decided to proceed with caution. "Have you been on top before?"

Nodding, her face flushed again as she bit down on her lip. I loved seeing that rose color fill her cheeks. "Did you like it?"

Brynlee covered her face and let out a groan. "Oh God, Brody, this is embarrassing!"

I pulled her hands away and took her chin in between my thumb and finger as I lifted her eyes to mine. "Don't be. Brynlee, I want you to enjoy yourself when we're together. I want you to feel like you can say or do anything you want with me and not be embarrassed about it."

She stared at me intently. Lifting her eyebrows, she asked, "Anything?"

"Anything."

"I've never given nor received oral sex. My last boyfriend wanted to, but it didn't feel right with him."

"Would it feel right if I asked you?"

Fire danced in her eyes and my dick instantly got hard. "Yes, very much so."

"Okay, that's the first thing on our list."

With a nervous chuckle, she asked, "We're making a list?"

"Hell yeah, we are. What's next?"

"O-okay, well, I've never had sex against a wall. I'd like to try that."

I lifted my hand and pretended to be checking off a list. "Got it. Keep going."

Brynlee's head lowered as she whispered. "Shower sex?"

"Are you asking me if I've ever had it?"

Her face instantly looked disappointed. "Have you?"

17

Smiling, I shook my head. "No. Nor have I ever fucked anyone against a wall."

Brynlee's breathing increased, and I wasn't sure if what I said excited her or scared her.

Her eyes closed as her lips parted open slightly. "Tell me what you're thinking about, Brynlee."

Keeping her lids shut, she said, "I'm thinking about how turned on I am by you saying that."

My hand caressed the side of her face as she opened her eyes again. "I wouldn't mind being ... well, um ... you know."

I lifted the left side of my mouth into a smile. Knowing what she wanted to say, I decided I wanted to hear it from her sweet lips. Her innocence was the biggest turn-on I'd ever experienced and her telling me she wanted me to fuck her was what I desperately wanted. "No, I don't know. Tell me."

Brynlee gulped as she looked into my eyes. "I wouldn't mind you ... fucking me."

She said it so low I could hardly hear her. My dick heard her loud and clear though and was ready for action.

Down boy. All in good time.

I lowered my head and leaned in closer to her as I pressed my forehead to hers. "What was that?"

Playfully hitting me on the chest, she laughed. "Brody! You know what I said!"

"No, no I don't think I did."

With a sexy pout, Brynlee whispered, "Please don't make me say it again."

Son-of-a-bitch, I loved this girl. "Okay, angel, I heard you and I wouldn't mind fucking you too. But before we do that, I want to make love to you first."

"Oh," Brynlee barely said. "Can we just skip your plans, Brody? I'm horny as hell now with all this sex talk."

I couldn't help but let out a chuckle as I stood up and brought

her with me. "I'm more than fine with that. But, we need to eat dinner. Are you ready?"

"Where are we going?"

With a wink and flash of my dimples, I kissed her quickly on the lips and said, "It's a surprise." That moment I realized I wanted more of Brynlee; I knew our first time together had to be special. I wanted her to remember this day for the rest of her life.

Three

Brynlee

I loved surprises. When I was a little girl, my father would tell me to hop in his truck and he would take me somewhere as a surprise. Whether it was an ice cream cone or shopping for a new pair of shoes, all of it was special to me.

Brody reminded me of my father. The way he treated me like I was his everything was exactly how my father treated my mother.

"So you're really not going to tell me where we're going?"

He turned and grinned as he took my hand in his. My stomach flipped as the entire world disappeared, leaving me with just the sound of my heart beating as I got lost looking at this man I was falling in love with. Something about being with Brody took the weight of the world off my shoulders. He made me feel relaxed and so happy. Like I could do or say anything and it would be the most beautiful thing ever to him.

"Somehow I get the feeling my Brynlee likes surprises."

I let out a laugh. "Oh yes, I love surprises very much."

As soon as Brody started driving, I looked around to see where we were going. I had been in Austin for almost four years and I still didn't know my way around too well. I did know we were headed out toward Lake Travis.

He turned off the main road and headed down a twisting, winding road. A few minutes later, he pulled up to the valet as I looked at the massive restaurant. "The Oasis?"

Brody looked at me, shocked. "You've never been here before?"

With a shrug and shake of my head, I said, "Nope."

He stepped out of truck as another valet opened my door and held his hand out for me. "Thank you," I said with a smile.

Brody walked up and took my hand from the valet. "I've got it. Thanks, dude."

My body ignited as I pressed my lips together to keep from smiling. It was clear Brody didn't like this guy taking me by the hand and that thrilled me. I loved that he was possessive of me. With our fingers woven together, we headed into the restaurant.

The hostess behind the desk looked up and smiled the instant she saw Brody. Clearly she didn't see me as she took in the sight of his body. Rolling my eyes, I looked around so I didn't have to watch her ogling my boyfriend.

"Hey there," he greeted her politely. "I've got a reservation under the name Miles. Brody Miles."

I glanced back over to the hostess as she ran her finger down her list. Her eyebrows lifted as she said, "Oh yes, the Starlight Terrace. Let me make sure everything is ready for you, Mr. Miles."

Pressing a button on the little mic she wore around her neck, the hostess began talking. "Is the Starlight Terrace ready for Mr. Miles?" With a cheerful nod, she looked at Brody and then me. She grinned bigger when she looked at me with excitement in her eyes, causing me to smile in return. "I'll send them up."

"Mr. Miles, Ms. Santos, please follow me and I'll show you to

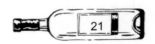

21

your private room."

My stomach dropped as I whispered, "Private room?"

Brody squeezed my hand and walked behind the hostess as we made our way over to an elevator. "If there is something not to your liking, please be sure and let Andrew and Rachel know. They will be working with you today."

"Sounds good," he replied as he glanced down at me and winked. *What in the world is this man up to?* Whatever it was, it felt like Christmas morning with how excited I was.

The elevator doors opened and revealed a huge open room. It was breathtaking. My eyes wandered everywhere as I took in all the beautiful natural wood and rock. White lights draped across the massive ceiling, giving it a romantic touch. When I finally saw a single table set up the middle of the room, I gasped and covered my mouth.

"Surprise," he whispered in my ear.

I quickly turned to face him. "Brody, it's beautiful."

"Mr. Miles, good evening. May I get you and Ms. Santos something to drink?"

I'm sure the smile on my face spoke volumes.

"I'll have a whiskey sour please," Brody requested.

The waiter glanced over to me and raised a brow while he waited for me to find my voice. "Oh um, I'll have an old-fashioned please."

The waiter gave a quick nod and turned to leave as I began walking around the giant room. Brody took my hand and led me to one set of doors that opened outside to the deck. We strolled to the edge and I peeked down, looking over lower decks that contained tables with patrons sitting at them.

"The sunset is going to be amazing out here. I can't wait to show you, Brynlee."

I pulled my head up and turned to him. "You rented out this whole floor? Why?"

Taking my hands in his, Brody gave me a panty-dropping smile

as his thumbs moved lightly over my skin, a trail of fire left in their path. My body was a tingling mess of happiness. "I wanted our first time together to be special for you."

My head was spinning. No guy ever did anything like this before for me. Usually it was a quick roll in the hay; they did their thing and either made an excuse to leave or they ordered pizza or something.

Tears pooled in my eyes as I peered out over the lake. "No one has ever done anything like this for me. I'm at a loss for words."

Brody pulled me closer to him as one hand landed on my lower back and the other slipped around my neck. His crooked smile had my heart beating faster than ever before as my eyes fell to his soft lips. "Then kiss me, sweetheart."

His eyes were inviting as our lips drew closer together. I couldn't help but lick them right before they pressed together. The feel of Brody's mouth on mine was amazing. My heart dropped, my stomach fluttered, and my knees grew weak. I couldn't imagine what making love to him would be like.

"Excuse me, your drinks."

Brody slowly pulled his lips from mine and I instantly missed the contact. If I didn't have any manners at all, I'd have told the waiter what my exact thoughts were of him at this very moment.

As I reached for my drink, I tried to get my breathing under control and get over the shock of Brody renting out an entire floor of the Oasis. I took a small sip and made my way back into the restaurant. "Brody, this is insane," I said with a giggle. Truth be told, I was feeling over-the-moon happy and beyond excited for what was to come.

Brody walked up to me and kissed me on the forehead. When he pulled back, his eyes met mine. Something in them was different; they were softer and full of something I'd never seen before. I watched as his mouth moved and I saw those damn dimples that made my insides melt. My skin tightened and the hair on my body rose as it reacted to those beautiful hazel eyes.

Oh. My. Goodness.

My head began to spin as reality hit me right in the heart.

I wasn't falling in love with Brody, I was already in love with him. So very much in love with him.

Is this happening too fast?

My eyes closed as he lifted his hand and placed it gently on the side of my face, stroking his thumb across my skin. When I opened them, Brody slowly shook his head as I leaned my head into his hand. My heart was racing, my stomach was in flutters, and my knees knocked together as I attempted not to drop to the ground.

"Brynlee, I love you."

Tears formed in my eyes as I shut them again, feeling one slip away. The moment would be etched in my memory forever. Opening my eyes caused my tears to fall freely as Brody cupped my face and softly brushed the wetness away with his lips. "Please tell me you're happy, sweetheart."

"Very happy. I love you too, Brody."

Before his lips could reach mine, the waiter cleared his throat and began talking. "Your dinner is ready, if you'd like to take a seat."

Brody sighed. "Save that kiss for me." His fingers gently skimmed over my lips as he took my hand and led me to the table.

Swallowing hard, I made a mental note to ask Melanie or Crystal if a guy had ever made them feel like they were walking on Cloud Nine. I knew if I had a mirror, my reflection would be beaming back at me. My cheeks felt as if they were glowing.

Brody pulled out my chair and as I sat. He gently ran his hand down my arm as he left to go to his chair.

My goodness ... does this man know how to swoon me or what? At the rate he was going, I was going to fall apart just from him looking at me.

With a flush of his own moving across his cheeks, Brody handed me my napkin before he sat. "I hope you don't mind, but I or-

dered for us."

My mouth watered as the waiter placed a plate with fish and steamed veggies in front of me. "Your redfish topped with cilantro lime butter and sautéed vegetables on the side."

Of course my stomach took that as a cue to rumble. Brody and the waiter both laughed as I felt my face warm. "I guess I'm more hungry than I thought."

Brody smiled so big I couldn't help but chuckle as the waiter asked, "Is there anything else I can get you right now?"

"No, thank you," he said.

After the waiter walked away, Brody lifted his glass of water in a toast. Following his lead, I raised my glass and grinned like a silly schoolgirl.

"To the start of one of the most magical nights of my life *and* to the most beautiful woman I've ever laid eyes on."

I pressed my lips together to contain the sob that was bubbling up in my chest as he winked and clinked our glasses together.

This night was more than magical.

It was a fairy tale come true.

Four

Brody

After eating, I stood and took Brynlee's hand. The moment our skin touched, I felt that familiar shock run through my body. I'd never had a girl cause that type of reaction. Then again, I'd never met anyone like Brynlee. She was the dream I had been waiting for.

We made our way out onto the deck as the sun began setting in the sky. With a quick peek over to Brynlee, my throat tightened as I watched her. She was stunning. The way the sun's rays were hitting her face showcased her beauty and made me realize how truly lucky I was to be standing there with that woman. Of course all my friends would be telling me how pussy whipped I was, especially Travis. He'd be first in line to take my man card from me if he ever found out all I had planned for Brynlee to make the evening special for her.

"It's so beautiful," Brynlee whispered as the wind lightly blew her brown hair around her face. My heart felt as if it was going to

beat right out of my chest.

What in the hell is this girl doing to me?

The sun was just about to dip below the horizon when I took Brynlee by the arms and turned her to face me. "This is crazy. This is probably the most insane thing I have ever done in my life."

Letting out a chuckle, Brynlee shook her head and asked, "What is?"

It was then I knew what I was about to do was far from insane. At least my heart was telling me that. I cupped her face within my hands and captured her beautiful hazel eyes with mine.

"Marry me."

Brynlee's mouth dropped open as her eyes widened in surprise. "W-what?"

I closed my eyes and shook my head before opening them again and searching her face. I needed to know how she felt in that very moment. "Brynlee, I've never in my life felt like this. I know it sounds crazy, and we're still in school and I have no idea what is going to happen in a few months when we graduate. But all I know is I want to be with you … forever."

Her hands came up and rested on my arms as she started crying. "Brody, this is crazy! We haven't even slept together. What if you suck?"

I pulled my head back in shock. "Bite your tongue. I'm going to be the best sex you've ever had."

Sucking her lower lip in between her teeth and gnawing on it, Brynlee finally nodded and released her poor swollen lip as she threw herself into my arms. "Yes. Yes I'll marry you!"

I was sure the whole restaurant heard her scream when I picked her up and spun her around as we both started laughing. I led her over to the outdoor sofa and pulled her onto my lap where we quickly got lost in a kiss. My hand traveled all over her body, stopping at her chest where I cupped her breast with my hand. When Brynlee moaned into my mouth I nearly lost all control.

27

Music started playing from inside the restaurant and I tried like hell to stand up and bring her inside to dance with her, but I couldn't. I needed to taste her. Feel her in my arms. I needed to make love to her … the sooner the better.

"Brody! You're going to get a ticket if you keep driving so fast."

I reached for Brynlee's hand and squeezed it. "You have no idea how badly I want to get you to a bed."

She giggled and said, "Oh, I'm pretty sure I know how you feel."

Thirty minutes later, I pulled up to the Hotel Ella as Brynlee sucked in a breath. Stopping at the valet, I quickly got out, gave my name and headed to my girl. Opening the door for her, she stepped out and looked at the giant mansion hotel. "What are we doing here?"

I placed my hand on her lower back and led her to the entrance. Leaning down, I whispered against her neck, "I wanted privacy. No roommates, no interruptions. Just you and me."

The excited look on her face caused my pants to grow smaller. "Oh, that sounds amazing."

After checking in, we headed up to the room as I carried the small bag I had packed. It only contained a change of clothes for each of us, one full box of condoms, and pajamas for Brynlee. I never thought to ask her what she liked to sleep in, so I'd bought her something at Victoria's Secret.

I unlocked the door and held it open as she walked in. The first thing we saw were floor-to-ceiling French doors that led out to a veranda balcony. "Oh wow," we both said as I shut the door behind us.

The massive king bed was to the left of us, with a sitting room to the right. Brynlee spun around as she dropped her head back,

swung her arms open and laughed. "Brody! This is so romantic."

I was internally fist pumping. Score one for Dad. One wouldn't think I would ask my father where to take a girl to sleep with for the first time, but Brynlee was different and my father was the grand-daddy of romance. Or at least my mother always said so. When he mentioned this place, I knew it would be perfect.

"You like it?" I asked as I dropped the bag to the floor and moved toward the French doors. With a slight push, the doors opened out to a beautiful view. Closing my eyes, I could picture Brynlee in a beautiful wedding gown standing out here.

"Like it?" she scoffed. "I love it! It's beyond perfect."

Pleased with her reaction, I rubbed my sweaty palms against the thigh of my pants. I hadn't been this nervous since I'd lost my virginity to Travis' older sister when I was sixteen and she was eighteen. Talk about being seduced. If Travis ever found out, he'd hang me up by my balls and leave me to die.

Pushing the memory from my mind, I stepped into the bath-room. *Holy Shit.* This room was worth every expensive-ass penny I was spending on it. Marble covered all of surfaces. My eyes wandered as I took in the giant soaking tub and then the huge separate shower. A wicked smile spread across my face. Not only was my baby going to get wall sex tonight, she was getting shower sex at the same time. Two things that I had yet to experience myself and I couldn't wait to share it with the love of my life.

I quickly exited the bathroom and headed back into the room, stopping dead in my tracks. My eyes widened as I felt a flash of adrenaline rush through my entire body and end up right at my dick. Opening my mouth to talk, my pitch raised and I felt like a teenage boy going through puberty again.

When I was finally able to find my voice, the only thing that came out was, "Jesus, you're … you're … you're gonna make me come in my pants."

Brynlee was standing at the end of the bed naked. She had her

legs crossed and she was covering her breasts, and I swear her entire body was flushed. It had to have been the most amazing sight I'd ever seen.

Slowly walking up to her, I let my eyes roam her body as I stopped right in front of her. She was perfect and I hated that she was trying to cover herself up. She wasn't a stick figure like most women. She had an hourglass figure with an ass I just wanted to grab and hold on to as I fucked her hard and fast. Hips that swayed when she walked and a chest I longed to touch every single chance I got. Jutting her lower lip out, Brynlee scrunched up her nose as she talked. "It's not really fair that I'm naked and you're not."

"Can't. Think. Straight."

Brynlee let out the sweetest laugh, and I let it settle into my heart and soul. "Undress me, sweetheart."

Her eyes burned with passion as she dropped her hands to her sides and licked her lips in anticipation of what was to come.

Placing her hands lightly on my chest, both our bodies shook. Brynlee took in a deep breath and slowly unbuttoned my shirt. I helped pull it off as I tossed it to the floor. It wasn't the first time she saw me without a shirt on, but her eyes took in every single ounce of me as her hands trembled while she unbuttoned my pants.

I was positive she could hear my heart beating in my chest. It was so loud it was beginning to drown out everything else. She pushed my pants down as she hooked her thumbs into the waistband of my boxer briefs and pulled them down as well.

My dick sprung free as Brynlee let out a gasp and quickly stood up. I'd give anything to have her take me in her mouth, but I needed it to move slowly. The last thing I wanted her to do was something she wasn't ready for.

It was my turn to suck in a breath of air when Brynlee took me in her hand and began gently stroking. I watched her face as her eyes focused on my dick in her hand. Her eyes were laced with worry.

"You're huge. It's never going to fit," she whispered.

As I chuckled, I lifted my hands and cupped her breast as I ran my thumbs over each nipple, causing them to harden instantly. I just wanted to spin her around and bury myself so deep inside her she would forget any other man before me. She was mine now. Forever mine.

Brynlee mumbled something I couldn't make out as she spread the pre-cum around with her thumb. My dick was painfully hard as I tried to ignore the fact that my balls were beginning to tighten up.

Reaching down, I grabbed her hand and pulled it up to her mouth where I placed her fingers inside as she sucked on them. My mouth parted slightly open as I watched what she was doing to her fingers.

"That's hot," I rasped with a smile on my face.

My right hand dropped as I made my way to what I knew was going to be heavenly. Brynlee slightly parted her thighs as her chest began heaving when I ran my fingers across her lower lips. I easily slid in as I cursed, "Fuck, you're wet as hell, baby."

Brynlee's hips pushed into my hand as she silently begged for more. I slipped another finger in and began pumping them fast and hard as Brynlee grabbed onto my shoulders and hissed, "Yessss."

I wanted her to come, but with my mouth on her. Withdrawing my hand from her pussy, I brought it up to her mouth where her eyes widened in shock when she realized what I wanted. With a quick lick of her lips, she parted them ever so slightly while I ran one finger along her bottom lip. Her eyes stayed fixed onto mine as I slipped it inside her mouth and she began sucking. My eyes rolled into the back of my head when she moaned slightly.

Hottest fucking moment of my life.

Wanting to sample her sweetness as well, I moved my fingers to my mouth and licked off her juices. Her breathing increased along with my pulse.

"So damn good. I want to taste you … now."

When I placed my hand on her shoulder and guided her down,

Brynlee quickly dropped to the bed and began moving back as I crawled over her. I spread her legs apart with my knee as I took her mouth with mine and kissed the living fuck out of her.

"Oh … God … Brody. What's happening to me?" she panted as I pushed my knee up against her pussy, provoking her to grind shamelessly. Dropping my lips, I kissed along her jaw and moved to her neck, where I made my way under her ear and began sucking on her earlobe.

"Feels so amazing," she said as she rocked against my knee.

I smiled into her neck. She hadn't even begun to feel amazing yet. My lips fell to her chest where I placed light kisses until I reached a nipple. Sucking and pulling on it with my teeth drove Brynlee crazy.

Jesus H. Christ. What type of fuckers had she dated that didn't worship her body like it deserved?

My lips traveled down her body to her belly button where I swirled my tongue. Brynlee dug her hands into my hair and pushed me further down, silently begging me to give her relief.

"Patience, baby. All in good time."

She whimpered as I kissed her gently along her hips. I settled between her legs as she lifted her head and looked into my eyes. "You're mine now, Brynlee Santos."

She absentmindedly nodded her head as she gripped the bed cover.

Never taking my eyes from hers, I licked between her lips and up to her clit.

"Oh God!" she called out as she dropped her head back onto the bed. It wasn't going to take her long at all.

I spread her lips apart and cursed, "Damn. That looks beautiful."

Brynlee thrashed her head back forth as she quietly begged me. "Please … please … Brody."

Giving her what she wanted, I buried my face deep into her core as I worked her up with my tongue. Her hips pumped as her hands

dug into my hair. I loved feeling her pressing my face into her, demanding for more.

"Oh God."

I moved my tongue up and began flicking her clit as I pushed my fingers inside of her. I could feel her body getting ready to release her orgasm. Her legs shook as her pussy pulsed against my fingers and her hands pulled my hair as she arched her back, screaming out my name.

I sucked and licked as much of her as I could while her body slowly came down from her climax. She tasted better than anything I'd ever tasted before. My dick was ready to explode as I moved over her body and watched her as she opened her eyes.

Brynlee panted as she tried to catch her breath. "Ohmygawd."

With a grin, I bent over and kissed her, surprised and thrilled all at once to see she let me. I wanted her to taste herself—taste her own desire for me.

Brynlee wrapped her legs around me and moaned as she pulled me back to her entrance. "Baby, I need to get a condom," I murmured.

Her legs dropped as I quickly jumped off the bed and found the bag I had dropped when we first walked in. Digging through it, I ripped the damn thing open and pulled out four condoms before crawling back over her.

I tossed three of them to the side of the bed and ripped one open with my teeth as Brynlee stared intently. Excitement danced in her eyes. Holding the condom out for her, she took it as I moved over her. Brynlee sunk her teeth into her bottom lip as she rolled the condom on me. My entire body trembled as I watched her.

Her eyes looked up into mine as she said, "I want to taste you too, Brody."

With a push of my knee, I opened her wide to me. "You will, baby, but I need to be inside of you before I lose control."

The innocent smile that slowly spread across her face killed me.

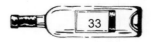

My stomach did that fluttering thing and my heart felt like I just plummeted down a roller coaster. My dick pushed against her as she sucked in a breath of air.

"Relax, baby," I whispered against her lips, working my way inside of her. With each inch I slowly crept into her body, I lost myself even more to her. *What would she feel like without a condom?* Fuck, I couldn't even imagine. If this felt amazing, what would bareback feel like?

Fucking heaven.

Brynlee's legs wrapped around me as she arched her back and I pushed all the way in. "Damn, you're so tight. I don't want to leave; I want to stay buried inside of you, Brynlee. Forever."

Fingertips lightly moved across my back as she drove her hips up into me, urging me to move. With each painfully slow movement, I soon found myself going faster and harder than I wanted to.

"Brynlee, I need to slow down."

Her legs wrapped tighter as she met me thrust for thrust. "No! Brody, don't stop."

A few more hard pumps and I was pushing myself into her, balls-deep as my cum filled the condom.

We both called out each other's names as she wrapped her arms around my neck and our mouths claimed one another. The kiss was beautiful. I'd never in my life experienced anything like what I just had with Brynlee.

This was it.

She was the one.

Five

Brynlee

My finger trailed lightly up and down Brody's arm as he slept peacefully next to me. I couldn't have wiped the goofy-ass grin off my face if I wanted to.

I felt alive. Like something inside of me had awoken. Was this what love felt like? Because if so, I was down for feeling like this for the rest of my life!

Brody rolled over and I gently kissed his shoulder before slipping out of bed. After a quick sweep of the room looking for my clothes, I reached for his t-shirt sticking out of the bag and slipped it on as I headed for my purse. It was killing me not to tell someone about the mind-blowing sex I'd had.

Twice.

Grabbing my purse, I dug down to the bottom for my phone as I quietly opened the French doors and stepped outside. My fingers came up to my swollen lips as I giggled and found my sister's num-

ber. Hitting her name, I walked up to the edge of the balcony and looked out into the night.

"This better be good, bitch."

"Hello to you too, Mel."

My sister, Melanie, let out a dramatic sigh. "Just get on with it. I have a four-year-old who will be up in mere hours to torture the living hell out of me."

Squeezing my eyes shut, I blurted it out. "I just had the best sex I've ever experienced in my entire life!"

Melanie gasped on the other end of the line. "What? You had sex? With Brody, the hotter-than-hot guy?"

I nodded like a giddy schoolgirl and did a little weird jump. "Yes! And he asked me to marry him and I said yes!"

"Whoa ... hold the fucking fort. You can't hit me with hot sex and tell me you're getting married all in one phone call. And wait, you just started dating this guy. Are you insane or just high from a good fuck?"

"Both!" I squealed with a smile as wide as the state of Texas.

Melanie let out a whistle and said, "He must have a big dick."

I hugged myself as I let the memories of earlier flood my memory. "He does and he knows how to work it as well as his mouth, if you know what I mean."

"Oral sex? Nice. My baby sister finally broke her oral sex cherry?"

Rolling my eyes, I peeked over my shoulder to check to see if Brody was still sleeping. Once I was assured he was, I sat down in a chair and gave my sister all the details.

"Oh my God, Mel. Why didn't you tell me it was so amazing?"

Melanie laughed. "Oh God ... it's been so long since anyone has given me oral sex. Hell, it's been so long since I've had sex, I think my virginity is coming back."

I pressed my hand over my mouth and chuckled. "I seriously doubt it, especially since you have a kid."

"Well, there are cobwebs down there for sure. Even my dildo has to push through them to get some action."

"You're so bad. Can we get back to my amazing sex life please?"

"Oh sure, go forth and rub the salt in my wound. So tell me, did he make love to you or did he fuck you?"

I could just imagine Melanie now, sitting on her bed wiggling her eyebrows as she talked.

"Oh, Mel. He made sweet beautiful love to me. Twice."

She gasped. "A big dick *and* stamina. Score! Are you sore?"

I moved about in the chair and shook my head. "No, not yet."

"Well, if Mr. Stamina keeps at it, you will be. Soak in a hot bath and that will help."

"You know, I've had sex before, Mel. It's not like this is my first time."

"Uh-huh. Okay, well, trust me when I say I didn't get pregnant with Jacob because I only fucked Dean a couple times. I really think it was the night he screwed me four times. Pretty sure it was the fuck against the wall that impregnated me."

"Eww. Like I said, can we get back to talking about me and how amazing Brody is?"

Melanie sighed. "Fine. But honestly, Bryn, married?"

My stomach dropped at the idea of becoming Brody's wife. The thought of waking up in his arms every morning caused my heart to skip a beat. Being wrapped in his arms every single night as we fell asleep? Oh yes, mark me down for one marriage please.

"Mel, I've never felt like this before. *Ever.* All he has to do is smile at me and my body comes to life. His touch sends a surge through me that has me longing for more. It's crazy and wonderful and magical all at the same time."

"Do you think maybe you guys got caught up in the moment of hot sex and he just blurted it out?"

I smiled as I dug my teeth into my lip. "He asked me after din-

ner when we were watching the sunset. We hadn't even been together yet."

She sucked in a breath of air. "Holy shit!"

"I know! It's so romantic it's unreal."

"No, you idiot! You agreed to marry him before you even knew how he was in bed? What the hell is wrong with you?"

I pushed a frustrated sigh out. "Melanie, seriously, it's not just about the sex."

"It's always about the sex. On another note ... Dad's going to freak the fuck out. You know this, right?"

For a moment, my eyes widened in horror as I thought about my parents, but then I realized their opinion didn't matter. "I don't care. It's my life and I'll do what I want. I'm graduating in a few months and there isn't a damn thing he can do about it."

"Yeah, he must have a magical dick because this is not my baby sister I'm hearing right now."

I stood up and wrapped my free arm around my waist. "Mel, this is it. I feel it in my bones. I love him. The things he whispered to me when he made love to me..." I shook my head as I smiled. "He makes me feel like I'm his everything."

The line was silent for a few seconds before I heard Melanie sniffle. "Are you crying, Mel?"

"No!"

"Liar," I said with a giggle.

"Fine! I may have had a few tears but I quickly got my head out of my ass. Honestly though, Bryn, if you say this guy is the one then you know I'll stand by you one hundred percent."

"He is, Mel."

"Can I ask just one more thing?"

It was then the hairs on my body stood as I felt Brody's presence. His arms wrapped around my waist as he buried his face into my neck.

"S-sure," I stuttered.

"Have y'all even thought about what happens after college ends in a few months and you're forced to decide other things?"

Suppressing the moan in the back of my throat, I closed my eyes and asked, "Other things?"

"Yeah, Bryn. Like where are y'all going to live? Texas? California? What are Brody's plans for after college? I know yours, but have you thought about his?"

Reality hit me for the first time since we started dating. I tried to think, but the way Brody was moving his hands over my body was causing my core to tighten with need again.

"We still need to figure all that out."

Melanie moaned and said, "Ugh. Brynlee, I'm just saying to not get caught up in the whirlwind of everything. Keep your head on."

Brody's hand slipped between my legs as I tried like hell not to whimper when he pushed his fingers inside of me.

"Promise, Mel. Um ... I have to go."

"The bastard woke up, didn't he?"

Laughing, I said, "Yep."

"You disgust me, you bitch. Tell him to fuck you this time."

I rolled my eyes. "Bye, Mel. I love you."

"Love you too, Bryn. Practice safe sex!"

Hanging up, I dropped my arms to my side as my head fell onto Brody's massive chest.

"Take a shower with me, Brynlee."

My stomach clenched as I said, "Okay." He had me in his arms before I even knew what was happening. Less than a minute later, I was standing under a hot shower as Brody pressed me against the cold marble. I sucked in a breath as the cold took me by surprise.

"Brody," I whispered as I reached down and began stroking his hard length. There was no doubt in my mind I was going to be sore as hell after tonight, but I didn't care. The only thing I could feel right now was the warmth running through my veins. "Make love to me, please."

The longing look in his eyes had my heart pounding. "Oh baby, I'm going to do more than make love to you."

My stomach fluttered as his words settled into my head. "What are you going to do?" I asked as I ran my tongue along my lips.

Brody lifted me up and pushed me against the wall of the shower again. I wrapped my legs around him as his mouth came down on mine. My hands pushed into his wet hair as we got lost in the rough, yet strangely gentle, kiss. We were desperate for each other. Brody's tongue danced with mine as we both moaned.

Brody pulled his mouth away as his eyes looked into mine. They were on fire as he pushed into me, and I inhaled a quick breath as he filled me completely. "Yes," I said as I squeezed my legs around him tighter.

"I'm going to fuck you, Brynlee, and show you what you've been missing out on."

I couldn't help but smile as I felt myself tighten around his dick with each movement he made. Each time, I felt the buildup.

"Feels fucking amazing, baby. My God, I've never felt like this before." Brody spoke as he buried his face in my neck and moaned.

"Shit, I can't get deep enough!" he shouted as he moved faster and pushed in deeper as my orgasm ripped through my body. I'd never had an orgasm during sex before Brody. I wasn't sure if it was just the raw passion and love we felt for each other, or if I had just been missing the hell out of great sex.

The faster he went, the more my body shook. Then I felt his dick swell as he pushed in hard and called out my name while I called out his. I loved that we came together. There was something so magical about it. I'd never had sex feel so damn good before.

So amazingly good.

Our breathing was labored as Brody held onto me tightly and I did the same. I could feel him twitching inside of me and it was the most amazing thing I'd ever experienced.

Pure heaven.

"I've never felt so amazing," I whispered.

Brody pulled back and smiled as his eyes searched my face. "That was beyond amazing. Being with you is like seeing and feeling for the first time. That felt so good, like nothing I'd ever experienced before."

Giggling, I scrunched up my nose. "We should add that to the top of our list of favorite things to do."

He laughed as he lifted me up and set me down. I think it was then we both realized what we had done. The look of horror on Brody's face said it all.

We had forgotten a condom.

I had never in my life forgotten to tell a guy to put a condom on. *Never.* Brody stumbled backwards and scrubbed his hands down his face as he began cursing up a storm. The memory of the night Melanie told our parents she was pregnant invaded my thoughts. *How could I be so foolish? So stupid? I know better!*

"I'm so sorry, Brynlee. Son-of-a-bitch what in the fuck did I do?"

My father's words raced through my mind. *"Don't you ever come home and tell me you're pregnant like your sister did. I will not have both my girls messing up their lives."*

Brody reached out for me and pulled me to him. Cupping my face with his hands, he kissed me over and over as he spoke against my lips. "I love you, Brynlee. Sweetheart, I love you so much."

Tears began to stream down my face because I knew what he was doing. "I love ... I love you too." I said between sobs.

"Sweetheart, are you on birth control?"

I was scared to death to answer his question. The moment I did, he was going to freak and then walk out. Melanie's voice invaded my thoughts.

"What are Brody's plans for after college? I know yours, but have you thought about his?"

Another sob escaped from my mouth as Brody kissed away my

tears as they mixed with the water from the shower. I was in a full-on crying fit while Brody turned off the shower and grabbed a towel. He quickly dried off, and then wrapped me up in the terrycloth and picked me up. My face smashed into his chest as I continued to cry. I was behaving like a baby, but I was scared to death. I had never been so careless before.

Brody set me gently down on the bed and forced me to look at him. "Talk to me, Brynlee. I don't want you upset after I just experienced something so beautiful with you. Please."

Pressing my lips together, I could feel them trembling. I swallowed and took a few deep breaths in and out of my nose until I got myself calm.

"I … I, um, I stopped taking the pill about six months ago because I hadn't been dating. I know it was stupid, but I'm so bad about remembering to take them, I thought it would be easier to just stop."

Even though he tried not to, Brody widened his eyes in alarm, but he quickly pushed it away. "It's okay, Brynlee. Whatever happens, we're going to be okay."

I shook my head and started crying again. "No it's not okay. We just had unprotected sex. I don't know if you've ever slept with anyone else like that before."

"Never. I swear to you."

"What if … what if I—?" I squeezed my eyes shut and covered my face while I let out a muffled scream.

"If you end up pregnant, then I'm going to be right there with you. Brynlee. When I asked you to marry me, I meant it. I will never leave your side. Ever."

My hands dropped to the bed as I stared at him. This man couldn't be real.

He just couldn't be.

Six

Brody

The fear in Brynlee's eyes killed me. This was my fault. I got so caught up in the moment, I completely forgot about a condom. I had never fucking forgot to wrap it.

Shit.

None of it mattered though. I knew whatever happened, I would never leave her side.

"What if … what if—?" Brynlee covered her face and screamed into her hands.

"If you end up pregnant, then I'm going to be right there with you. Brynlee. When I asked you to marry me, I meant it."

Dropping her hands down to the bed, Brynlee gave me a look of disbelief.

"Are you for real?"

I pulled my head back and nodded. "Yes. I would never walk away from you no matter what. Matter of fact, you're going to have

to push me out the door and tell me you no longer love me if you ever want me gone."

With a slight giggle, Brynlee put her hand on the side of my face as I leaned into it. "What about after college, Brody?"

"What about it?"

She sniffled and looked down at her hands that she was nervously rubbing together. "What plans did you have?"

I shrugged and said, "I was just going to go work for my father."

It dawned on me then that I'd never told Brynlee anything about my family. Here I asked the girl to marry me and she knew nothing about my family.

"My father owns a company that designs energy-efficient products, mostly solar stuff."

Her eyes widened. "Wow. What would you do for him?"

"Analytical stuff. Problem solving and figuring out how to make designs work better. Save the world because we're depleting our natural resources. Shit like that."

"Brody!" Brynlee said as she slapped my chest. "That sounds interesting."

"What about you? You mentioned once wanting to take over your parent's vineyard."

The smile that spread across her face was infectious. I couldn't help but smile back at her. "Ever since I can remember I've wanted to run the vineyard. My great-grandfather brought over a vine from Portugal and planted it on the land he bought in California. Our whole vineyard was made from that one vine."

A piece of hair was hanging down in Brynlee's face. I gently pushed it behind her ear as I smiled. "That's cool."

She barely spoke the next words. "Yeah. It is."

Brynlee began worrying her lip as she looked into my eyes. "If you want to be here in Texas, and I want to be in California, how are we ever going to make this work?"

I shook my head as I took her hands in mine. "Don't you see,

sweetheart? The only place I want to be is with you. I don't care if it's here in Texas, in California, or in fucking Alaska. You're the only thing that matters to me."

"We hardly know each other. What if you hate California?"

I flashed her my dimples as I kissed her forehead. "Nonsense. Wherever you're happy, I'll be happy. I just made you officially mine, Brynlee." Her cheeks flushed as she smiled.

"You certainly did. I'd even go so far as saying you marked me."

My eyes caught the condoms on the bed. I reached out for one and held it up. "And I'm not done with you."

Brynlee unwrapped the towel from her body and winked. "I'm all yours."

Three Months Later...

"**D**ude, seriously, why the fuck are we at a damn workout class?"

Women began streaming in as Travis and I stood in the back left corner.

Slapping him on the back, I laughed. "Because I want to see my future bride in action."

Travis rolled his eyes. "I still say you're crazy for getting married. And moving! Let's not forget you're leaving me to go halfway across the damn country."

I pretended to act like I was about to cry as I said, "Aww, don't worry about it, buddy. We'll Skype every day."

Travis pushed me, causing me to stumble backwards. "You say that now, but you know you won't."

My mouth fell open as I stared at him. I had been kidding, but apparently I underestimated how much Travis was going to miss me.

Women walked past us on their way to pick up the hand weights and a bar. Travis gave a blonde a quick head nod and hello as she smiled at us. "Jesus, I haven't been eye-fucked this much since that sorority party we went to a couple years ago."

A low chuckle slipped from my mouth. "See. You just might meet someone and have yourself a little afternoon delight if I know you."

Waving me off, he looked around the room. "Nah, I'm not interested in that shit anymore."

My head snapped over to him. It wasn't like Travis to turn down a potential hook-up with a hot girl. "What's this I hear from you? You're not interested?"

"Have you forgotten about your fiancé's best friend? You know, *my girlfriend*, Crystal?"

Grinning from ear to ear, I shook my head. "Dude, you're in love with her."

Travis let out a gruff laugh. "What? You're fucking crazy. I haven't been drinking from the love mug like you."

"I call bullshit."

Brynlee came walking into the room. I hadn't told her I would be coming today, and this would only be the second class I'd been to that she taught at Life Time Fitness. The other class was yoga. Yeah. No, thank you. There was no way in hell I was doing yoga.

"Speaking of bullshit, you haven't forgotten again to wrap the stick, have you?"

I had told Travis about my fuck-up on not wearing a condom a few months back. When Brynlee was late on her period, we went to HEB and bought two of every kind of pregnancy test. All of them came back negative and the next day she started. "No, I haven't, dickhead. Brynlee is now on the pill. Once we get married though, I'm tossing those damn condoms into a fire pit and watching them burn."

Travis laughed as he shook his head. We only had three weeks

of school left. The day after we graduated we were getting married at the Oasis. Brynlee wanted to keep it small. The only people attending were our parents, Travis and Crystal, Brynlee's sister Melanie and her young son Jacob, and my younger sister Katherine.

"All right! Let's get started ladies and—"

Our eyes met and Brynlee did a little hop of joy.

"Ugh. You both make me sick with your whole love-fest bullshit."

A girl with red hair turned and glared at Travis. Lifting his hands he apologized, "Sorry. Didn't mean to say that out loud."

Brynlee clapped her hands together to get everyone's attention. "Anyway, let's get started ladies, and the gentlemen hiding in the corner back there."

A few girls turned and cheered us on as we both lifted our hands in embarrassment. "Dude, she called us out. I'm taking a point away from her."

I rolled my eyes and followed along as Brynlee did a few stretches and started explaining to the class, which neither Travis nor I were listening to.

"You can't take points away from her. I'm marrying her."

Travis awkwardly did the stretches as he turned and looked at me. "The hell I can't, douche-lover."

"Fuck off," I said as I grabbed some hand weights when Brynlee told us to.

"The moment you say 'I do' is when the point-tracking stops. Up until then, I will give and take points as I see fit. Where she stands with points on your wedding day will depend on if I object to the marriage or not."

I stopped what I was doing and glared at him. "I'll kill you if you open your mouth at my wedding."

"You'd kill me? Really? Dicks before chicks, Brody. Remember that little saying? Yeah, she must have a magical pussy or something that made you forget the golden rule."

I couldn't help but start laughing. Everything about Brynlee was magical, and I wasn't gonna lie, her pussy was fucking amazing. And it was all mine.

With a quick push on Travis' shoulder, he lost balance and bumped into the girl next to him. She turned to bitch him out, but when she saw him, she replaced her pissed off look with a come-stick-your-hand-in-my-panties look.

"Oh. Did you need help with something?"

Normally Travis would have been all over that. If there was one thing my best friend could do, it was attract girls. It would have been all but guaranteed he would be walking out of the class with her.

"No. Sorry, I just lost my balance." Travis turned and shot me a dirty look. Ah, the new Travis ... the one in love with Crystal seemed to be monogamous now.

Impressive.

An hour and a half later, Travis and I were hanging onto each other for dear life. "My fucking legs won't stop shaking. I think she damaged my lungs, dude. I can't breathe right!"

"What in the hell just happened in here?" I asked as I watched all the women bouncing by us like Brynlee didn't just attempt to kill us all.

"Hey guys. How did you like *advanced* BodyPump?" my fiancée asked with a knowing smirk.

Still trying to breathe right, I gulped, "Advanced? Like how advanced? Cause I feel like I'm gonna die, baby."

Brynlee threw her head back and laughed. "Oh, come on. You two aren't that out of shape, are you?"

Travis picked up the step and the weights, glaring at Brynlee as they shook in his arms. "You're evil. Has anyone ever told you that? I heard the one girl say you kicked it up a few notches today. You. Are. Evil."

With a tilt of her head and an innocent smile, Brynlee looked between Travis and me. "I don't have any idea what you mean,

Travis."

With a brush off of his hand, he walked toward the corner of the room as he mumbled, "That's another lost point."

My phone rang as I forced my body to roll over and grab it. "Hello?"

"I can't fucking shit."

I snarled my lip at the visual. "Metamucil, dude."

"No, I can shit just fine, Brody. I can't fucking sit on the toilet to shit."

I knew exactly how he felt. My legs hadn't hurt like that since after the first day of high school football practice my freshman year.

"Dude, I can't get myself out of bed, so shut the hell up."

"Fuck you! I can't sit to shit! Do you have any idea how long it took me to get out of my car last night? My legs have never felt such pain. You're marrying the devil incarnate. She just lost like fifty points. Fifty!"

Moaning, I hung up and dropped the phone to the floor. I wasn't sure how long I was going to have to lie there.

Possibly until someone came to find me.

Seven

Brynlee

With a deep inhale, I held my breath for a few moments, and then slowly blew it out. *Stay calm. Breathe. Relax.*

There was a light knock at the door and I heard my sister's voice. "Bryn?"

Breathe in. Breathe out. I just need to relax.

The knob shook and Melanie called out my name again. "Hey, Brynlee, not to cause you any additional stress, but your future husband is kind of expecting you to head on down to the altar in a few minutes. Locking yourself in here is somewhat of a worrisome thing."

I took another deep breath as I stood up and rolled my head around a few times to loosen my stiff muscles.

With a quick turn, I opened the door and exclaimed, "I'm ready!"

Melanie looked at me like I had grown two heads. "Weirdo.

How do you do that?"

Another quick glance in the mirror to make sure my makeup was okay and I was ready to do this.

"Do what?" I asked as I looked back at my sister.

Melanie's eyes widened in surprise. "Um, oh I don't know. Freak the hell out and lock yourself in a bathroom, only to come popping out ten minutes later looking like all refreshed and ready to go."

With a shrug, I smiled and blew my sister a kiss. "I'm getting married today! I'm getting married today!"

Melanie snarled her lip as she rolled her eyes. "Yes, I know, sweet sister."

My mother walked into the room and let out a gasp. "Oh look at my *garotinha!*" She quickly walked over to me and wrapped me in her arms as she spoke in Portuguese. "*Eu não posso acreditar que você está se casar.*"

My eyes quickly began to fill with tears as I pulled back and nodded. "I know, Momma. I can't believe I'm getting married either."

Placing her hand on the side of my face, her eyes locked onto mine. "Brynlee, I see how much you love Brody and the same goes for him. He is a *bom homem,* and oh my does he *amo você.*"

I couldn't help but laugh. My parents had both grown up with Portuguese-speaking parents. They often mixed both English and Portuguese. I nodded and said, "Yes, Momma. He is a good man and he does love me. Very much."

My father cleared his throat as the three of us turned to look at him. "*Meu amor*, you look beautiful."

For some reason, seeing my father made me even more emotional. I pressed my lips together in an attempt to keep from crying as I blinked back my tears. Melanie walked up to our father and said, "Don't make her cry, *Papai.*"

With a chuckle, my father kissed Melanie on the check. "Be-

have, Melanie."

My sister turned and looked over her shoulder as she gave me a wink. "Always, Papai. Always."

I turned back to my mother. "I'm nervous."

She gave me an understanding look as she smiled. Her green eyes sparkled and I noticed how breathtaking my mother was. Her light brown hair was pulled up into a neat bun on the top of her head and her makeup was light and airy. My mother never needed makeup though. She was naturally beautiful. She said it was her Portuguese heritage. She was forty-six years old but didn't look older than her early thirties. People always thought she was Melanie's and my sister.

"You love him. He loves you. You are about to start an amazing journey together, Brynlee."

As I blew out a breath, I watched my father approach us. "You will have trying times. Every couple does."

Nodding her head, my mother whispered, "*Sim.*"

"Times when you will both fight. Say things you don't mean, question your love for each other, but you have to let love find the way. After all, that's what love is for, to show you the way when other things have blinded you. It has a way of opening your eyes when you need it the most."

My father engulfed me in a hug. "Papai, I love you so much. I only pray I have a marriage like yours and Momma's."

After holding me for a few moments, my father took a step back. "You will."

My heart was racing and I was trying to make sense of the emotions I was feeling. Excited, scared, nervous, and doubt all rolled up into one big giant knot in my stomach. *Where is the doubt coming from?* It scared me the most. I didn't doubt my love for Brody, or his love for me. There was something lying under the surface that kept trying to show its ugly head and I couldn't figure out what it was.

Shaking my head, I pushed it aside and said, "Papai, will you do

me the honor of walking me to the love of my life."

He smiled bright and big as he held out his arm for mine. My mother kissed me on both cheeks and turned to give my father a loving look as she headed for the door.

"Smile for the picture!" Melanie called out, as the photographer snapped the picture right as Brody pushed a piece of cake into my mouth. I was almost positive my sister knew what I would do next. I grabbed a piece of cake and pushed it into his face as he busted out laughing.

"Oh Brynlee, you're going to ruin your dress," my mother called out from somewhere. I didn't care. I was deliriously happy. My wedding dress was beautiful and I really didn't want to ruin it, but at the same time I wanted to enjoy every single minute of my wedding day without worrying about my dress or my hair.

Brody and I said our vows right at sunset on the same deck he proposed to me on. It was simple, yet romantic, and the perfect way to start our new life together. One day we graduated college, and the next we were getting married while overlooking Lake Travis during the most breathtaking sunset I'd ever seen.

Perfect didn't even begin to describe the day.

Being ever the "hostess with the mostess," my mother ushered everyone back into the restaurant for cake. My body felt as if I were walking on a cloud. By the look on Brody's face, I'd say he was feeling the same way. As he reached for my hand, he gently kissed the back of it and then pressed his lips to my neck. The feel of his hot breath on my skin instantly kicked my libido into gear. My stomach tightened with the idea of Brody sinking deep inside of me. "I can't wait to peel this beautiful gown off your body."

With a smile and a quick squeeze of his hand, I whispered,

"When do we get to leave?"

"Not soon enough."

Travis and Melanie both stood up at the same time, hitting a spoon to the side of their drinks. Brody and I laughed as Melanie shot Travis a dirty look. "I'll go first, hotshot."

Travis chuckled while shaking his head and staring at Melanie. "Travis, let the bride's sister talk first," Brody said.

"The hell with that! I'm his best friend. We've known each other since we were babies."

Melanie glared at Travis and I was pretty sure if she had magical powers, daggers would have shot from her eyes and pierced Travis in the heart. "Well, I've got you beat, buddy. I've known Brynlee since the day she was born. So I get to give the first speech."

"Mommy! Mommy!'

The attention was quickly turned to my little nephew, Jacob, as he came running out of the bathroom with the nanny Melanie had hired to help her for the day.

"Mommy!" Jacob stopped right before he slammed into Melanie. "There's a bone in my pee-pee!"

The look of mortification that spread over Melanie's face was priceless and I secretly hoped the photographer captured it.

Snap.

The sound of the camera going off caused me to bust out laughing. Never mind the fact that my nephew just figured out his pee-pee gets hard.

"Holy shit. That trumped anything I could've ever said." Travis laughed as he picked up Jacob and spun him around before setting him back down and prompting him for a high five. Since Crystal came down with the flu and had to miss the wedding, Travis spent most of his time getting to know Jacob.

While Melanie stood there stunned, the room erupted in laughter as Jacob realized he was the cause of all the fun. He immediately ran around the tables, pointing at his privates and yelling out, "My pee-

pee has a bone! My pee-pee has a big bone in it!" Travis followed, chanting the same thing, as Melanie looked like she was about to pass out before she snapped out of it.

"Travis! Stop running! He thinks you're playing, you jerk!" Melanie shouted as Travis turned and ran backwards while sticking his tongue out at Melanie. "Real mature, you ass."

"Jesus H. Christ," Brody said. "This is the shit we'll be talking about for years to come."

Tears streamed down my face as I watched Melanie and my mother chasing after Jacob. Melanie stopped and pointed to my father. "Papai! You need to talk to your grandson. I was *not* prepared for this! Not prepared at all."

"Can't breathe!" I said as I wrapped my arms around my waist and laughed.

Brody stood up and walked over to the DJ and told him to crank up the music. Before long, my mother caught Jacob, Melanie retreated to the bar for something "stiff," while Travis mentioned something about getting matching T-shirts made for him and Jacob, and Brody and I glided along the dance floor in each other's arms.

Life didn't get any more perfect than this.

Then our wedding song came on. Brody was left up to the task of picking out the wedding song. The moment it started, my heart beat faster as tears began flowing from my eyes.

"Dance with me, sweetheart," he said with a smile.

I walked into the arms of the man I loved more than anything as Faith Hill's "It Will Be Me" played.

I was wrong.

Life just kept on getting better and better.

Eight

Brody

Six Months Later... Napa California

The moment I stepped through the door, I let out a sigh of relief.

Home.

Thank fuck I'm finally home.

"Brody? Hey baby! Was traffic bad?"

Rolling my eyes, I let out a curt laugh as I dropped my keys and wallet onto the side table near the front door.

"You could say that."

Five months of this bullshit and I was already getting tired of it. I hated my job. Working for a semiconductor company was not what I thought I would be doing with my career. They were demanding and thought my world should revolve around work and nothing outside their walls.

Brynlee was in the kitchen and I was trying to decide what I

wanted to do first. Take a hot shower or wrap her up in my arms. Deciding I needed to feel her near me, I headed to the kitchen. As I rounded the kitchen, I stopped in my tracks.

"Happy almost six-month anniversary."

My eyes roamed over her body. The only thing she had on was a tiny little apron and red fuck-me heels.

"Holy shit." My dick hardened in my pants and I was thanking God I decided on my wife over a shower.

Brynlee chewed on the corner of her lip as she held a cupcake in her left hand and handcuffs in her right hand. "Are you ready to play, Mr. Miles?"

"Hell yeah, I am, Mrs. Miles."

Two long strides and I slammed my mouth to hers. Our tongues moved against each other with fury as we moaned in one another's mouths.

"Brynlee, I just want to bend you over and fuck you right here."

Her eyes lit up with a passion I hadn't seen in a few weeks. Life had become busy with her starting to do more and more at her parents' vineyard, and me working like a fucking dog six days a week. We hardly ever got to see each other.

My knees went weak and my heart dropped to my stomach as I watched Brynlee take a step back while licking the frosting off the cupcake. "I'm all yours tonight."

My pants were down and kicked off to the side in record speed. Brynlee swiped frosting off the top of the cupcake and fell to her knees as she wiped it over the head of my dick. The moment her tongue licked up my shaft my entire body shuddered. "Ah, baby that feels so damn good."

Brynlee licked the frosting off my dick while it jumped with each touch of her tongue. Taking my balls in her left hand and wrapping her right hand at the base of my shaft, she took me inside her mouth, moving in and out so damn slow I wanted to grab her head and start fucking her mouth.

Breathe in. Shit ... don't come yet.

Brynlee moaned and I felt the vibration throughout my whole body. Reaching down, I grabbed her shoulders and pulled her up as I huffed, "Stop!"

The smile on her face told me she knew I was close. Then she took another bite of the damn cupcake and winked.

"Fuck this."

Brynlee's eyebrows rose as she waited for me to take control. Turning her around, I pushed her legs open and teased her pussy with my dick.

"Oh God. I've been dreaming of you all day."

My lips began kissing her back as I slipped my fingers inside of her. She was soaking wet. "Feels like it, baby. Have you been horny?"

"Yes," she panted out as she pushed back into me. "I want you."

I worked her up until her body began to shake, and then I pulled my fingers out as she let out a frustrated moan. "Brody! I was about to—"

Before she finished her sentence, I pushed my cock into her hard and fast. "Oh God!" she cried out as I grabbed onto her hips and began pumping as hard as I could.

"Feels so fucking good to just fuck the shit out of you."

Brynlee dropped her head and met me thrust for thrust. Each time I pushed in, she arched back into me. *Fuck, this was making it deep.* My balls were slapping her over and over as I gave it everything I had.

My eyes landed on her ass as I thought about exploring with my finger, but decided that was something we needed to talk about first.

"I'm going to come. Oh God, yes!"

Brynlee called out my name as her body trembled with her release. I could feel her squeezing down on my dick as another orgasm hit her when I reached around the front and rubbed her clit. I couldn't even understand what she was saying as I let out a moan

and then called out her name as my orgasm hit me. She was milking me for every last drop as I kept fucking her. When it finally stopped, I slowed down but stayed buried inside of her. It felt too amazing to stop. If only we could stay like that always. Together as one.

"That was fantastic."

I peppered her back with soft kisses and grinned with satisfaction. "Yeah, it was. We need to do that more often."

My chest tightened when I pulled out of her. I missed her warmth immediately. While I looked for something to clean Brynlee off with, she held up the handcuffs and said, "Rest up, baby. We still need to play with these."

I could feel my cheeks burning with how hard I was smiling. "If this is what you give me at six months, what's a year going to be?"

"My ass," she whispered, her eyes darkening with desire as I cleaned her off.

My whole body froze as I stared into those sparkling hazel eyes. "W-what?"

"I want you to fuck me in the ass," she answered with a naughty smile.

It didn't take long for me to fall back onto my own ass and stare up at her. "Best. Fucking. Anniversary. Ever."

"How do you know, since you don't have any others to compare it to?" she asked with a laugh while bending over to kiss me.

Slowly shaking my head, I licked my lips and said, "I'm talking about our one year. I already know. It's gonna be the best one yet."

Her mouth looked heavenly as she moved closer to me. Stopping right at my lips, I felt her hot breath as my stomach dipped. "Oh yes, it is for sure going to be a good one."

Two Months Later…

Travis: *Hey dude. How's Cali?*
Me: *Sucks. I hate my fucking job, which in turn is making me*

hate it here.

Travis: *Have you talked to Brynlee about it?*

Me: *No. Her father has been riding her ass about the vineyard. Last thing I want to do is stress her out. That place is fucking huge and he wants her help more and more. I haven't even had time off work to check the place out all the way.*

Travis: *Look for something else.*

Me: *I am. Brynlee and I have been fighting a lot the last month. I have to admit, I've been egging her on and I don't know what the fuck is wrong with me. I can tell she is stressed and not sharing with me, which pisses me off.*

Travis: *Dude, you need some bro time. You free this weekend? I could fly in Thursday and you could show me what Napa offers.*

Me: *FUCK YES. I need to see someone from home!*

Travis: *Done. I'll book my flight and see you soon.*

I stepped out of the shower and grabbed a towel as I dried my hair and wiped my body down.

"Brody, seriously, how could you forget to tell me that Travis was coming for a long weekend?"

"What's the big deal?"

Brynlee sighed as she stopped putting her hair up in a ponytail and turned to look at me. I knew she would be pissed by me not telling her, but a part of me didn't want to tell her. I didn't want her knowing how much I was looking forward to Travis coming so I could escape for a bit.

"It's not a big deal, but the least you could've done was told me so I could've made sure the guest room was clean."

With a shake of my head, I laughed. "Because it's so dirty from all of our friends coming and staying with us. Fuck, we don't even

have any friends. At least in Texas we got together with people. Had a good time and didn't act like fucking fifty-year-old people."

Brynlee's mouth dropped open. "Why haven't you mentioned feeling like this before? If you want to go out more we can. You never let me introduce you to my friends. The only people you know are stupid people I went to high school with."

"Oh you mean Janet or Jean or whatever the fuck her name was. She was so damn depressing she made me want to rip my hair out and dig my eyes out of my head with a spoon."

Brynlee put her hands on her hips. "Jane was her name. She just got a divorce and had a new roommate move in with her. She was sad."

"Okay, Brynlee, do you have any other friends who might actually want to go out and grab a beer? See a movie, play a little poker?"

Her eyes widened as her chest began heaving up and down. "What, are we still in college? Is that what you want? To go hang out at bars and get fucked up? Would that make you happy?"

Slamming my hands down on the counter, I yelled out. "No, being in Texas at a damn bar on Fourth Street getting fucked up would make me happy. I can't take it any more. I hate my fucking job so much I want to quit every time I walk into the damn building. My boss is an asshole, and if the receptionist tries to show me her tits one more time, I'm going to just rip her goddamn shirt open and get it the fuck over with so she'll leave me the hell alone. Let's not forget how your dad is working you to death and making you work weekends, so we never see each other. Oh wait—you're learning the family business, so that's okay if I never get to see you anymore. The vineyard is more important than your fucking husband. You've been withdrawn the last few weeks and I have no idea why. I'm tired of it, Brynlee, so yes! Yes I want my best friend to come into town, and I want to take him to a bar and to get fucked up because my life is sucking right now."

Brynlee stood there staring at me with her mouth wide open. When her eyes looked down at my hand, it was then I realized I was bleeding. I had been so pissed off I grabbed my razor and was squeezing the hell out of it.

I dropped the razor and lifted my eyes back to hers and about dropped to the floor.

Her eyes were filled with hurt as she fought to hold back her tears. "You said wherever I'm happy, you'll be happy. Was that all a lie, Brody?"

Nine

Brynlee

My body was trembling as I let Brody's words sink into my head. Of all the times for him to lose it. My head was spinning. I was already scared, confused, and after his blow up, I was really pissed off.

"You want to go out and have a good time? Go." I relented as my voice cracked. "I'm sorry I didn't realize how miserable you were in your life here with me."

Brody closed his eyes and shook his head, "Wait, Brynlee, let me explain."

My heart was breaking as I realized what was happening. I was slowly pushing him away the last month not realizing I was doing it. I just needed to make it past tomorrow. Once I found out what the lump in my breast was, I could move on. I hadn't mentioned anything to him because I knew he was stressed out with work, and I didn't want to worry him if it turned out to be nothing.

I held up my hands. "No. There really is no need to explain any further to me. You made it pretty damn clear just how unhappy you are."

"Fucking hell, let me just … let me just have this weekend with Travis. That's all I want."

I couldn't believe what I was hearing. My heart was pounding in my chest so loud I could hardly hear Brody talking. Lifting my chin, I glared at him. "Go have your fun night. Get fucked up. Hell, for all I care, why don't you fuck someone while you're at it."

Turning on my heels, I grabbed my purse and stormed out of the house. The only place I knew to go was to my sister's. She lived on the vineyard in the guesthouse. It was perfect because she was able to have her privacy, yet still have my parents close by to help them out and for them to help out with Jacob.

With a deep breath in, I knocked on the door lightly. Melanie opened it and took one look at me and shook her head. "Oh fuck. The first fight."

Pursing my lips together to keep them from trembling, I shook my head. "You guys have been fighting? What the hell is wrong with him? Doesn't he know what in the hell you're going through right now, that fucker?"

Breaking down into tears, Melanie wrapped her arm around my shoulder and guided me into the small cottage. Jacob came running out. "What's wrong with Bryn-Bryn?"

Only Melanie and Jacob called me Bryn. Of course Jacob had to double it to make himself different from his mother. This kid was going to be a handful, that was for sure.

"She stubbed her big toe, buddy."

Jacob's eyes widened in horror. "Oh, Bryn-Bryn, that hurts like a mofo."

"What?" Melanie and I both said at once as Jacob laughed and ran to his room.

"God is punishing me for getting knocked up so young. That's

the only thing I can think of."

Melanie sat me on the sofa and headed into the kitchen. I knew what she was doing. Opening a bottle of wine. According to my family, especially my father, all your problems can be solved with a good bottle of wine.

She handed me a glass of red wine as she sat down next to me. "So, tell me what happened."

I pushed out the breath from my lungs and slowly pulled in a deep cleansing breath. "Travis is coming in today. They're having a guy's weekend, but Brody failed to tell me until he got off from work early and called to announce he was picking Travis up from the airport. Of course, I came home and things just blew up."

A sob escaped my lips as I covered my mouth and started crying again. "Oh God, Mel. He said he hated it here. He hated his life."

"He said he hated his life?"

A quick wipe with the back of my hand showed my black mascara on my fingers. I probably looked like a mess. "Well, not in those words, but he might as well have. Said he missed Texas and his friends and going out and having fun. He said we were like an old couple." I set my wine glass on the coffee table and cried into my hands. "This is all my fault."

"What?" Melanie shrieked. "No fucking way. He's acting like a dick. How could he do this the night before you get your results back?"

I dropped my hands to my sides as my body slumped over and I looked at Melanie with a scared face.

"Oh. My. God. You didn't tell him?"

Slowly shaking my head, I whispered, "No."

"Jesus, Brynlee! Don't you think your husband should know that you found a lump in your breast? What did you tell him when they did the procedure?"

I swallowed the lump in my throat as I said, "I didn't tell him about it. I avoided him touching me for a few days. I've been work-

ing late and getting home late and telling him I was too tired. I just didn't want him to worry. He's been so stressed at work, and if I had known he hated it so much, I would have told him to quit and now … oh God, now he's talking about Texas. What have I done?"

Melanie pulled me to her as I cried. I cried so hard I was sure I wouldn't have any tears left.

"Listen to me. You need to go back home and tell him the truth, Bryn. This isn't fair to him. For all he knows, you're tired of him like he's tired of his job."

"No!" I insisted, shaking my head frantically. "I love him more than ever."

"Then tell him the truth. I know he loves you. This is part of marriage, sweetie. It's not always pretty and fun. It's hard work and take it from me, if you don't work at it and fight for it, you lose it forever before you even knew it was lost."

In that moment it all made sense. I knew Melanie was right. I needed Brody with me tomorrow. I had planned on telling him when he got home and asking him to go with me before he announced Travis was arriving.

Standing, I gave Melanie a slight smile. "I'm going to head home." Kissing my sister on the forehead, I reached for my purse and made my way out the door. The vineyard wasn't far from our house so it only took me a few minutes to get back home. Pulling my phone out, I hit Brody's number. It rang and rang before his voicemail picked it up.

"Hey. I'm sorry, baby. I'm so sorry for the way I've been acting. I, um, I have something I need to talk to you about. Will you call me when you get this? It's really important. Tell Travis I said hi. I love you, Brody. I love you so very much."

I hung up and pulled into the garage and parked. Walking in, I turned on the TV and waited for Brody to call me.

My body jerked and woke me up as I looked around trying to figure out where I was.

The living room.

The TV was still on HGTV, playing some House Hunters rerun I had seen a million times. Picking up my phone, I looked at the time. One in the morning. I had no messages or missed calls from Brody. Now I was getting scared. Hitting his number, it rang twice before Brody answered it. "Hey, it's Brynlee!"

My heart fell as Travis yelled out for Brody. "Dude! It's the wife!"

All I could hear was music playing. "Sorry, Brynlee, he's getting fucked up currently, like you told him to do."

"Travis, put Brody on the phone now."

Travis laughed. "He's kind of busy right now."

I slowly stood up as my stomach felt sick. "What do you mean?"

"He's doing shots with Buck. His new best friend in California."

"Put him on the damn phone, Travis!" I shouted.

I heard a loud crash as I placed my hand over my stomach to calm my nerves. "She wants to talk to you, dude."

"Yello!"

"Brody? Baby, I think you should come home."

Brody laughed. "You were the one who told me to go out and get fucked up. Let me tell you baby. I. Am. Fucked. Up."

Tears began to spill over onto my face as I shook my head. "I need you to come home. I have a doctor's appointment tomorrow and I need you there with me."

"What? Oh now you want to spend time with me, Brynlee? Well, sorry baby. It's boy's weekend."

My body collapsed onto the sofa as I cried harder. "Brody, *please*. I'm begging you to come home."

"Bar closing in an hour baby. Be home then."

The line went dead as I pulled my phone out and looked at it. "Oh God. Oh God," I said as I began pacing back and forth. Where in the hell could they be? There were so many places, and for all I

knew, they drove to Santa Rosa.

Dropping my head back, I closed my eyes and said a silent prayer Brody wouldn't drive and that they would call a cab.

By five a.m. I couldn't keep my eyes open any longer. Brody's phone was either dead or turned off. As I dragged my feet to the bedroom, I sent my sister a text.

Me: *Will you go with me to the doctor tomorrow? If yes, meet me here at eight am.*

I fell onto my bed and cried myself to sleep. Again.

Ten

Brody

My mouth tasted like fucking cotton as I rolled off my stomach and onto my back. Opening my eyes slowly, I looked up at the ceiling. "Motherfucker. How much did I drink?"

I forced myself to sit up as I pushed the sheet away from my body and scrubbed my hands down my face before dropping them to my side. With a quick release of breath I looked around.

"Oh, fuck."

My eyes roamed around the strange room as I looked down and saw I was naked. Jumping up, I felt my chest squeezing tightly. "No. No, no, no! What in the fuck did I do?"

My clothes were in a pile at my feet as I quickly got dressed. My head was pounding so hard I felt sick. I sat back down on the bed and pulled my boots on as I took another look around the room.

Bras. Panties. Skirts. "Oh my God. I couldn't have. I wouldn't

do that to Brynlee."

Turning to the side, I saw a note with my name on it.

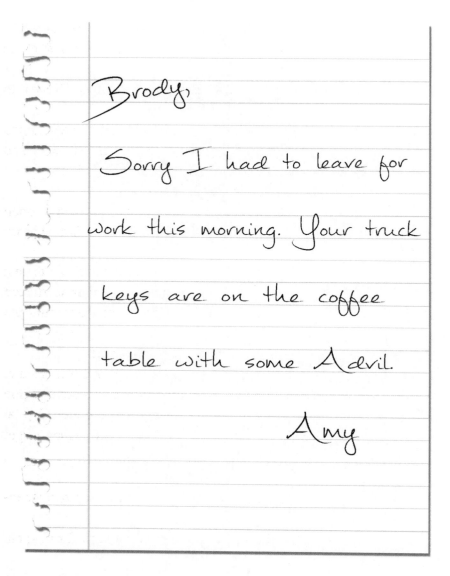

Brody,

Sorry I had to leave for work this morning. Your truck keys are on the coffee table with some Advil.

Amy

Amy? Who in the fuck is Amy? I cheated. Holy fucking shit, I cheated on my wife with some girl named Amy. NO! I would never cheat on my wife.

I jumped up and made my way to the bedroom door. When I opened the door I turned down the hall and stopped in my tracks. Travis was fucking some girl in the kitchen.

"Travis!" I yelled as he spun around and I saw the girl. "Jane?"

Travis turned and gave me a look of horror. "Did you just come out of that bedroom, dude?"

I shook my head as I looked between Travis and Jane. "I have to get home."

Looking for my keys, I spotted them on the table and grabbed them. Travis was right by my side as he pulled up his pants and yelled over his shoulder. "Thanks for the ride, baby!"

Jane laughed and said, "Anytime, cowboy!"

The front door couldn't open fast enough as I pushed it open and headed to my truck. "You fucked her?" I asked as I jumped into the truck.

"I guess a few times. Hell, I don't remember fucking her last night, but according to her, we fucked a few times. I was so fucked up I don't think my dick could've worked once, let alone multiple times."

I shook my head. "What about Crystal, you asshole?"

Travis jerked his head over and looked at me like I was insane. "You are seriously calling me out when you just walked out of some girl's bedroom? You fucking cheated on your wife, dude! Crystal and I broke up last week. That was the whole reason I needed to get away and wanted to come here."

My mouth fell open. "You broke up? Why?"

With a small shrug, Travis said, "She wanted to see other people."

My heart hurt for Travis. I knew he had fallen hard for Crystal. "Damn, dude. I'm sorry."

"It doesn't matter. All that matters is what happened last night between you and that blonde."

My hand pushed through my hair as I cursed under my breath.

"I don't remember. I don't remember anything after those last shots with Buck. All I know is I woke up fucking naked and some note from a girl named Amy was on the side table."

"Damn, dude. Fucking hell."

Tears began to build in my eyes as I hit the steering wheel. "I'd never cheat on her. I don't care how drunk I was. I love her. I fucking love her!" I shouted as I drove as fast as I could to the house.

"Dude, your phone is plugged in and on the floor down here," Travis said as he reached for it. "Shit, Brynlee called you a ton. There are a couple messages."

Travis hit play as he handed me the phone. The first message was Brynlee saying how sorry she was and something about needing to tell me something important. The next message was her begging me to come home. She had a doctor's appointment she wanted me to go to this morning.

My eyes glanced quickly over to the clock. "Fuck." It was almost noon.

Pulling into the driveway, I saw Melanie's car parked there. Throwing the truck into park, I jumped out of the truck and ran to the front door. Unlocking it, I tore through the house calling out Brynlee's name.

Travis and I made it into the kitchen when I rushed past him and into the master bedroom. I stood there for a few minutes trying to make sense out of what happened over the last twenty-four hours.

"Hey, Travis."

"Hey, Brynlee, Melanie."

Brynlee!

Running down the hall, I stopped dead in my tracks when I saw her. Her eyes were red and swollen and I wanted to kick the living shit out of myself for hurting her.

"Travis, I think we need to step outside to let Brynlee and Brody talk."

"Um, yeah, sure, Melanie."

My eyes darted over to Travis as he gave me a look of sympathy. When I looked back at Brynlee, she had tears in her eyes. "Where were you all night?"

My heart felt as if someone was twisting a knife into it as my breathing slowed. I made a promise to Brynlee I would never lie to her, no matter how bad the truth was. She deserved the truth.

"I don't know. I don't remember anything after doing shots with some guy named Buck."

Brynlee blinked back her tears. "Do you remember talking to me on the phone? When I was begging you to come home?"

My knees buckled and I stumbled, as I whispered, "No."

"Were you at the bar all night?" she softly asked.

I felt a tear slowly roll down my cheek as I shook my head no. "I, um … I woke up this morning in someone's bed."

A sob escaped through her lips as her hands covered her mouth. "Oh God, no."

Shaking my head, I took a step toward her as she backed away and held up her hand. "Don't. Don't come near me."

"Brynlee, I swear to God, I don't remember anything, but I know I would never hurt you."

Her lips trembled as she tried to talk. "Was there a girl in bed with you?"

Looking down, I said, "No, but I was naked and I was in a girl's room."

Brynlee broke down crying as I walked over to her and pulled her into my arms. "Baby, please don't cry. I swear to you I didn't do anything. I know it in my heart I could *never* do that to you. I love you!"

Brynlee buried her face into my chest and sobbed. Her hands came up and rested on my chest as she attempted to stop crying. She took in a shaky breath before pushing me as hard as she could.

"Get out."

"W-what?"

"Get out of this house and don't ever come back. I needed you today and you were sleeping in some whore's bed! Get. Out!"

Panic began setting in as my throat constricted and I fought to pull air in. "Brynlee, no. I swear to you, I didn't cheat on you."

Brynlee roughly wiped her tears away and laughed. "How do you know what you did, Brody? You don't even remember me begging you to come home! You fucking bastard. Get out of this house! I never want to see you again."

Falling to my knees, I cried as I begged her. "Please. Please don't do this. I love you, Brynlee. I love you and only you. I swear to God I would never hurt you."

The look in her eyes killed me. Disappointment along with hurt. "You hurt me when you walked out of this house yesterday."

"No, baby, I had no intentions of getting shitfaced. I swear I—"

"Just get out! Get out! Get out! Get out! Get the fuck out!" Brynlee screamed.

"No. I'm not leaving."

Brynlee glared at me as she slowly shook her head "I don't want you here. I don't even want to look at you. Get out!" Melanie and Travis came running back into the house. I dropped my head onto the floor and began crying. "Brynlee no. Please no don't do this. Baby, *please*."

"Travis, get him out! I never want to see him again. Take his ass back to Texas to rot!" Brynlee screamed as she cried.

Travis stood me up as I looked at Brynlee with pleading eyes. "I told you I would never leave you unless you told me you didn't love me. I'm not leaving."

Brynlee's eyes widened in horror as she swallowed hard. Tears streamed from her face again as she spoke the words I never in my life wanted to hear. "I don't love you, Brody. Please … just … leave."

Brynlee collapsed into Melanie's arms as I cried out her name.

The only thing I remember after Travis pulled me from the

house was sitting on an airplane. My father was waiting when we walked out of the airport. I had nothing with me. No clothes. Nothing.

"Dad, I didn't cheat on her."

My father had never looked at me the way he was looking at me now.

"Let's just get you home. You need sleep."

Turning to Travis, my father nodded. "Thanks for calling me, Travis. Let's give it a few days."

Travis looked between my father and me. "Right. I'll, um, I'll call you in a couple of days, Brody."

Lifting my hand, I mumbled a goodbye and followed my father to his Audi.

I spent the next four days in bed crying and feeling sorry for myself. I called Brynlee at least twenty times a day. She never returned my calls.

My life was over.

Without Brynlee, I didn't want to live.

Eleven

Brynlee

"*L*ife isn't fair."

If one more person said it to me, I was going to scream. I dropped my head back against the swing and sighed. The screen door creaked as it opened and I prayed like hell it wasn't one of my parents. There was no way I could take another lecture or pep talk from them. I was tired of talking.

"Want a glass of wine? I heard it cures all that's fucked up in your life."

Not moving my head, I smiled and let out a chuckle. "Tell me why you're not married again?"

Pulling my head forward, I watched as Melanie set the bottle of merlot on the table, along with two glasses.

Plopping down in the chair, my sister shrugged. "Someday my prince will come. He better have some plywood, a hammer, and some nails. And a huge dick."

With an incredulous stare, I slowly shook my head. "What? How do you even put plywood and nails in the same sentence as 'He has to have a huge dick'?"

Melanie's smile widened as she looked at me like I had just asked her the stupidest question ever. "First off, I need that back deck of mine fixed. And second, after he fixes it, he's going to fuck me until I can't move. In order for that to happen, he needs a huge dick. Not a big one, a *huge* one."

As I poured myself a glass of wine, I laughed. I loved my sister, but she was all things dicks.

"It's nice to hear that."

My eyes looked up to meet hers. "Hear what?"

"Your laugh. Dad would say it was the merlot."

My smile faded and thoughts of Brody swarmed my mind. Quickly looking back down at the wine, I took in a deep breath as I leaned back in the swing and took a sip. My heart physically hurt anytime I thought of him.

"Bryn, you need to talk to him."

The heaviness in my chest appeared for the hundredth time today as I attempted to hold back my tears. "I can't."

Melanie let out a frustrated moan. "Damn it. He needs to know what is going on."

Anger boiled in my blood as I quickly finished off my wine in one drink. I leaned forward and poured another glass as I asked, "Why? Why does he need to know what's going on? He cheated on me, Mel. Did you forget that? He wasn't there for me when I needed him the most."

"Maybe if you had told him what in the hell was going on, he would've been."

Wincing at her words, I swallowed hard. "Are you on his side?"

Melanie rolled her eyes. "Oh for fuck's sake. There are no sides here, Bryn. I love you, you're my sister and I will stand by you whatever you do, but I also know that I've never seen a man break

down before like he did. Travis said Brody hasn't gotten out of bed in three days."

I pulled my head back in surprise. "You've talked to Travis?"

"Yeah, he called to ask how you were doing."

Panic shot through my body. "You didn't tell him did you?"

"Calm down. No, I didn't tell him you have cancer. I wanted to, but I would never do that to you."

My phone buzzed and I saw Crystal's name scroll across. "It's Crystal."

"You haven't told her either?"

My chin trembled as I thought about the last few days. Everything was moving quickly and I wasn't sure what I was feeling. Scared. Angry. Frustrated at myself for keeping this from Brody. If I had only told him, he would have never gone out.

"You can cry, Bryn."

Pressing my lips together, my throat ached as I tried to hold back.

"Damn it, Brynlee. Let it out. Scream. Yell. Do something other than keep it in."

A single tear rolled down my cheek as my sister jumped up and ran into the house. Less than thirty seconds later, she was back on the porch and grabbing my hand. "Let's go."

"Where?" I asked as she pulled me toward our father's truck.

"You'll see."

I jumped into the truck and fought like hell to keep my emotions in. I had allowed myself to cry the first day. I wasn't sure if I was crying over Brody or the cancer. A combination of both, I'm sure.

Lost in my thoughts, I wasn't paying attention to where Melanie was going. When the truck came to a stop, I glanced out the window.

"The old windmill," I whispered.

"Get out of the truck and follow me," Melanie said with authority in her voice.

I did as she said, but my feet moved slowly. It felt as if I were

walking in mud as my heart and head argued back and forth.

Call him.

Don't call him.

Call him.

Don't call him.

It hadn't stopped in the almost four days he had been gone. The constant battle in my head and the endless doctor appointments were beginning to wear me down physically and emotionally. Today we decided on my treatment plan. A mastectomy. The pathology test result on the tumor would decide whether I would have to start chemotherapy.

I reached up and felt my long brown hair. I clutched my arms around my body and finally asked the question I was trying to avoid.

Why? Why me?

"This type of cancer is rare in women your age, but we found it in time."

Melanie stopped abruptly and turned to face me. "Let. It. Out."

I shook my head. "I don't know how."

Melanie's eyes softened as she took my hands in hers. With a slight squeeze she asked, "What do you think of cancer?"

My vision blurred and my body turned cold. "I hate it."

"Good. So do I. What are you going to do about this cancer?"

"Beat it."

Melanie's eyes pooled with tears. "Damn straight, you are. Who is going to help you fight it?"

A sob pushed from my pressed lips as I barely got the words out. "My family."

Melanie shook her head. "Who else?"

It was my turn to shake my head. "I'm angry."

"At who?"

"Brody. Myself. Cancer. God." Tears spilled down my face. "I'm so fucking angry!"

Melanie nodded. "Say it again, Bryn."

79

"I'm angry and I'm so scared, Mel. I'm so damn scared."

"Don't tell me, Brynlee."

When we were little, Melanie and I used to come to the old windmill. It was from when our great-grandfather started the vineyard. It overlooked the entire valley. When we were angry or upset, this was our thinking spot. Or as Melanie called it, "Our pissed-off-at-the-world spot." We would stand and look out over the valley and scream as loud as we could, casting our anger away. Melanie said it worked on anything—fear, anger, hate. All you had to do was scream and the wind carried your burden to God. She spent a lot of time up here after her divorce from Dean.

"I'm too mad at God to give him this," I whispered.

"He knows. But you have to, because you can't carry all this on your own. Tell him."

I slowly turned and faced the valley. As I looked out over our family's beloved vineyard, everything bubbled up to the surface. My hands clenched as I let it all come to life.

"Why did you do this to me?" I shouted. My pulse elevated and all I could hear was my heartbeat, pounding in my ears.

"I was happy! Why did you take that from me?" Closing my eyes, I planted my feet further apart. "Why … Why?" I screamed out as loud as I could. Then I just screamed. As loud and as hard as I could until my throat began to ache. Melanie wrapped her arms around me as I cried harder.

"I can't do this without him, Mel! Oh God … Brody, I need you! I don't want to die!"

My legs gave out as I slowly sank to the ground, taking my sister with me. I wasn't sure how long we sat up there, but once the sun started going down, I had a sensation of increased strength. I could feel God's presence within my soul. I was going to fight this and I was going to win.

"I told him I didn't love him."

Melanie was resting her chin on my shoulder as we watched the

sun slip behind the red and pink clouds.

"You didn't mean it."

A sick feeling moved into the pit of my stomach. "His face when I said it, Mel. He looked—destroyed."

"You have to call him."

The thickness in my throat grew, the sure sign I was holding back my onslaught of tears. "I will. I'll call him once I get through the mastectomy. I just … I just … he's gonna ask to come home, and I don't think I can forgive what he did to me."

Melanie began brushing her fingers through my hair as she whispered, "Shh. One thing at a time, baby sister. One day you will. I promise you. Just keep holding on, Bryn. Love has a way of healing."

My head dropped back against my sister as we sat and watched the sky change colors.

Just keep holding on…

Twelve

Brody

I walked into the kitchen to find my parents and Travis sitting at the table. Groaning, I shuffled over to the refrigerator and pulled it open. What I really wanted was something to erase my memory of the last week and a half. Me waking up in some woman's fucking bed naked. I knew in my heart I wouldn't ever cheat on Brynlee. I'd never hurt her.

Grabbing the orange juice, I headed over and grabbed a glass from the cabinet. The heat from their eyes staring at me was starting to piss me off.

Maybe I should call Jane. Ask to talk to this Amy. Fuck. What good would that do?

"It's good to see you finally got out of bed at a decent time," my mother remarked with a raised eyebrow.

My eyes darted between the three of them. My father shook his head, a look of disappointment washed over his face. "What are your

plans, son?"

I shrugged. "I have none."

"Well you better make some, and quick."

I took a drink of orange juice and chuckled. "What, are you going to kick me out, Dad?"

My mother stood. "Of course we would never do that, but Brody Gregory Miles, this is not how we raised you."

I let out a frustrated sigh while my hand pushed through my hair. "I know, Mom. But I'm telling you, I feel it in my heart. I didn't cheat on her."

The chair my father had been sitting in abruptly fell to the floor as my mother jumped. "Then do something!" he shouted.

"Like what, Dad? She told me to leave. She said she didn't love me anymore."

Travis shook his head as he folded his arms. "I call bullshit."

My head pulled back as I stared at him. "What?"

"Bullshit. You know damn well that Brynlee was hurt. She said the only thing she knew to say at that moment to get you to leave. That girl loves you. You can see it in her eyes."

I looked away as I pretended to kick something on the floor. "All I saw in her eyes was hate and disappointment."

"Then do something," my father said again with a huff. "Brody, you have to decide. Are you going to sit here and feel sorry for yourself, or are you going to get back on a damn plane and go fight for your marriage? I know I didn't raise a damn quitter."

I stood taller, the realization of the last few days hitting me like a brick wall. "No sir, you didn't."

Then a strange feeling moved over my body. Brynlee. Something was wrong. I felt it in my heart. She needed me.

Pushing off the counter, I walked over to Travis. "She had a doctor's appointment. Something's wrong."

Travis stood as something moved across his face. "Oh man. Son-of-a-bitch."

My mother reached over and slapped Travis on the back of the head. "Mr. Woodward, I don't think so."

"Sorry, Mom."

Travis has called my mother "Mom" since the first day I dragged him home so she could look at the bloody nose I gave him when he called me a sissy for not climbing a tree fast enough.

Swallowing hard, I asked, "What? What's wrong?"

Travis shook his head as if he was trying to get his thoughts together. "Melanie."

"What about her?" I asked as my pulse quickened.

"I called her the day we got back to make sure Brynlee was okay. She kept talking in code. I didn't understand what she was saying, but now that I think back on it, I think she was trying to tell me something."

I swallowed hard. "What? Jesus, spit it out!" I shouted as my mother glared at me.

"Um, she said something about Brynlee needing you now more than ever. That, um … shit, what was it she said?"

I wanted to walk up to Travis and shake him like a rag doll. "Travis, think! What did she say?"

Pushing his hands through his hair, he dragged them down his face and let out a frustrated moan.

"Oh! She said you needed to come back and stand by her side while she went through this. I figured she meant the whole thing with you cheating."

"I need to get back to California." I turned and quickly headed out of the kitchen, but not before looking back over my shoulder and shouting, "I didn't cheat on her!"

"First class, Travis? Those were the only seats you could get?"

With a shrug and smirk, he pulled out his phone and sent some-one a text. "Hey, you said get us on the next flight out and I did. If you want to bitch about the price, you should have booked it your-self."

Travis' head snapped up the moment he saw the flight attendant coming. "Gentlemen, is there anything I can get you to drink?"

He cleared his throat and leaned closer to her. "I know some-thing you can get me, but it's not a drink."

I rolled my eyes and waited for her to set him straight. She didn't. She smiled, licked her lips, and then purred, "We'll talk after the flight lands."

My mouth fell open. "How do you do that?"

"Do what? Attract women to me? I think they can sense I have a big dick."

My head dropped back against the headrest. "Oh Christ. Tell me again why you're coming with me?"

"Because you've missed the hell out of me. Because I pulled you off the floor of your house and dragged you out while you still had a shred of manhood left in you."

"Fuck you. You have no idea what I'm going through."

Travis sighed and looked at me. "Dude, I know. I'm giving you a hard time."

I attempted to give him a grin, but failed.

"I've been thinking," Travis said as he smiled at another girl walking back to her seat.

"Don't hurt your head."

"Seriously, Brody. I think you need to go back to what's her name's place and talk to the girl you, um, spent the night with."

"I didn't sleep with her. I believe it in the depths of my soul."

I could feel Travis' stare. Peeking over to him, he looked at me with a stunned expression on his face. "What the fuck is that? In the depths of your soul? Dude, that's deep shit right there."

Pushing out a frustrated breath, I sat up and looked for the flight attendant. "I wonder if it's too late to get your ass kicked off the plane."

"Ha ha. I'm being serious, Brody. One talk with that girl and this whole thing gets straightened out."

The hair on my body rose as I thought back to that morning. None of it made sense. Why was I naked if I hadn't slept with the girl? Maybe I thought it was Brynlee? Squeezing my eyes shut, I shook my head. "I'm afraid if I talk to her, she'll tell me the one thing I don't want to hear."

"So you'll go the rest of your life wondering if you cheated on your wife?"

My eyes caught Travis'. "I don't know, man. I really don't have a fucking clue about anything anymore. I'd like to just forget that night ever happened."

He sighed. "Well, I think you're doing the right thing by going back to California. Have you tried calling Brynlee today?"

My head turned as I looked out the small airplane window. "No. She's not responding to any of my voicemails."

"I *really* think you need to call her or text her, dude."

Glancing back over to Travis, I noticed he had a sense of urgency in his eyes. "Why? I'll be there in a few hours. She isn't bothering to listen to them, so what's another few hours."

"You don't know that. Text her, dude. Trust me."

The gruff laugh that crossed my lips was followed by this sarcastic response: "Like you know about relationships."

Travis' eyes filled with hurt as he narrowed his eye at me. "No, I don't. But I know you love her and she loves you. And if you've been going after her heavy each day, and then all of sudden she gets nothing from you, it's going to play with her head."

My stomach felt sick just thinking about this whole mess I got us into. "You're right."

Pulling out my phone, I sent Brynlee a text before the plane took off:

Hey, sweetheart. I miss you so much and wish you would call me back. It kills me knowing I hurt you. I love you so much.

My finger hovered over the send button for a few seconds before I pushed it. I set my phone to the side and closed my eyes.

"It's all going to work out, Brody."

My head lifted as I turned to my best friend. I wish I had his confidence. Something told me I wasn't going to just walk back into the picture and have Brynlee act like everything was okay. I was going to have to work at winning her trust back. There wasn't anything I wouldn't do to get her back.

"I hope you're right."

The flight attendants notified everyone that we would be pushing back from the gate any moment. I picked my phone up and stared at it, willing Brynlee to text me back. My heart sank while a feeling of dreadfulness passed over my body as I went to shut my phone off. The vibration of my phone caused me to hold my breath. Brynlee's name scrolled across the screen.

"Breathe, dude. The last thing I want is for my hot flight attendant to give your ass mouth-to-mouth when you pass out."

With a smile, I shoved the phone into Travis' face. "She texted back!"

Travis smiled and motioned toward the phone. "Read it."

I can't talk right now, but I'll call you tomorrow. I didn't mean it when I said I didn't love you, Brody. I just can't say it right now.

My body felt alive for the first time in days. She responded! I read her text again. At least she still loved me. I'd work at earning it all back. I texted back:

It's okay, baby. I'll say it enough for both of us.

Travis leaned back into the chair and let out a contented sigh. "I knew she didn't mean it when she said that."

The plane jerked as it backed up. I looked out the window and said a silent prayer that Brynlee wouldn't be upset to see me.

By the time the plane took off, I couldn't fight how tired I was. Closing my eyes, I drifted off to sleep and dreamt of the most beautiful girl in the world.

Thirteen

Brynlee

My hand shook as I read Brody's text message over and over.

Hey, sweetheart. I miss you so much and wish you would call me back. It kills me knowing I hurt you. I love you so much.

"You're going to burn a hole in your phone if you keep staring at it like that."

With a sigh, I set my phone on the side table. Today was my first round of chemotherapy, and I had to admit I was scared shitless. I loved my sister, but I wished more than anything it was Brody sitting next to me. The treatment plan changed and now we were doing chemo first and radiation to shrink the tumor, and then doing the double mastectomy.

"What are you reading?" I asked as I tilted my head to read the

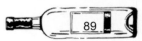

book my sister was holding.

Her face constricted as she turned it over and read the title out loud.

"*The Grocery Store and Single Men.*"

I couldn't help but chuckle.

"Hey, don't laugh at me. It says in here that single guys go to the grocery store at night, so guess where I'm going tonight?"

My head tilted as I raised my eyebrows. "Um, the grocery store?"

Melanie pointed to me and said, "Bingo. You need some food for the next few days."

"I'm staying with Mom and Dad."

Melanie dropped her book to her lap and sighed. "Bryn, you're going to have to go back to the house at some point."

With a shrug, I turned before she could see the threat of tears in my eyes. "He's everywhere in the house."

Melanie pulled her phone out and sent someone a text before pushing her phone back into her pocket and standing up.

"How are you feeling, sweetie?"

"Fine. The doctor said everyone responds differently, and it would be a few days before I saw any effects."

Melanie walked up and began twisting my ponytail with her fingers. "Do you remember when we were little and we used to have a crush on Brett Sumners?"

My face turned up in a smile. "I remember *you* having a crush on Brett. I didn't."

"Bullshit. You said he was hot in his football pants."

I rolled my eyes. "All guys are hot in football pants."

Melanie gave me a blank expression. "Not if they have no ass. A flat ass doesn't look good in football pants. Period."

With a wave of my hand, I brushed off the silly conversation as I glanced around the room. There were three other people all getting chemo treatments. "Why did you mention him?"

"Oh, no reason really. I happened to have run into him at the *grocery store* the other night. He owns a construction company. It was the perfect excuse to get him to come out to my place."

Melanie flopped down onto the chair across from me and grinned from ear to ear. "Uh, what was the perfect excuse?"

"Me remodeling my kitchen."

"You're remodeling the kitchen?"

An evil smile spread over my sister's face. "I am now that I saw Brett in his softball uniform and his ass looked better than ever."

"You whore," I whispered.

Melanie scrunched her nose up as she leaned forward and whispered back, "Hey, I'm tired of feeling like Snow White without the dick."

"Don't you mean *prince*?"

"Dick, prince, it's all the same thing."

The nurse walked into the room with a cheery smile. "Brynlee, you're about done and can leave soon. I'm sure you're ready to head home after sitting here for almost three hours."

With a polite smile, I nodded and said, "Yes, ma'am."

The thought of coming back in three weeks and doing this again should have turned my stomach. Being in the hospital with poison pumping into your body gives you time to think. I had let myself fall apart up at the windmill, but I had a new energy.

Cancer was getting ready to have me kick its ugly ass.

If only Brody were here …

"**M**elanie, why are you driving so fast? Are you trying to make me sick for Pete's sake?"

"Sorry! Shit, I'm sorry, Brynlee. Mom said she had some home-made soup ready for you. I think she's upset you didn't want her at

the hospital."

My head rested on the back of the seat as I inhaled a deep breath and slowly pushed it out. "Mel, you know she would have fussed over me, and she would have made me nervous with her busy energy. You're easy. You just read about how to meet guys."

Melanie laughed and then took my hand in hers. "Everyone loves you and cares about you, Bryn. That's all."

I lifted my head and looked at my sister. "I know. I'd be lost without you guys." My heart ached in my chest as I thought about Brody. My heart and head were in a constant battle. I wasn't sure anymore if I was more upset about Brody sleeping with some stranger or the cancer.

Pulling up to the gate, Melanie's phone went off. I glanced down and swore I saw Travis' name. Melanie quickly pulled it up and slowly pulled in a deep breath as she punched in the code for the gate.

"Where's your remote for the gate?" I mindlessly asked.

"Jacob lost it, I think. Little shit."

With a smile, I leaned my head back again and thought of my little nephew. He was a handful, and I wasn't sure how Melanie did it, but he brought such a joy to our family and I knew Melanie would be lost without him.

As Melanie drove down the driveway, she took my hand in hers again. "I want you to know something, Brynlee."

Keeping my eyes shut, I mumbled, "What's that?"

"Love is a powerful healer. Never forget that."

Smiling, I nodded and said, "So is laughter. Maybe I should have you cut my hair before it starts falling out. Everyone reacts differently. It could fall out in a few days or after the second or third treatment."

"Sure, Bryn, we can have fun with it. Maybe dye it purple or something."

The car came to a stop and I exhaled as I lifted my head. Before

I had a chance to say anything else about my hair, my breath hitched. Brody was standing there, staring at me. His face was laced with fear.

"B-Brody," I whispered.

Melanie squeezed my hand. "He came for you, Brynlee."

My head snapped over as I gave her a dazed look. "Did you know he was here?"

Melanie pressed her lips together and glanced back over to Brody.

"Melanie! How could you tell him?"

"I didn't tell him anything! Travis told me that Brody said he felt like something was wrong. He was worried about you and told his parents he was coming back to California to fight for you. Travis texted me and I told him you were staying here at Mom and Dad's. That's all."

My chest felt light as my stomach dipped.

He came back for me.

For us.

"Oh God. Did Mom and Dad tell him about the cancer?"

"No. That's your place to do that."

I glared at my sister as I pushed the car door open. "Don't you dare utter one word about where we've been."

"Brynlee, he's going to know something is up. You haven't slept in twenty-four hours. You look exhausted."

Ignoring my sister, I got out of the car and tried to put on a show for Brody. The moment his eyes locked onto mine, I knew that he knew something was wrong. My legs felt weak as I moved toward him.

"Please don't be mad that I'm here. I'm not giving up on us, Brynlee. I love you too much to just walk away from our marriage."

I blinked rapidly, trying to keep from crying. "I'm not sure I'm ready to just move on. You did the worst possible thing you could ever do to me."

He shook his head and wiped a tear from his face as I placed my hand over my stomach. I could see the regret pouring from his body. *I'm not ready to just move on and forgive. He needs to see how badly he hurt me.*

I'm so tired.

It was as if everything hit me all at once. I'd only been getting two to three hours of sleep a night since Brody left almost two weeks ago.

"I know I can't just walk back into your life and pretend like nothing is wrong. I realize I need to earn your trust and love back. I'll do whatever I have to do, Brynlee. If I have to be only your friend, that's what I'll be. I'm here for you, not only as the man who loves you, but also as your best friend." His eyes roamed over my body before looking back up to my face. "I see it in your eyes—something's wrong and I want to be by your side, sweetheart. Please let me make it up to you, Brynlee. Please."

Brody's words swirled around in my head as I fought to figure out how my heart was feeling. I didn't want to cry. I was done crying over the cancer and I was ready to hit it head on. Brody standing here telling me he was here for me brought another wave of emotions racing through my mind. I wanted to hate him for betraying our love, for sleeping with another woman. If I had the strength to hit him in the chest, I would have, but his eyes spoke of how much he loved me.

Best friend.

Brody was my best friend, if only I could push the pain of what happened from my heart. Everything started to go fuzzy as my legs wobbled. As I said Brody's name, everything went black.

Fourteen

Brody

Brynlee whispered my name then collapsed as Melanie called out her name. I was at her side and grabbing her before she hit the ground.

"Get her to her room," Melanie said as she rushed into the house.

My body felt alive with Brynlee in my arms as I carried her into the house. "Something is wrong with her. Melanie, what's happening?"

"You cheated on her, Brody. How was she supposed to act when you just show back up?"

Travis snapped his head over and looked at Melanie, "Melanie you said we should just—"

Holding up her hand, Melanie shook her head. "I know ... I know, Travis. It's just been a long day. I'm sorry, I know I told you to just come here."

Angelo and Catrina, Brynlee's parents, had already had a little talk to me privately after I showed up at their house. Angelo made it clear he was pissed as hell at me and wanted to knock my front teeth out. Catrina seemed a little more understanding. I still refused to believe I slept with another woman. I loved Brynlee too much to hurt her like that, yet I was scared to death to go back to Jane's place and ask Amy what exactly happened.

I was afraid of finding out a truth I didn't want to believe.

"Get her to her room. She was probably exhausted from not sleeping well and then with the—"

My eyes snapped over to Catrina. "With the what?" I asked as I gently laid Brynlee on her bed and sat down next to her, pushing her hair away from her face.

Brynlee's parents and Melanie all exchanged a look before looking back at me. Melanie cleared her throat. "Um, it's not our place to tell you, Brody."

My chest tightened as fear washed over my body. I knew something wasn't right. "She had a doctor's appointment she wanted me to go to," I said as I looked back down at Brynlee sleeping.

"She's sick?" I wasn't sure if I was asking them that or stating the obvious.

Melanie walked up to the side of the bed. Looking up at her, I was stunned to see tears in her eyes. "Yes, but that's all I can say. She needs to talk to you herself."

I squeezed my eyes shut. "I'm going to stay in here until she wakes up."

Angelo moved over to the other side of the bed and glared at me. "I meant what I said, Brody. I'm angry as hell with you, and it's taking everything out of me not to pound your face into the ground." Glancing down at Brynlee, he smiled weakly. "She needs you, so this is what you're going to do. You'll move into the original house on the property. My grandfather built it with his own two hands and it's stood strong ever since. But it needs a lot of work; we're thinking of doing a bed and breakfast and using that house. Starting to-morrow, you'll start helping me with the vineyard and then in the afternoons, you'll work on the main house. I'll pay you, you'll accept it, and you will be begin to fight for your marriage."

I swallowed hard. "Yes, sir. I'll do whatever you need, and the whole reason I'm here is to fight for our marriage. To make up for the mistake I made."

Angelo turned and looked at me. Sadness swept across his face as he said, "You're here for a lot more than that."

Without giving me a chance to respond, Angelo turned and headed out of the room, followed by Catrina, Melanie and Travis.

Brynlee started to stir as she stretched her arms and let out a soft moan. I had been sitting in the reading chair that was in corner of the room. When her eyes opened, she looked around and then smiled when she saw me. Reality must have set in seconds later because her smile rapidly faded.

As I stood, I stretched and made my way over to her. Sitting on the side of her bed, I placed my hand on the side of her face. She didn't pull away, which gave me a small glimmer of hope.

"Brynlee, please tell me what's going on. No one will tell me anything and I know you're sick."

Brynlee cleared her throat as she pushed herself up in the bed to sit up. "I'm so thirsty."

Jumping up, I held out my hands to keep her from moving. "I'll get it! Hold on!" I shouted as I practically ran out of her room and down the stairs. I slid to a stop in the kitchen and looked at Melanie and Travis sitting at the small table. I didn't have time to wonder what I ran in on when I saw them pull their hands away from each other.

"She's thirsty. I need water."

Melanie grinned at me as she stood and got a glass out and filled it with ice water. "I take it she just woke up."

Nodding, I took the glass and said, "Yep," as I turned and headed back to Brynlee.

Not wanting to spill the water, I slowed down but still took the stairs two at a time. Brynlee was walking out of the bathroom that was attached to her old bedroom when I came back into the room.

"Hey," I said as I smiled and walked up to her.

Her eyes looked so sad as she tried to give me a smile. "Hey," she whispered and then sat down on her bed with the water.

When I sat on the bed, she turned and faced me, sitting with her legs crossed. "I need you to know something."

"Okay," I said with a nervous nod.

"When I, um … when I told you to leave and that I didn't love you, I didn't mean it. I knew it was the only way to get you to leave. When you said earlier you needed to win my love back, well, I just wanted you to know that I didn't mean that. It doesn't mean I'm not angry and hurt though."

My body felt cold as I thought about how badly I had hurt the only woman I'd ever truly loved. "I know you are and you have every right to be. I fucked up so bad and I'm not sure if I'll ever be able to win your trust back or your forgiveness."

Something passed over Brynlee's face. "Life is too short to hold onto that. I forgive you, Brody, but I'm not sure I can forget just yet."

I attempted to swallow the lump in my throat as I took in her words. "Please just tell me we're not over, Brynlee, because I don't think I could ever live a day without you. These past two weeks have been fucking hell."

Brynlee let out a gruff laugh. "Tell me about it."

I reached for her hand and she pulled away, causing my stomach to recoil and an overwhelming fear to burn into my heart.

I blinked back the tears and tried to push the rejection away. "Will you tell me why you went to the doctor?"

Brynlee turned and looked out her bedroom window. With a deep breath, she slowly blew it out.

"I found a lump in my breast a month or so ago. I went in to the doctor and they did some tests. A mammogram and then a sonogram."

My breath caught in my throat for a few seconds before I found my voice. "W-why didn't you tell me?"

A tear rolled down Brynlee's face as she shrugged. "I didn't want to worry you with how stressed you had been at work. I didn't … I didn't realize how much you hated your job and life here."

Guilt flooded my body as I fought to keep from punching myself in the face. "I don't hate my life here, Brynlee. I didn't mean the words that were coming out in anger. I did hate my job, and I should have told you but, sweetheart, I would never want you to keep something like that from me."

Brynlee nodded and continued to look out the window as she talked. "In hindsight, I know it was so wrong of me to keep it from you. That day we fought, I was going to tell you and ask you to go with me to the doctor's appointment. I was going to find out if it was cancer or not. They had done a biopsy a few days before I found out."

Bile rose to my throat.

Cancer.

Please God no.

"W-what … what did they say?"

Brynlee turned and looked into my eyes. I had already known. Deep down inside I knew something was wrong with her. I felt it and that was part of the reason I rushed back to California.

She fought to keep her tears back as she lifted her shoulders and sat up straighter. As if making a statement before she spoke the words. "I have stage one breast cancer."

My head dropped and I silently began to cry as my body shook. I wasn't there for her. I wasn't there when she found out the worse possible news any person could ever hear.

Oh, God. Please forgive me.

"I'm so sorry I wasn't there for you," I cried as I buried my face in my hands.

No.

No, this is not about me. This is about Brynlee.

Everything her father had said to me earlier made sense. I quickly wiped my eyes and looked up at her. "I'm here now and I'm not leaving your side. I swear to you … I'm not leaving you ever again, and this time I don't care if you tell me you hate my guts."

A soft smile spread over Brynlee's face before it faded and she retreated back to looking out the window. "I started my first round of chemotherapy today. I have six rounds total. I go back every three weeks."

I wanted to pull her into my arms and hold her. I wanted to make love to her, kiss her, shower her with the love she deserved.

"Then what happens after that?"

"Radiation."

A tear slowly made its way down her cheek as she shook her head and wiped it away. "I chose to have a double mastectomy. I wanted to talk to you about it, but … but there were so many things I wanted to talk you about and I couldn't." Instead of holding her tears back, she let them fall and a part of me died watching them. "I'm so sorry I didn't tell you about the lump before, but damn it, Brody! I'm so mad at you right now!"

Brynlee sobbed as she looked at me with pleading eyes. I followed my instincts and got up, pulling her into my arms where she cried harder and hit my chest a few times.

"I'm so mad at you! I'm so damn mad at you!" she sobbed out as I held her tighter to me.

The lump in my throat and the pain in my chest kept me from

talking. Maybe I needed to be quiet and just let Brynlee get out what she needed to get out.

"I had to make all these decisions, and I couldn't talk to you about it because I pushed you into someone else's bed."

I pulled back and took her face within my hands as I frantically shook my head. "No. No you did not, Brynlee. I acted irresponsibly and made a decision that I will regret for the rest of my life. This is my fault, sweetheart, not yours. I'm the bastard who got shitfaced and doesn't remember anything. This is all on me, not you."

Brynlee's eyes searched my face as she fought to speak. "I'm not sure if we will move past this. I love you, Brody, but my heart hurts so bad and I'm so scared. I'm trying to be positive, but … I may never be able to have kids."

My knees buckled. "W-what?" I asked, my voice barely above a whisper.

Brynlee closed her eyes. "I'm throwing all of this at you at once and it isn't fair to you."

"Yes, it is. I'm the one who wasn't here for you and I want to know everything. I *need* to know."

My hands were still holding her face as I wiped my thumbs across her skin. "Because I'm younger, the chemo might cause me to become infertile." Our eyes locked as my heart beat loudly in my chest. "I have to take pills to help me from getting too sick, and…" Brynlee started crying harder. "I'm going to lose my hair."

My lips crashed to hers as she grabbed onto my arms and held on while I kissed her with everything I had. I knew it was wrong of me, but the fear in her voice was more than I could bear.

I needed her to feel my love. I needed her to know she was the only woman I would ever love. Pulling my lips away, I whispered, "Look into my eyes closely, sweetheart. There is nothing for me to hide. I love you and I'm here for you, mistakes and all. I would rather die than live a single moment without you in my life. Whether that means we move on as husband and wife or as best friends. I

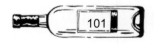

don't know. All I know is what my heart feels and I know there's no love like ours. Our love and your strength will pull us through all of this. I swear it."

Brynlee smiled, and for the first time since I woke up in that bed, I had a sense of hope.

Fifteen

Brynlee

A week had passed since Brody had come back from Texas. My father was working him like a dog and I knew what he was doing. I made a mental note to talk to him and tell him to take it easy on Brody.

As I sat on the back porch, I looked out over the vineyards. I loved it here. There was something about this place that warmed me through and through. My eyes caught sight of the truck Papai used for work on the vineyards. Leaning forward, I smiled when I saw it was Melanie and Travis.

Huh.

Interesting.

The truck pulled up and Melanie and Jacob jumped out. *Oh. Oh, this is super interesting.*

Smiling, Melanie walked up to the back porch as she told Jacob to run in and say hi to Grammy and Grandpa.

Jacob ran past me with a huge smile on his face. "Hey, Bryn-Bryn! Travis took me fishing! I caught dinner tonight."

"Wow!" I said as he pushed through the door and called out for my parents. Turning back slowly, I raised an eyebrow as I looked at my sister.

"You've been spending a lot of time with Travis this past week."

Melanie constricted her eyebrows and looked at me with a shocked expression. "No I haven't."

With a tilt of my head and that I-know-better look, I laughed. "Really? Okay, if you say so, but I thought I heard Travis telling *Papai* last night about how he was helping you with a broken faucet last night."

Melanie threw her head back and laughed. "Oh my gawd! Puhlease. That boy wouldn't know how to find his dick with a road map."

"That's not what I remember Crystal saying. Seems like Travis was pretty handy with his little guy."

A look of jealousy moved across my sister's face before it was replaced by a look of disgust. "I have no interest in Travis. None. He was nice enough to be there for me when I needed him, and he's great with Jacob, but that is as far as it goes. Besides, he has no one else to hang out with. Dad is working Brody into an early grave."

Ugh. I rolled my eyes and looked over to the original house that our great-grandfather built. It was about eight hundred feet from my parents' house. Brody and Travis were both staying there. When Brody was done helping my father around the vineyard, they came to eat dinner with us, and then he and Travis left to go work on the house.

"I need to talk to him about how hard he is working Brody."

Melanie laughed. "I'd say leave it be. You could be a widow right now if Dad had done what he originally wanted to do when he saw Brody."

My stomach dropped as I looked at my sister and carefully asked, "What did he want to do to him?"

"Let's just say Momma was making phone calls to people I don't think she normally talks to."

Raising my eyebrows, I asked, "What kind of people?"

Melanie lifted her hand and inspected her fingernails. "The kind that bury bodies after someone's been killed."

With a sharp intake of air, I dropped my mouth open. "You lie!"

Melanie cocked her head over at me and lifted her eyebrows. "Seriously? You think I'm lying?"

Looking out, I saw my father walking up with a scowl on his face. "Crap. I really need to talk to him about Brody."

"Yeah, you do. Travis said Brody has been falling asleep every night as soon as he sits down on the sofa."

Jacob came running out of the house. "Grammy says she needs help with dinner, Mommy."

Melanie moaned as she stood up and I followed. "Grandma said you relax, Bryn-Bryn." My eyes met my sister's as she laughed and shook her head. My mother had been treating me like a baby for the last week. I loved her and I knew she was just worried, but I was about to go insane if I had to sit at that table one more night and be waited on hand-and-foot.

My father walked onto the porch and said, "*Meu amor*, Brody is about to cause Lenard to blow. He argues with him about the grapes. I've thrown my hands up with that boy."

"What?" I asked with a confused expression.

Throwing his hands up in the air, my father shook his head. "Grapes! He thinks he wants to learn the business." He laughed like he couldn't believe his own words. "Brody wants to know all about the winery."

A smile spread across my face at the idea of Brody being interested in the winery. It slowly faded as I let the truth seep back into my memory.

With a knowing nod, my father headed into the house, but not before adding over his shoulder, "Head on down there and have him come for dinner before he drives the only decent wine master in California away."

With a chuckle, I nodded and made my way to the vat room, which contained six stainless steel vats used for fermentation.

As I walked up, I could hear Lenard arguing with Brody. I couldn't help but let a smile play across my face.

"You don't know shit about grapes!"

"I'm trying to understand, Lenard. You have zero patience," Brody huffed with frustration.

"Gah. Go and build something, and stay out of my way."

"Just tell me what it is you do when you taste the flavors? Is it just a gift or are you blowing smoke out of your ass?"

My hand covered my mouth as I tried to keep the laughter inside. Rounding the corner, I cleared my throat.

Lenard raised his hands and eyes upwards. "Ah, an angel has come to save me." Brody turned around and smiled the most beautiful smile. I hadn't seen that smile in a long time as his dimples were out full on. His eyes moved over my body, and for the first time in two months, my body felt alive.

"Hey," he said as he approached me.

"Hey. It's time for dinner."

Brody's eyes lit up. "It is time for dinner, yes."

Turning, he started walking in the opposite direction of the house and headed to the original house he was staying in. My heart dropped when I realized he wasn't eating with us. My mind quickly went in a thousand different directions as I tried to figure out why he wasn't eating with us tonight.

I wasn't sure what I expected from Brody. He was trying his best to be there for me without crossing any lines that I put up between us. As much as I wanted him with me, I was still confused about where we were going in our marriage. We had yet to talk any more about that night. It was the elephant in the room, and at some point it needed to be addressed.

Closing my eyes, I took in a deep breath and turned to head back to my parents' house.

"Brynlee," he called out.

Stopping, I turned to face him. He motioned with his hand for me to follow him. Chewing on my lip, I fell in step next to him. We walked side by side to the original house. "I'm sure my mother has dinner about ready if you want to head on up there."

"I'm eating at my place this evening."

My stomach clenched as my heart felt another small break. Was Brody going to start distancing himself from me? From the family? Maybe he wanted to keep this strictly a friendship and eating every night with my family was making that impossible?

"I can't wait to show you how much Travis and I have done in just the last few days to the kitchen. Your dad's going to be happy with it, I think."

I nodded and remained silent.

Brody opened the door to the old house and stepped aside for me. I walked in and quickly looked around as my breath caught in my throat.

A picnic was set up on the floor of the living room. My eyes widened in shock as I looked back at him. "What is this?"

Brody motioned with his hand to the blanket that was spread out on the old wood floor. A wicker basket sat in the middle, along with a bottle of wine.

"It's dinner. I figured you might need a break away from your mom this evening. Don't get me wrong, I love your mother, but anyone can see she is weighing on your last nerve."

"Yes. Yes, she is," I said with a giggle.

Brody placed his hand on my lower back and the familiar warmth spread through my body like a wildfire. There was a constant battle between my heart and my head. My heart was telling me

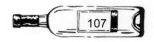

to just ask Brody to make love to me, and my head was telling me we needed to move slowly. I couldn't just forget everything that happened. Brody did the ultimate wrong when he slept with another woman, regardless if he remembered his actions or not.

"Smells like barbecue," I said as I inhaled deeply and dropped to the floor.

Brody's face beamed with excitement, which caused me to giggle. "I had a little something delivered especially for you."

When he opened up the basket, it revealed food from one of my favorite places back in Austin. Rudy's.

"Tell me there are baby back ribs in this basket," I said as I licked my lips.

Laughing, he nodded and said, "Yes ma'am." He nodded with a warm laugh. There's also brisket and creamed corn, and even a pickle in there."

My face blushed as a memory surfaced.

"You keep sucking on the pickle like that, and I'm going to take you right here on the table."

Giving a sexy, yet wicked, smile, I put my mouth completely over the pickle and moaned as I closed my eyes. "I can't help it. I love their pickles."

When I opened my eyes, Brody was staring at me with a wild look in his gaze. My heart started beating faster as I felt the pulse between my legs.

"Of course, I've always wanted to try public sex."

Brody leaned in over the table. "Really?"

As I nodded my head, I said, "Yep. You up for it?"

"Hell yeah I am."

My eyes quickly looked around Rudy's as I took everyone in.

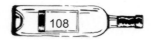

Damn it. A table full of cops was behind Brody and a family of six was to my right.

"We may get arrested if you keep looking at me like that with the fucking pickle near your mouth."

With a quick bite of the pickle, I winked as I giggled. "Next time."

"So how are you feeling?" Brody asked, pulling me from my memory. I was positive he knew where my mind had drifted by the way he moved about on the blanket.

"Okay. I was really tired yesterday."

"Yeah, Melanie said you slept a good portion of the day. That's good. Rest as often as you can, sweetheart."

My chest fluttered. I'd always loved how Brody called me sweetheart. When we were in bed, it was baby. It always made me feel special. *I wonder what he whispered to the girl he was with that night?* I prayed like hell he hadn't called her sweetheart.

Ugh. Stop this Brynlee. It does no one any good to have thoughts like this.

"Melanie said Dad's been working you pretty hard. I was going to talk to him about it tonight."

He smiled and gave me a wink. "Nah, I enjoy it. I've learned a lot already and find it all fascinating. So far, I think how they do the toasting of the barrels is the coolest thing yet. I think Angelo was getting tired of my questions earlier. Tomorrow he said he'd show me how the bottling line worked."

I leaned back on my hands and watched Brody talk while he took all the food out and set it up. I tried not to read too much into the excitement I heard in his voice, especially when he mentioned the barrels. With his degree in chemistry, I could see why he found it

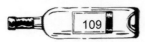

all fascinating.

"You sound like you're enjoying it."

Brody looked up from where he was scooping out creamed corn. "I am. I really am. It's different from anything I've ever done before. I'm fascinated by the science behind it all."

He handed me a plate filled with ribs, brisket, and corn. He then pulled out the wine and poured me a glass, then himself.

"Did he tell you the story behind why we still use barrels?"

Laughing, he nodded. "Yes. I think it's pretty awesome that that tradition is still so rich in this community. I'm a little more than pissed I missed out on the wine stomping last fall."

Taking a bite of my ribs, I closed my eyes and moaned. "Holy crap. This tastes so freaking good."

When I opened my lids, Brody was staring at me. Pulling his eyes off me, he looked down at his food. "I was thinking it might be kind of neat to do some kind of event that centers around the grape stomping. I mean, I know the machines do all the work now and y'all mainly do it just for tradition with your family, but think how neat it would be to make a whole weekend out of it."

I raised my eyebrows and looked at him. He really was interested in this. "A lot of vineyards hold some kind of grape stomping event. My parents' have talked about it, but just haven't wanted to take on that side of the business. That's where I come into play now that I'm here."

There was a sparkle in his eyes. "I'd love to help you figure it all out."

Butterflies danced in my stomach at the idea of Brody working alongside me here at the vineyard. Turning my attention back to my food, I nodded and said, "That would be fun."

"First though, I need to learn about grapes."

Laughing, I shook my head as I tilted it and gave him a questioning look. "Grapes?"

His dimples appeared and I fought like hell to keep my ass

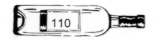

planted onto the blanket and not leap up and throw myself at him.

"Yep. Tonight is our first lesson of me learning more about the vineyard and winery."

The idea of spending alone time with Brody like this was bringing a new energy to me. There was a sense of ease between us, almost as if we were staring new, at the beginning.

"I like the sound of that, Mr. Miles."

Brody's smile faltered for one quick second before he nodded and asked, "Then it's a date?"

Smiling and feeling happy for the first time in a long time, I nodded. "It's a date."

Sixteen

Brody

After eating, Brynlee and I took a walk and ended up in the winery. "The process of fermenting the grapes is cool."

Grinning, Brynlee agreed. "Yeah, it's a neat process."

"What do they do with the skins of the grapes?"

"Dad has them throw it out to the deer on the other side of the vineyard. They love 'em!"

With a nod, I looked up at the giant steel tanks. Glancing back over to Brynlee, I winked. "So, I'm ready for my lesson."

Laughing, Brynlee looked at me. "Hmm, let's see. Where should I start? How about a quick history of wine?"

Smiling, I motioned for her to continue. "Well, I'm sure you know Jesus had wine at the Last Supper."

The small chuckle that burst from my chest felt good. "Yeah, that's pretty well known."

Brynlee laughed, and I could tell it felt good for her as well. "I

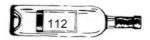

guess so. Well, the Jewish people have used wine for years. I know the oldest winery found has been dated back to 4100 BC. The Bible talks about wine in Genesis."

"Noah getting toasted after the flood and being up to no good."

Brynlee lifted her eyebrows. "Someone knows his Bible stories."

"Hard to forget when your Sunday school teacher does a whole cool lesson on the flood and the animals and the rainbow. Then throws in how Noah got drunk and showed his dick to his sons."

Brynlee's mouth dropped open as she slapped me on the chest. "Your Sunday school teacher did not say it like that!"

"She might as well have."

Shaking her head, Brynlee headed to the door that led down to the wine cellar. "The ancient Egyptians used it for ceremonial things."

"Okay, so I get it—wine has been around a long time. How did your family get into it?"

Brynlee's face lit up. "Port."

"Port?"

"Yep, it's a type of wine that became very popular in Portugal a few hundred years ago. My great, great, great ... um ... great-grandfather started a vineyard after England demanded more of the wine. Ever since then, wine has been a part of my father's family as well as my mother's."

"Really?"

Brynlee nodded her head. "My father tells the story so much better than I ever could. I've heard it for years, but honestly I half-heartedly listened to it."

As we walked toward the barrel cellar, I wanted so badly to take Brynlee's hand in mine. I followed her down the stairs as I fought the urge to beg her to forgive me.

Clearing my head, I focused on where we were headed. I had been down here a few times, but didn't really pay that much atten-

tion to anything. There were three rows of barrels lined up and down a room that was at least a hundred feet long.

A giant wall was built on one side that held hundreds of bottles of wine. Turning the corner, we came to another room that housed a mesquite table that fit at least twenty to thirty people.

"Wow. I don't ever remember seeing this room."

Brynlee smiled. "That's because it's new. I had the room remodeled and this is now called the library."

Narrowing my eyebrows in confusion, I asked, "The library? There are no books, Brynlee. It's all wine."

With a sweet laugh that caused a humming sensation throughout my body, Brynlee shook her head. "It's a wine reserve library. The plan is to begin tours of the winery. People will get to see how we make and produce wine by touring the tank room, the process of bottling the wine, why we still use oak barrels, how to read wine labels, and then finally they will come down here for taste testing. It will be for groups of twenty people or less."

The look of excitement on Brynlee's face was unbelievable. "So will you still do the taste testing upstairs in the main building?"

"Yep. Seven days a week except Thanksgiving, New Year's and Christmas day."

"I think that's a great idea, Brynlee."

"Thanks, I've been wanting to do something like this since I was in high school. I knew Daddy wouldn't go for it unless I was here to oversee it."

Her smile faded as thoughts of uncertainty filled her eyes. Smiling, I walked up to her and took her hands in mine. "It's going to be a huge success, sweetheart."

With a grin, Brynlee let out a breath. "So, the grapes. You have Zinfandel grapes, which are common here in California. It's sold as a pale-pink White Zinfandel. Lenard will tell you it has a warm berry flavor and a good sweetness to it."

I watched as Brynlee talked about the grapes as she walked to

different bottles of wine.

"Touriga Nacional. This is Portugal's most widely known grape and the vine my great-grandfather brought with him to America."

"The port wine?" I asked.

Brynlee nodded. "Yep."

"Then you have one of my favorites. Viognier."

"The Shiraz," I said as I wiggled my eyebrows. I knew it was one of Brynlee's favorite wines.

With a giggle, she nodded her head as she gave me the sweetest look. "Yes. I'm impressed."

I flashed her the smile I knew she loved so much, the one that first caught her eye.

Brynlee's mouth parted open as her eyes darted across my face. The electricity dancing in the air was unmistakable.

"I want to kiss you," I whispered as I closed my eyes.

"Open your eyes, Brody, and look at me."

My eyes snapped open as I looked deeply into Brynlee's eyes.

"I want more than anything for you to kiss me, but I'm afraid to open up to you again."

The stabbing in my chest was almost unbearable. "I swear to you, I'll never hurt you again."

"How do you know you won't? How do you know we won't fight again and you'll get drunk and ... and ..."

Tears spilled from her eyes.

Taking her face into my hands, I shook my head. "Brynlee, I will pay for my mistake for the rest of my life. We're gonna fight again, that's part of marriage. But I promise you I will never do what I did that night ever again."

Brynlee looked down as I kept her face secure in my hands. "Maybe we rushed into marriage. Maybe we should have lived to-gether or you should have moved to California first to see if you would like it here."

My heart dropped to my stomach. "No. Marrying you was the

best damn thing I've ever done. Brynlee, I love you." Bending down to look into her eyes, I silently pleaded with my gaze as I slowly whispered. "I. Love. You."

Her eyes caught mine as she looked up at me. "I love you too."

The need to kiss her was overwhelming.

"Brynlee? Brody? Are you two down here?"

I dropped my hands to my sides as Brynlee wiped her tears away. "Yeah, Mel. We're heading back up."

My heart couldn't have ached any more than it did that moment. Brynlee turned and moved toward the stairs as I slammed my fist against the brick wall and cursed under my breath.

I'm going to win her trust back. Losing her is not an option.

"**Y**ou did all this yourself, Brody?"

I pulled my head back and looked at Brynlee's father with a shocked expression. "Yes, Angelo, I did. Well, I had Travis' help with some of it."

Angelo looked around the kitchen as he nodded his head. "I'm impressed. You're very good with your hands and you have good taste."

I couldn't help but laugh. "I'll take that as a compliment."

"Do, I don't give them out often."

With a quick nod of my head, I followed Angelo out onto the back deck that overlooked the west side of the vineyard. My heart began to feel heavy as I looked out over the vineyard. It always made me think of Brynlee. "May I ask you something, Angelo?"

He didn't turn to face me as he stared off over the vineyard. "*Sim.*"

It was taking time, but I was slowly beginning to pick up some of the Portuguese language. I knew *sim* meant yes.

"Do you think love can overcome anything?"

Angelo nodded his head. "*Sim.* If the love is true and strong, *ele pode superar qualquer coisa.*"

Okay, I didn't have a damn clue what he said. "What did you say, sir?"

"If the love is true and strong, it can overcome anything."

The small rock on the deck caught my eye as I kicked it. "I see it in her eyes. She hasn't forgiven me and I'm not sure she'll ever be able to."

Angelo turned to face me. "It's only been a little while. Forgiveness takes time." He took three steps closer to me and placed his hand on my shoulder. "*Seja paciente,* Brody. Be patient. I see the regret weighs heavy in your eyes."

The weight in my chest only grew. I was trying to be patient and I knew I needed to let Brynlee come to me on her terms.

I would stand by her side as her best friend and pray that her father was right and that our love would overcome everything that had been thrown at us.

Seventeen

Brynlee

Melanie stood in front of me and smiled as I looked at myself in the mirror. The next day was my second chemo treatment and the doctor said my hair would start falling out probably after the second or third treatment.

"Pink or purple, Bryn?"

Chewing on the corner of my lip, a slight chill ran through my body at the idea of my hair falling out. This was silly. It was just hair. It would grow back.

Glancing sideways at my mother, I shrugged. "Pink?"

She nodded her head and said, "Streaks. Pink streaks."

Melanie started to laugh as she said, "Hell yes! Mom knows the way to go!"

A chuckle escaped from my lips as I nodded. "Okay. Cut it just to my chin in a bob and let's do pink streaks throughout."

Melanie picked up the scissors and looked at me in the mirror. I

saw it in her eyes, even though she didn't vocalize it. She was just as scared as I was, but we stayed positive. That was the only way I was going to get through it.

"Here we go!" Melanie exclaimed as she moved the scissors to my hair, and I held my breath while my mother started filming. My brown hair was down to the middle of my back. I'd worn it long since I could remember.

Change is good. Change is healing.

The front door flew open and Brody practically fell into Melanie's living room. We all turned and looked at him. He was trying to catch his breath as he held his hand up as if asking us to wait until he caught his breath.

"Didn't. Want. To. Miss. This."

My posture instantly relaxed as I took in a deep breath and slowly let it out.

Brody was here.

I became hyper-aware of how my body felt as he looked at me with so much love and concern in his eyes. My stomach fluttered as my pulse began to race.

As he looked around before he brought his eyes back to mine and smiled. "I wanted to be here when you cut it. What did you decide to do?"

Those dimples. That smile. His voice. The idea that he wanted to be here pulled hard at my heartstrings.

With a grin, I looked up at Melanie. "Cutting it to my chin and then putting in some pink."

Brody laughed and sat down across the room as my mother kept filming. "I love it. You're going to look beautiful, sweetheart."

My smile faded as I looked back into the mirror. I use to love it when Brody called me sweetheart. Now when he said it I couldn't help but picture him whispering it to some other girl.

"Ready?" Melanie asked, pulling me from my thoughts.

"Yeah," I whispered as I tried to push the thoughts of Brody

cheating on me away. Glancing over at him, I couldn't help but grin. He was wringing his hands together. It was a nervous habit he had. "Want to dye it?" I asked Brody as Melanie stopped cutting.

"Hell yeah, I do!" he said with a smile from ear to ear.

"What? You can't have him dye it. Are you insane?"

With a shrug of my shoulders, I asked, "Why not?"

"He doesn't know what he's doing. He will screw it up, Bryn."

I laughed and shook my head. "It's gonna fall out anyway."

Brody tried not to let the look of sadness pass over his face, but he failed. Quickly pushing it away, he stood up and clapped his hands together. "I can do it! How hard can it be?"

Glancing up to Melanie through the mirror, I saw her shooting daggers at Brody. "It's harder than it looks, prickface."

"Melanie, watch your language!" my mother said with a giggle.

"Prickface? That's all you got, Mel?"

"Oh trust me, I have a lot more for you. Would you like me to go down the list of names Brynlee and I came up for you?"

"Melanie!"

"Girls, stop arguing and let's do this."

Jacob came running out of his room and right up to Brody. "Brody! Do you have a bone in your pee-pee like Travis and me?"

My mother, Melanie, and I all shouted, "Jacob!"

With a laugh, he ran back into his room as Brody shook his head and laughed.

"Let's do this!" I said with a smile.

Ten minutes later, my hair was at my chin as I stared at myself in the mirror. "You look so much younger," Melanie said as she squeezed my shoulder.

It wasn't so bad, I thought as I looked at my much shorter hair.

"Looks beautiful," Brody said as he walked up to Melanie. "Let's dye it now!"

Melanie rolled her eyes as she walked into the kitchen. "Do me a favor prickface, dry her hair."

I glared at Melanie. "Mel, stop calling Brody that."

Brody picked up the hairdryer and stuck his tongue out at Melanie. "Oh, really mature, Brody."

Brody turned the dryer on and began running his fingers through my hair as I attempted to hold back the moan I wanted to let slip through my lips. My mother was still filming, so I didn't want it to be caught on camera how Brody's touch was affecting me.

"Brody, I can dry it."

"Nonsense, I want to do this, sweetheart."

Ugh.

Pushing out a frustrated sigh, I looked down and let him dry my hair as my mother said she needed a minute to run to the restroom.

My hair was so short it didn't take long to dry. Brody turned the dyer off and smiled as he looked at me in the mirror. "It's so wavy."

"I guess 'cause it's so much lighter it makes it wavy."

His hand moved through my hair again as he whispered, "I like it this short."

My voice cracked as I nodded and said, "Me too."

Our eyes met as we stared at each other, lost in the moment. Neither one of us was really sure what to say to the other.

Brody opened his mouth to talk when Melanie came back into the room. "Okay. Here we go. Are you sure you want Brody to do this, Bryn?"

Nodding and giving Brody a wink, I said, "Yep. Let's see what he's got."

Melanie began to show Brody what to do as he slowly began taking pieces of my hair and brushing on the dye. My heart was pounding and I wasn't sure what I was supposed to be feeling. I knew I had the right attitude to fight cancer, but I was so confused by how I should be feeling about Brody. I needed to focus on fighting the cancer, but all I was focused on was my feelings toward Brody. One minute I was angry with him and the next minute I craved his touch and fought the urge to beg him to kiss me and hold

me in his arms.

After sitting there for a few minutes, Melanie led me go over to the sink, where she washed out the dye. Thirty minutes later she turned me around and I looked into the mirror. My hair looked adorable as streaks of pink curls framed my face. Melanie had curled my hair, claiming it had to be styled.

Smiling, I bit down on my lip and said, "I love it!"

"Me too!" my mother and Melanie said at once.

Turning around, I came face to face with Brody. "It looks beautiful, sweetheart."

My smile dropped and I balled my fist. "Stop calling me that."

It was as if the entire feel of the room changed as Brody's smile dropped and he tilted his head at me with a confused expression.

"What?" he asked as Melanie took a step closer to me.

"Stop calling me sweetheart. Every time you say it, it makes my skin crawl."

"Brynlee," Melanie whispered as she walked up to me.

"I ... I didn't realize you didn't like me to call you that, sweet—"

I shook my head. "Ugh. Damn it! Just stop it, Brody."

A look of hurt washed over his face as I felt a sense of satisfaction. It hurt my heart to know I was glad that my words hurt him.

"Don't ever call me that again."

As I walked to the door, Brody took me by the arm. "Why are you taking this out on me?"

"Brody, why don't you head on back to your place. I think Brynlee's had a long day."

With a quick move, I jerked my arm from his hands. "Why am I taking this out on you? Why is everything always about you? You fucked her, Brody, and you probably whispered that stupid word in her ear!" Placing my hands on his chest, I pushed him as hard as I could, a stream of tears falling down my cheeks. "Please don't call me that again."

Brody stood taller and didn't move. Not even when my mother and Melanie told him to leave. He slowly shook his head as he walked up to me and lifted me up into his arms. Burying my face into his chest, I cried harder.

The moment Brody started walking toward the door, I felt at ease. I knew it was because I was in his arms. "I'm going to bring her back up to the house."

Everything faded away. My sister and mother's voice slowly faded as I grabbed tighter onto Brody's shirt. His smell invaded my senses as I cried harder. I wasn't angry with Brody. I was angry with the situation we were in. Angry that I couldn't move past the mistake Brody made that night.

I was angry with cancer. I hated it. I wanted to beat it into the ground and stomp on it until I had no more energy to move.

The sound of Brody's heart beating slowly relaxed me. My eyes opened when I felt Brody putting me into bed. When he lifted the covers over my body, I reached out for him.

"Don't leave me. Please don't leave me."

Brody looked at me with an uncertain look on his face. "But I thought..."

I tried to wipe away the wetness from my cheeks but the tears wouldn't stop. "I feel like I'm hanging on by a thread. I need you, Brody."

He quickly walked around the bed and climbed in. It wasn't lost on me that he stayed completely dressed.

"We're going to fight this together, Brynlee. Our love is strong enough to overcome all of this, and you're going to trust me again."

A sob escaped my lips. "Don't let go of me. Please don't let go."

Brody wrapped his arms around me and pulled me to him as I felt the heat from his body spread over me like a warm blanket.

"I love you, sweetheart."

My body completely relaxed as everything faded away. Every-

thing except for the feel of Brody's body next to mine.

"I love you too," I barely whispered as exhaustion claimed my body.

Eighteen

Brody

Brynlee reclined in the oversized chair with her legs crossed reading a book as I sat across from her. I couldn't help but watch the chemo as it slowly entered her body. I tried to push the sick feeling from my stomach but I couldn't. Melanie sat next to Brynlee as she typed away on her laptop, working on the books for the vineyard.

She must have sensed my eyes on her because she lifted her head and looked at me. With a grin, I nodded to her. "Are you bored yet?"

Shaking my head, I forced the words from my throat. "Never."

With a quick wink, she went back to reading.

The past week had been both blissful and awful. Brynlee telling me not to call her sweetheart gutted me to the core, but each night she couldn't fall asleep unless I was holding her in my arms. I'd force myself to stay awake until she drifted off. Once I knew she was

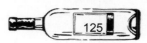

sleeping, I would get up and head back to my place. The walk to the original house every night gave me plenty of time to think and get my head together. I needed to know the truth and the only way I could find that out was to go see Amy. The girl whose bed I woke up in that fucked-up morning I changed my marriage forever.

The nurse walked into the room as we all looked up at her and smiled. "You're almost finished, Brynlee. How are you feeling?"

"Okay."

"Are you nauseous at all?"

She shook her head. "No, not yet anyway."

The nurse smiled as she turned to me. "You have a very brave and strong wife, Mr. Miles."

With a grin, I nodded and said, "I know I do. She amazes me every single day."

The look on Brynlee's face said it all for me. For the first time in weeks, I saw something spark in her eyes that had been missing.

Two days had passed since Brynlee's second chemo treatment. She was sleeping on the sofa when I walked into the living room. I'd been helping Angelo all day as we built new cabinets for the master bathroom in the original house.

The house had been added on to twice over the years. It was now a three-bedroom, three-bathroom house. I was slowly falling in love with it and hated the idea of Angelo and Catrina renting it out as a bed and breakfast. Every night I walked over the old wooden floors and wondered if the walls could speak, what they would say.

"She's been so tired today. Barely able to keep her eyes open."

"I'll bring her up to bed," I said as I glanced over to the clock on the mantel that read nine.

Catrina placed her hand on my arm. "Brody, eat something.

You've been working yourself too hard. You didn't come for dinner and I know you must be hungry."

"I'm fine, Catrina. I made a tuna fish sandwich earlier." I said as I smiled and gave her a light pat on the hand.

Snarling her lip, she made a tsk sound and rolled her eyes. "That's not food. That's junk!"

"Thank you for caring." I said with a chuckle as I kissed her forehead. "Let me take care of your daughter, and I'll come back down for something to take back to the house with me."

Sadness filled her eyes as she shook her head. "You leave every night and go back to that house all alone. *É tão triste.* My heart hurts for you both."

"It makes me sad too, Catrina."

Lifting her eyebrows, she smiled, and pointed to me with her index finger. "Someone has been studying his Portuguese."

A small chuckle escaped my lips as I nodded my head and then held up the t-shirt and sweatpants I was holding in my hands. "The water is turned off in the house. Would you mind if I took a quick shower in Brynlee's bathroom?"

"Brody, this house is your home. You don't have to ask permission to use the shower," she said with a wave of her hand.

Another kiss on the forehead and a thank you in Portuguese to my sweet mother-in-law, and I walked over toward the love of my life.

I scooped Brynlee up and carried her up the stairs to her room. She woke up and changed into her pajamas as I took a shower in her bathroom.

A small knock on the bathroom door had my heart beating harder in my chest. "Yeah?" I called out.

"I'm waiting for you."

Smiling, I felt a lightness in my chest. "All right, I'll hurry, sweet—. Um, I'll be out in a few minutes."

Ten minutes later, I was walking out of the bathroom and into

Brynlee's childhood bedroom. Smiling, I looked at her sitting up in the chair with her head bobbing around.

I dropped my dirty clothes onto the floor and walked over to her. "Baby, let's get you into bed."

Brynlee slowly stood up and let me guide her over to the bed. "Don't leave me, Brody."

My stomach lurched as I thought about how she never said anything about me getting up and leaving every night. "I won't. Let's get you under the covers."

As I pulled the covers over Brynlee, she reached for my hand. "Don't leave at all. I need to be in your arms when I wake up."

"I promise I won't leave," I said as I pushed a strand of her pink hair behind her ear.

A smile spread across her beautiful face as she let out a contented sigh. When I pulled my hand back, I sucked in a breath as I looked down into my hand.

Pink strands of hair.

My eyes closed as I said a prayer to God that Brynlee was ready for this next step in her fight against cancer. Turning on my heels, I reached down and grabbed my phone out of my jeans.

> **Me:** *Her hair is starting to fall out.*
> **Travis:** *Fuck.*
> **Me:** *Travis, I'm freaking the fuck out dude.*
> **Travis:** *Do it away from her. She needs you.*

My face constricted as I forced the tears to stay back as I stood in the middle of the bedroom, listening to Brynlee's soft breaths as she slept.

> **Me:** *I know. It just sucks.*
> **Travis:** *I know dude. I know.*
> **Me:** *I'll call you tomorrow. Later.*

Travis: *Later dude.*

My hands shook as I pulled up a message for Melanie.

Me: *Her hair is starting to fall out.*
Bitch-sister-in-law: *Fuck. Is she okay?*
Me: *I don't think she knows. I pushed a piece of hair away from her face and some of it came out.*
Bitch-sister-in-law: *Brody, don't leave her tonight.*

A single tear finally got free as it rolled down my face. I'd never felt so helpless as I did in that very moment.

Me: *I won't.*

I slid the button up on the side of my phone and silenced it as I walked around the bed and set the phone on the side table. With a soft fluid movement, I slipped under the covers and pulled Brynlee against my body.

"Brody," she whispered as I squeezed my eyes shut and fought like hell not to cry.

I fucking hate you, cancer.

I hate you so much.

Nineteen

Brynlee

T he sounds of the birds singing outside caused my eyes to open. Brody had stayed last night. My heart felt as if it was about to leap from my chest.

He stayed.

I attempted to roll over without waking him up, as I turned to face him. With a smile, I lightly ran my finger along his strong jawline. The pull of his lips was strong as I stared at them. My lips tingled as I remembered what the feel of his kisses were like. I slowly rolled onto my back and sat up. As I turned to get out of bed something pink caught my eye.

The moment I realized what it was, I started crying. The next thing I knew, Brody was sitting next to me, pulling me into his arms as I silently cried into his chest.

No words were spoken between us. It was part of the process. Part of the fight and it wouldn't take me down. That didn't mean it

didn't hurt. It hurt like hell. I didn't give a crap about my hair; it would grow back. I worried about what Brody would think. Would he still look at me with lust in his eyes if I were bald? Would he still want me if a part of me were missing?

Brody pulled back and dropped down in front of me as he took my hands in his.

"Look at me, Brynlee."

His eyes pierced mine. "This is not a defining moment in this fight. Cancer is not going to win."

I nodded my head as I whispered, "I know."

"You're so fucking beautiful."

I needed to feel his lips on mine. I needed to feel his love. I dropped down onto my knees as Brody cupped my face within his hands. "So beautiful."

"Kiss me."

The moment his lips touched mine, a new energy surged through my body. I wrapped my arms around his neck and we quickly got lost in the kiss. It was slow and passionate. Not rushed and crazy like so many of our kisses in the past had been.

The love I felt pouring from his body into mine caused goosebumps to break out over my skin.

When both our lungs desperately needed air, Brody pulled his lips away slightly. "I'll love you forever."

A sob escaped from my lips as I said the only thing my voice would let me say, "Love me."

Brody slowly stood up, hauling me up with him. His eyes never left mine. His lips kissed me gently along my face as I lifted my head to give him access to my neck.

His one hand dropped to his side as it slowly moved to my lower back and pulled my body closer to his. His hard length was pressed into my stomach as I moaned and Brody crashed his lips to mine again.

After another mind-blowing kiss, Brody took a step back. I

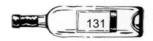

knew what he was doing was the right thing to do, and I also knew it had to have been hard for him not to make love to me when I had just asked him to. I loved him for knowing that when we finally decided to make love, it needed to be about us and not about the cancer.

Brody swallowed hard then cleared his throat. "I'm going to go make you breakfast."

With a nod, I gave him a knowing look. "Okay."

Quickly walking into the bathroom, Brody turned on the water. I knew he was splashing his face and getting himself together. My hands went to my stomach as I tried to calm the mixed feelings I was experiencing.

For five minutes, there was no cancer.

No cheating.

My fingers grazed across my lips. It was love flowing between our bodies.

It was beautiful.

It was healing.

The sound of the buzzer caused me to jump as my stomach flipped.

"Ready?"

Glancing up to Melanie, I nodded and smiled. "Ready as I'll ever be."

Melanie walked around to stand behind me. We had a chair in the middle of my parents' kitchen as I sat waiting for my sister to shave off my hair.

After waking up this morning and seeing my hair on the pillow, I decided to just shave it all off. Melanie had bought three different wigs that were sitting on the counter.

Brody stood to my left as my parents stood to the right. Jacob

stood directly in front of me with one of the wigs now on his head. It was the shoulder length brown wig. It looked exactly like my real hair.

I couldn't help but laugh when he pushed it over his shoulder with his hand and mumbled something about Travis wearing one too.

"Here we go," Melanie said as she ran the shaver over my scalp.

Seeing the brown and pink hair fall to the floor on my own terms was freeing. A weight was lifted off my shoulders and I laughed. The more it fell to the floor, the more I knew in my heart I was going to beat this.

I was going to win back my life.

Brody walked up to me and took my hand. I hadn't even realized Melanie had finished. Pulling me up, he placed his hand on the side of my face as I leaned my head into it. "You're my everything."

Tingles raced over my body as Brody gazed into my eyes. It might take us a while to get back to who we were, but I knew we would.

"Promise me?"

Brody's breathing increased as he fought to hold back his tears. "With every breath in my body."

Reaching up on my toes, I brushed my lips across his as he pulled me in closer and deepened the kiss.

"Gross! Bryn-Bryn and Brody are kissing!" Jacob spun around and started jumping. "Mommy, I want my hair shaved too!"

The room erupted in laughter as Melanie walked over and hit her iPod that was in the docking center. Music started playing as Jacob started jumping. "Let's dance!"

"Shake" by Victoria Justice started playing as Melanie grabbed Jacob and began dancing with him. Turning, I looked as my father and mother started to dance.

Brody took me in his arms and said, "Dance with me, Brynlee."

Giving him a grin, I said, "I'd rather you call me sweetheart."

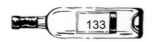

His eyes lit up as he showed me those dimples I loved so much. He spun me around as I broke out in laughter.

"Get your shake on, *Papai!*" Melanie called out as my mother and father cut loose like I'd never seen before.

Brody pulled me into his arms and kissed me quickly before spinning me back out. I'd never felt so free in my life. In this moment with my family, everything was perfect.

Jacob jumped up on the table and began shaking his little bottom as Melanie yelled out, "Shake what your momma gave you, baby boy!"

Brody sung the words as he started dancing with my mother. My heart literally felt as if it was soaring as I watched him. My father walked up and held his hand out for me as I walked into his arms and we danced.

After the song stopped playing, Jacob began clapping as I raised my hands to my face. My cheeks were sore from smiling so big. Brody winked at me and mouthed, *You've got this.*

I nodded as I pressed my lips together.

We were going to be okay. For the first time since this hell began, I knew deep in my heart and soul, we were going to be okay.

Twenty

Brody

S tanding next to one of the stainless steel fermentation vessels, I asked Michael, the other winemaker at Santos vineyard, another question.

"How do you taste the wine and know what you're tasting?"

Michael was a patient man, thank goodness. With a shrug, he said, "A gift maybe."

"Huh. So when the new oak barrels come in, what is the process to get them ready for the wine?"

Michael checked something off his list and began talking. "Have you seen them putting the steam into the new barrels?" He looked up and lifted his brow. "Why do you think they do this, Brody?"

After thinking about it for a few seconds, I said, "They're dried out after the toasting. You have to get them wet again or I would imagine the wine would soak right through the wood."

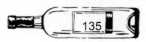

The grin that spread across his face made me smile. "That's exactly right. Follow me."

Michael headed down to the wine cellar as I followed. He walked down the room a few feet, looking for a particular bottle of wine. "Ah, here it is."

With a flick of his hand, he motioned for me to follow him into the other room. Stopping at a table, he pulled a drawer open and took out a bottle opener.

The pop from the cork echoed throughout the library as Michael poured two glasses of a white wine. He picked up a glass and handed it to me.

"Close your eyes, Brody."

Doing as he said, I closed my eyes.

"Bring it up and smell it deeply. Let it in and study it."

I did as he said. It was that familiar smell I got every night when Angelo opened a bottle of wine at dinner.

"Taste it, but taste it with your palate. Not your mind."

I opened my eyes as I brought my eyebrows in together tightly. "Not my mind?"

"Trust me. Close your eyes and drink."

With a forceful push of air out of my lungs, I took a sip and let it rest in my mouth for a few moments before I swallowed it.

"Tell me what you taste."

I could hear the smile in Michael's voice. He loved his job, that much was clear.

Swallowing, I kept my eyes closed. "I taste vanilla. It's a dry wine. I, um, I taste peaches with a slight taste of pears maybe."

The room was dead silent. Opening my eyes, I looked at Michael, who stood there staring at me. "Have you done taste tests with Angelo?"

"Um, no. I mean, I've drunk plenty of wine with him before." I laughed nervously, not really sure how to read the look Michael was giving me.

Michael nodded slowly. "That was a Chenin Blanc. Stay here."

My eyes widened in surprise as Michael quickly headed back into the barrel room and grabbed another bottle of wine.

"Turn away from me, young Brody."

With a shrug of my shoulders, I did as he asked.

First, came the pop of the cork and then, the chug of the wine being poured into the glass.

Michael walked around and stood in front of me. Lifting his eyebrow, he simply said, "Drink and tell me what you taste."

My hand reached out for the glass as I smiled and said, "Okay, boss man." Closing my eyes, I took a drink and let the wine sit for a few seconds in my mouth before swallowing it.

With a huge grin, I said, "Ahh, I've had this wine a lot. First thing I taste is fruit followed quickly by an espresso taste for sure, and then a slight hint of chocolate. Like a dark chocolate though."

"Avete il regalo!"

My eyes sprung open as I watched Michael dance around the table speaking in Italian. "I knew it the moment I met you. *Avete il regalo*!!"

You couldn't help but laugh at his excitement. "Michael, what in the hell are you saying?"

Michael grabbed me by the arms and kissed one cheek and then the other. I still wasn't used to the ways of these old-school Europeans.

"Brody, you have the gift. *Avete il regalo."*

Talk about being confused. Michael kissed both cheeks again as he laughed and said something else in Italian.

"I don't even want to know why this dude has already kissed you four times."

My head turned to see Travis standing in the doorway shaking his head with a look of pure disappointment on his face. "I know it's been awhile dude, it has for me, too, but this—"

Motioning with his hand between Michael and me, Travis shook

his head.

"Michael is the winemaker here at the vineyards. He was having me tell him what I tasted in the wine."

"He is a natural! Brody, we must start your training right away."

"What?" Travis and I both asked at once.

Michael started speaking in Italian again as he headed for the stairs. "This is wonderful! This is amazing. *Avete il regalo!*"

Travis and I stood at the bottom of the stairs and watched Michael head up laughing and speaking between English and Italian.

"What in the fuck did you do to him down here?"

My head snapped over to Travis. "I didn't do anything but taste some wine."

Travis shook his head and added, "And kiss him."

"I didn't kiss him. *He* kissed *me*. On the cheeks!" Throwing my hands up in frustration, I bumped Travis as I headed up the stairs. "Besides, that's what they do when they're happy."

"Uh-huh."

"No, I mean excited."

"That ain't any better, dude. You should have stuck with happy."

I moaned in frustration as I headed outside and toward my place. "Son-of-a-bitch. You haven't even been here ten minutes and I already want to punch the fuck out of you."

Travis laughed. "I guess I shouldn't tell you I accepted a job in Santa Rosa then."

I came to a halt and turned to face my best friend. "What?"

With a shrug of his shoulders, Travis grinned. "I missed you. Sue me."

Pulling Travis in, I hugged him and patted his back hard and fast before pushing him away and hitting him on the arm. "Dude, that is the best news I've heard in a long time."

Travis tried not to smile as he said, "Just don't kiss me, asshole."

"Well, well, well. If it isn't the king of manwhores. What are you doing here?"

Melanie walked up and smirked at Travis as she tried to act like his presence sickened her. In all honesty, I don't think I'd ever seen Melanie's eyes light up like they were when she stared at Travis.

Glancing back over to Travis, I was stunned to see he had the same damn look in his eyes.

"Well, if it isn't the Wicked Witch of the West. Good to see you too, Melanie."

With a roll of her eyes, she bumped his shoulder as she walked past him and called over her shoulder, "Please tell me this is quick stopover on your way to Hell."

Travis laughed. "If Santa Rosa is hell, I'm almost home."

Melanie stopped walking and spun around, her mouth practically to the ground. "W-what?"

Travis walked over to her and pulled her into his arms, as she was stunned into silence. "That's right, baby. I'm moving here."

"No," Melanie whispered.

"Oh yes."

"Fuck."

Travis lifted his eyebrow and said, "I'm down for it if you are."

Melanie quickly came back to her senses as she pushed Travis away and then slapped him. "Ugh!"

She took two steps backwards and then turned and starting mumbling every curse word known to man.

Travis laughed as he headed back over to me. "Damn, this is gonna be fun living here in good ole California."

"Wow!" Travis said as he walked into the house. "It looks great. You've done a lot, Brody."

With a smile and push of my hand through my hair, I nodded as I looked around. "So you're really here to stay?"

"You bet I am. I figured there was really nothing in Texas for me. I really love it here and could totally see me making a life here. Hey, your mom said they are still planning on coming out to visit. They want to see Brynlee something terrible."

I sighed. "Yeah, I know they do. Katherine is still planning on coming too."

"I'm sure Brynlee will be excited to see them. Speaking of Brynlee. How are things going?"

"Slow, but that's good. She's been through a lot the last few weeks. We had a few setbacks, but I think the healing between us is going pretty damn good."

Travis smiled. "Be patient."

"Ha! That is what everyone keeps telling me. I'm trying to be patient, trying to be strong, trying to be positive. All I really want is to reverse the clock and change all of this."

Travis nodded and placed his hand on my shoulder. With a slight squeeze, he gave me a sympathetic look. "Nothing worth having ever came easy. The fight will be worth it in the long run. I promise."

With a smile and a nod of agreement, I said, "California has already made you smarter."

Travis threw his head back and laughed. "Come on, let's open a bottle of wine and catch up."

I wasn't going to admit it to Travis, but having him here meant the world to me. He was more than my best friend. He was my brother and I would never forget what he had done for me.

My mind drifted to Brynlee as I popped open a bottle of wine. For the next few hours, Travis and I talked on the back porch.

Twenty-One

Brynlee

Three Months Later...

I sat at the table and ran my finger along the rim of the glass as I watched Brody talking to Minnie Zello. He was smiling politely as she talked his ear off.

Melanie sat down next to me and bumped my shoulder. "He's just being polite talking to her."

With a fake smile, I nodded. "I know."

Melanie pulled her phone out and smiled as she looked at a picture the babysitter had sent her of Jacob.

"There is nothing more I hate than sitting at these benefit dinners."

I lifted the corner of my mouth and nodded. "I agree, but you know how special this is for Momma and Papai. Plus, we're hosting it this year here and we probably should be walking around doing the whole hostess thing."

Melanie chuckled. "To hell with that. I've been hit on by at least six different guys who wouldn't be able to find their dicks even with a GPS tracking device. I'm pretty sure Dad had something to do with at least three of them approaching me with that look in their eyes."

A smile slowly built as I asked, "Why do you say that?"

Melanie took a sip of wine. "'Cause two of them cut right to the chase, telling me how I'd been single long enough and something about them being able to fulfill the hole in my life."

I busted out laughing. "Seriously? They said that to you?"

Melanie nodded. "Yep," she said as she popped her p. "How are you feeling, Bryn?"

The thin glass that held my ice water hit my lips as I took a drink and set it back down. "I feel good. I'm glad the chemo treatments are over and we're onto the next step."

Melanie looked at me as if she was trying to read my answer. "The radiation making you sick or tired?"

Pushing my lips out and looking up as if I was thinking, I shook my head and said, "Nope, not yet."

"Good. You're almost done, baby sister."

I let out a gruff laugh. "A couple more hurdles."

Melanie took my hand in hers. "I know, sweetie. I know. But you are rocking that wig if I do say so myself." Removing her hand, she reached for her glass of wine and drank it in one drink.

"What about you, Mel? How are you doing?"

Melanie let out a fake laugh. "I'm about as good as I can be. My vajayjay has been neglected for far too long." Turning to look at me, her face became serious. "Do you know I passed a giant dildo on the side of the road getting onto the highway? Just when you think you've seen it all."

My hand covered my mouth as I giggled. "Maybe it's a sign."

With a lift of her eyebrows, Melanie flashed me a dirty look. "A sign, huh? What kind of sign?"

"Oh I don't know, a sign that your dry spell is about to be over."

I motioned with my head over to where Travis was standing.

Melanie's eyes looked over my shoulder as she busted out laughing. "Travis? You think I'm about to start something with Travis?"

The energy around my sister changed the moment she looked at Travis.

"You guys hooked up once before. Why not Travis?"

"Because the boy can't do anything right. He practically needed me to hold his dick for him while he fucked me."

My mouth dropped open as I felt a sick feeling wash over me. "Gross. I didn't need that visual."

Melanie smiled. "Actually, the boy is good with his parts."

"Oh yeah?" I asked as I lifted my brows with a look that told her I wanted to know more. "Do tell."

My sister blushed, which was not something I was used to see-ing. "He's fun to talk to, Bryn. That's all. We were both lonely and let things get out of hand. It's not ever going to happen again. He has too much of a roaming eye."

I tilted my head and stared at my sister. "Not when he was with my friend, Crystal. He was very faithful. Speaking of Crystal, you get to meet her."

Melanie snapped her head and shot me a dirty look. "What?"

I was slightly taken aback by Melanie's reaction. "Um, yeah, she's coming to visit me in a few days."

Something passed over my sister's face, but I wasn't sure how to read it. Motioning to one of the waiters, Melanie took another glass of wine as she asked, "Does Travis know?"

"I'm not sure. I mentioned it to Brody yesterday after my treat-ment. I fell asleep almost right after that so I can't remember if he said he'd let Travis know or not."

Brett Sumners walked by and smiled at Melanie and then me. "Evening, ladies."

With a polite smile back to him, I stole a peek at my sister. Her

posture straightened as she slowly stood up. Looking down at me she said, "I think I'll go see if I can break this dry spell for my vajayjay. Later, little sis."

I rolled my eyes and shook my head as I watched Melanie walk up to Brett. One quick look over to where Travis had been standing and talking, and I couldn't help but notice how he was eyeing Brett like he wanted to pound his face in.

The hair on my neck stood when I felt Brody's warm breath on my neck. "Hey, beautiful."

My entire body came to life with just the sound of his voice. Closing my eyes, I savored the feeling. After weeks of chemo and now radiation, having something affect my body like this was something I relished.

Dropping my head back, I grinned wide as I looked up into his green eyes. Brody had been amazing the last three months. Never leaving my side and going to every appointment with me. He took me on picnics, we went for long walks, and he immersed himself deeper into the winery, where he sucked up as much about it as he possible could.

I thought back to one of the long walks as I felt my chest get lighter.

"So the wine is aged in the oak barrels for how long?"

"Around eighteen months," I said as I let the cool evening breeze hit my face.

"And you have to top off the wine in the barrels."

I nodded my head. "Yep, that's why you see the barrels stained like they are."

"So freaking interesting."

With a smile, I glanced over to Brody. "Then you bottle it and

bottle-age it."

Brody reached down for my hand as we walked side by side in silence before Brody stopped and turned me to face him. "I think your father may never let me near that process. I touched one thing and it broke."

With a giggle I shook my head. "Don't kid yourself. Papai loves how interested you are. So do I."

Brody's eyes lit up. "It's a part of you and that makes me love it even more."

My heart skipped a beat as my stomach fluttered. I knew he meant what he said.

A part of me wondered if this was just him trying to make up for the cheating and all the hurtful things that were said. The other part of me saw the true passion of knowledge in his eyes.

"All these beautiful lights twinkling, the music playing, and you're sitting here drinking water."

The lights reflected in Brody's eyes as I stood and let him lead me out to the little makeshift dance floor. My parents had transformed our house and the winery to feel as if you were stepping back in time. I imagined if you were to go back in time to the days when my family started in the wine business, this was what it would feel like.

Brody took my hand in his has he gently pressed his lips to the back of my hand. My heartbeat quickened as every nerve ending in my body tingled. "Tell me what you're thinking."

I let out a soft sigh and smiled. "Portugal."

"Portugal?"

"Yeah, the ambience of how everything looks makes me think of Portugal and maybe my great-grandparents throwing a party back

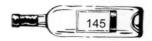

in their home country. Can you imagine how much simpler times were back then?"

Brody smiled and held up his finger. "Don't move. Wait right here."

I watched as he walked quickly over to the DJ. The left corner of my mouth rose into a smile as I wondered what he was up to. Giving the DJ a thumbs up, he made his way back over to me.

Stopping in front of me, Brody gave me that smile that had been melting my heart since the very first time he flashed it my way. Those dimples, oh my, I had missed seeing them every night and every morning.

My body jumped when Brody reached down and took my hands into his. "Dance with me, sweetheart."

My heart leapt into my throat as I struggled to find my voice. My lips parted slightly as my eyes stared into his.

"There isn't any music."

Brody lifted an eyebrow and right then the music began playing. Tears built in my eyes as I realized what song it was. With a soft tug, Brody pulled me against his body as I listened to Lady Antebellum's "Can't Take My Eyes Off You" while we slowly danced.

As I pressed my lips tightly together, I fought to keep from crying as the words of the song filled my head.

Brody placed his hand on my lower back and brought me in closer to him. The rest of the world disappeared and it was just the two of us. Pulling my head back, I gazed into his eyes. His thumb gently wiped my tears away as he looked at me with so much love.

"You're so beautiful. I love you so much."

A sob pushed past my lips as my throat tightened as my voice cracked. "Brody, I want to leave."

You couldn't mistake the look in his eyes as his mouth parted open. I was positive it matched my own. Lifting me into his arms, Brody carried me as he made his way away from everyone and started toward the original house.

Burying my head into his chest, I attempted to calm my heartbeat down. I wanted this. I needed this.

It was time to move on and put the past where it belonged.

In the past.

Twenty-Two

Brody

My heart was pounding in my chest as I carried Brynlee into the house and shut the door. We didn't say a word to anyone as we walked away and headed to the home I had been staying in and remodeling. Brynlee's face had been buried in my chest the entire time, neither one of us uttering a single word.

"Brynlee, you have to talk to me."

Lifting her eyes to mine, she smiled and my knees wobbled. "I miss my husband's touch."

Swallowing hard, I closed my eyes and let the tears fall. I didn't deserve this amazing woman.

My eyes opened to see Brynlee crying as well. I slowly set her down and cupped her face within my hands. My thumbs moved across her soft skin and wiped away the tears.

"Tell me what you want me to do. I'll do whatever you want, sweetheart."

"Make love to me. Please."

With a quick lick of my lips, I kissed her softly. This needed to be slow. I wanted to give her the attention she deserved. The love I was dying to give her.

Picking her up again, I made our way through the house and to the master bedroom. I carefully set her down as I captured her lips again and reached around her back. My hands were shaking as I tried to unzip her dress.

I never stopped kissing her as I slowly pushed the dress from her body. The dress fell and pooled at her feet. Brynlee wrapped her arms around my neck as she deepened our kiss. Her body trembled as I placed my hands on her back and softly moved them up her back to her bra. One quick move and the lacy piece of lingerie fell to the floor. I knew she had to have been sensitive, so I tried like hell to be careful.

My lips moved to her jaw as she dropped her head back. I placed gentle kisses along her neck as I moved further down. Soft kisses were placed above her breasts as her body shook from crying.

I dropped to my knees and placed my hands on her hips and kept kissing her body. My lips pressed against her flat stomach as I hooked my fingers in her lace panties and pulled them slowly off.

Her crying about killed me as I looked up at her. Her head was dropped back with her hand covering her mouth. Squeezing my eyes shut, I kissed along her hips as her other hand laced through my hair.

Brynlee stepped out of her panties as I tossed them to the side and then stood back up.

Tears were streaming down her face as I shook my head, fighting like hell to keep my own at bay. Reaching up, I took her wig off and set it down on the chair next to us. Taking her face in my hands, I kissed her tear-soaked face over and over.

"B-Brody," she whispered as I walked her slowly back toward the bed.

"I love you. You're my entire world, sweetheart."

Brynlee grabbed onto my arms and smiled. "I love you too. So much."

I unbuttoned my shirt and tossed it to the floor as I watched her suck her lip between her teeth. I was breathless as I looked into her eyes.

"I'm nervous," she whispered as her chest heaved with each labored breath.

Giving her a smile, I lifted her hand to my mouth and brushed my lips against her soft skin. "Me too."

Brynlee giggled and it warmed my body. My breath hitched when she began to take off my pants. With one push, they fell to the ground, and I was trying like hell to get my shoes off and kick them away.

"Lie down, baby."

Brynlee's mouth parted open as she sat on the bed and moved back until she was lying down. Her breathing was labored as she took in one deep breath after another.

"Don't touch them, Brody."

My eyes looked down to her breasts before looking back up into her eyes.

She was biting down on her lip so hard it was turning white. "They … I won't have them … and I'm not sure how I feel right now."

"Don't think, Brynlee. Relax for me, baby."

Taking her hands and pushing them above her head, I kissed along the top of her breasts. I wasn't sure if she was sore anywhere from the radiation and I didn't want to hurt her.

My lips moved up her neck while my knee nudged her legs apart. Dropping my hold on her hands, I positioned myself over her, keeping my weight off of her as I slowly pushed into her body.

When Brynlee moaned as she arched her back, I died and went to heaven.

My eyes rolled to the back of my head as I moved ever so slow-

ly in and out of her. "You're where I belong. You've always been where I belong," I whispered as I looked deep into her eyes.

Brynlee's hazel eyes burned with passion as she lightly ran her fingers across my back.

"I've missed you so much," she whispered.

My lips moved across her neck as we totally lost ourselves in each other. I never wanted the moment to end. To be buried deep inside my wife was the most amazing feeling in the world.

The burning in my chest was beyond my control. While I made love to Brynlee, I prayed a silent prayer.

Please don't take her from me.

Please.

Brynlee lay sleeping in my arms as I stared up at the ceiling. So many emotions were running through me I didn't know how to sort them out. The idea that she forgave me was more than I could bear. The guilt would always live deep within me. All the nights I tossed and turned thinking about Brynlee and praying she would believe in our love again would never be forgotten.

Closing my eyes, I tried to push away the fear bubbling up. I had prayed so hard each night that God wouldn't take her from me.

"What are you thinking about?" she asked as I opened my eyes and gazed down at my beautiful wife.

"That forever could never be enough time."

Resting her chin on my chest, Brynlee lifted her eyes. "Enough time for what?"

"For me to love you."

Her eyes pooled with tears as we locked eyes. "I'm going to beat the cancer. Do you know why?"

"Tell me."

With a smile that had my stomach flipping, she simply said, "Because you and I have so much to do still. We're just getting started."

The love that flowed from her body into mine left me speechless as my desire to be closer to her overwhelmed me. I moved Brynlee until she was flat on her back as I hovered over her. "Are you too tired, sweetheart?"

With a wicked smile on her face, Brynlee shook her head and said, "No. And this time, don't be so gentle. I'm not going to break."

With a grin spreading across my face, I thrusted into her and made love to her until I could no longer hold back. Pouring myself into her for the second time tonight, Brynlee wrapped her arms around me weakly and called out my name as I buried my face into her neck and cried while reality flooded my heart like a storm.

Twenty-Three

Brynlee

"Oh. My. God."

Melanie stopped dead in her tracks as Jacob ran around the kitchen island saying something about going fishing with grandpa.

I had been leaning against the counter drinking a cup of tea when Melanie and Jacob came into the kitchen. Brody would be picking me up to take me to my radiation treatment soon.

"What's wrong?" I asked with a confused expression on my face.

Melanie's eyes widened in surprise as she pointed to me. "You had sex!"

My mouth fell open as I shook my head. "What? Do you have some kind of sex detector?"

"Who had sex?" Travis asked as he walked into the house.

"Well hello, Travis. Just make yourself at home, why don't

you?" Melanie said as she softly shoved him, causing him to lose his balance for a brief moment.

"Your dad invited me to go fishing with him and told me just to walk in, if you need to know, bitch face."

Melanie's eyes widened as she placed her hands on her hips and slowly shook her head. "Oh … oh, you want to see a bitch face? I'll show you one, you son-of-a-bitch!"

"Travis!" Jacob called out as he ran back into the kitchen.

Travis beamed as he squatted down and opened his arms just in time for my little nephew to run into them. "Hey there buddy. Whatcha up to?"

"Going fishin' with my grandpa!"

Travis smiled bigger. "Me too!"

Jacob fist pumped. "Yes!" Then took off running to find my father.

I stole a peek over at Melanie. She tried not to let the exchange between Travis and Jacob get to her, but I knew it did.

"Morning y'all!" Brody said as he walked into the kitchen. My stomach danced with butterflies as Brody winked at me.

"Holy shit," Travis said as he looked between Brody and me.

Brody walked up to me and stood directly in front of me. His eyes searched my face before they landed on my lips. I ran my tongue along the top and then bottom of my lips as I watched Brody's mouth part open.

"Y'all had sex. Finally—it's about fucking time!" Travis said as Melanie started laughing.

"I said the same thing!"

Brody rolled his eyes as he leaned closer to me and kissed me softly, yet quickly. "You ready?"

Fatigue rolled over my body as I nodded and said, "Yeah."

I set the cup in the sink and turned to face Melanie and Travis again. "I guess I'll see ya later."

Melanie walked up to me and placed her hands on my upper

arms. "If you're not too tired, we could go out to dinner tonight. Just you and me. Girls' night."

My heart felt as if it was going to burst. "I love you, Mel."

Tilting her head, Melanie pursed her lips together to keep her emotions in check. "I love you too, babe. Now go kick cancer's ass."

"**Are** you sure you feel up to this, Bryn? Brody said you feel asleep in the car and then slept the rest of the afternoon."

I laced my arm through Melanie's as we walked down Main Street. "Yes, I'm sure. I'm tired, but I want to spend some time with you."

As we walked along the street, I took in a deep breath. Fall was in the air and I couldn't wait for the grape stomp festival that Brody and I had been planning.

"So ... you and Brody, huh?"

My cheeks warmed as I looked away while Melanie started laughing.

"Why are you blushing? He's your husband for Pete's sake."

"I know. It's just everything we've been through the last few months. It almost felt like my first time all over again."

Melanie smiled as she pressed her lips together. "Wow. He must have a magical cock to make you blush like that."

"Oh my gosh! Melanie, do you really have to talk about my husband like that?"

Melanie shrugged her shoulders and said, "All I'm saying is the boy is gonna be needing some Gatorade to make up for all that lost time."

Melanie and I fell into a laughing fit as we walked into the restaurant.

Stopping at the hostess station, Melanie smiled at the blonde and

said, "My sister Brynlee and I are needing a table for two."

The hostess looked at me with a stunned look on her face. "Oh my gosh, Brynlee Miles?"

I nodded my head as I looked at her. "Yes. Have we met?"

The blonde laughed and said, "Oh, no, I'm sorry—we've never met. Your husband told me all about you. I'm so glad I finally get to meet you. You're so lucky to have a husband love you as much as Brody does. He talked so much about you in his drunken state it was cute."

My smile faded as I reached out to hold myself up. *Oh God. Oh God. Oh God.*

Melanie must have caught on to who this girl was as well. "I'm sorry, how do you know my husband?" I asked as my voice cracked. Melanie grabbed my hand.

"Oh, I'm sorry. I'm Amy."

She said it like I should have known who she was. Putting a face and name to the woman who Brody slept with made me sick to my stomach.

"Brody talked nonstop about you. It was nice to hear a guy talk about his wife like that. I had just left my husband, he cheated on me and Jane said I could stay with her while I got back on my feet."

Melanie squeezed my hand tighter as my throat felt like it was closing. This Amy girl just kept talking like nothing at all was wrong.

"They were all so drunk when Brody and Travis came home with Jane. After Jane and Travis went into Jane's room, Brody told me about your fight. I've never seen a guy cry before." Amy chuckled as I continued to stare at her in disbelief. "He felt so terrible and I tried to see if he wanted me to call you, but he got sick and started throwing up. I helped him to my bathroom and the next thing I knew he was passed out on my bed. I tried to find his phone to call you, but he didn't have it on him."

My eyes widened more as Melanie and I both said at once,

"Wait ... what?"

"You didn't sleep with him?" I blurted out.

Amy looked between us with a confused expression that quickly turned to a stunned one. "What? No, my God, no! I slept on the sofa, and then left him a note telling him I had to leave for work. When I returned, both he and Travis were gone, and I figured you two had made up and he headed home. I ... I didn't think twice about it."

Melanie grabbed Amy by the arm and called over her shoulder, "Chuck, it's important that I talk to your hostess!"

Chuck lifted his hand went back to talking to some guy at the bar.

"Brynlee! Come on!" Melanie shouted, and pulled me out of my stupor.

Once we got outside the restaurant, Melanie turned to Amy. "Let's cut to the chase. Did you sleep with Brody?"

Amy looked horrified as she took a step back and covered her mouth. Dropping her hands, she said, "No! I would never sleep with a married man. I'd just left my husband for cheating." She turned and looked at me. "Oh my God. Did Brody think that we slept to-gether?"

I swallowed hard. "He, um, he couldn't remember anything about that night and said he woke up in your bed naked."

Amy shook her head and said, "I swear to you that nothing hap-pened. The man couldn't stop talking about how much he loved you! I'm almost positive if I had made a move on him no matter how drunk he was, he wouldn't have done anything."

Melanie waved her hands around and said, "Wait. Travis said Jane saw Brody come out of your room. Jane knew Brody thought he cheated. Why wouldn't she say anything to you or ask you?"

Amy looked so confused I almost felt sorry for her. Looking at Melanie and then me she said, "Jane did ask me. The moment I walked into the door from work she practically attacked me, asking if I had slept with Brody. I told her nothing happened and that he

passed out and I slept on the sofa. The pillow and blanket were still on the sofa when I pointed to it and showed her where I had slept."

Melanie looked at me. "That bitch. She knew the truth all along and never said anything. I knew she had the hots for Brody."

Amy reached out for my hand. "Please believe me, nothing happened. The only reason I knew who you were was because Brody talked so much about you and your name is so different. I swear, nothing happened."

My head was spinning as my heart pounded against my chest wall. All those times Brody swore to me he would never do something like that. "Brynlee, why didn't Brody just come talk to me? I could have cleared this up months ago."

I was at a loss for words as I absentmindedly shook my head. "I … I don't know. I guess with the cancer and everything he—" I looked into her eyes as they filled with horror.

Amy covered her mouth. It was then her eyes moved up and she must have noticed I was wearing a wig. "I knew I recognized you. I work at the hospital too, Brynlee. I'm so very sorry."

"Oh my God." The reality of what was happening hit me like a brick wall as my body began to shake. "He didn't cheat on me?"

A tear rolled down Amy's cheek as she took my hands in hers. "No, honey. That man loves you so very much. He was destroyed that night about the fight you both had. He most certainly did not cheat on you. I'm so sorry you've both gone through so much pain. Had I known he thought that I would have cleared it up. I'm so sorry."

Amy pulled me into her arms and held me while I cried tears of joy for the first time in months.

Melanie let out a frustrated sigh as she said, "I'm going to kick Jane's ass."

Twenty-Four

Brody

Angelo walked around the house as he took everything in. Every now and then he would nod his head and mumble something under his breath.

Glancing over to Travis standing in the kitchen, I lifted my eyebrows as if saying I had no idea what Angelo thought of all the work we had done on the old house.

After walking through the whole house, Angelo stopped in the middle of the living room and stared at the fireplace as he took in a deep breath and blew it out.

"This house holds many memories. *Memorias bonitas.*"

With a smile, I nodded my head. "I can only imagine the memories shared in this house."

Angelo turned to face me as he slapped his hands together and smiled. "Then it is done."

My heart slowly ached at the idea of taking this old house and

turning it into a bed and breakfast. Travis sighed as he walked up to me and placed his hand on my shoulder. "This was fun, remodeling this place. We should do it again."

Angelo lifted an eyebrow and nodded his head in agreement as he pointed to Travis. "I like the way he thinks."

I looked at Travis and said, "Yeah. That might be something fun to do." Turning back to Angelo, I tried to swallow the lump in my throat. This house had become a part of who I was. My own memories were made in this house over the last four months. From a picnic in the living room, or Brynlee sitting on the floor watching me paint the rooms, to making love to her last night, I had laid claim on the house and hadn't even realized it.

Angelo reached into his pocket and pulled out a picture. When he handed it to me, I sucked in a breath. It was a picture of Brynlee and me sitting on the back porch. We were both laughing and I knew exactly what we were laughing at.

"I had just stepped into a gallon of paint." I looked up from the picture and asked Angelo, "Who took this picture?"

"Melanie took it while she was out taking some publicity shots for the winery and saw the two of you. She snapped a few photos and showed me this one. Do you see it?"

With a frown, I looked at him with confusion. "See what?"

"The love. The love between you and my Brynlee is unmistakable."

My fingers ran lightly over the picture as I looked at her smile. There was no doubt about it—she looked happy in the picture.

The words barely came from my lips. "I see it."

Angelo walked up to me and lifted my hand. Pressing an object into my palm, he smiled the warmest smile I'd ever seen. "I see it too, *meu filho*. Now it's your turn to make *memorias bonitas* with your family."

Opening my hand, I sucked in a breath as I looked at the key in my hand. "W-what is this?"

Angelo laughed as he threw his head back. "You always were a little slow. It's the key to your new house. The paperwork has already been taken care of and the deed is now listed in both your names. I'll let you tell Brynlee. Now, let's go have a glass of wine to celebrate this new chapter in our lives."

Angelo walked past me and headed out the door as I stood there stunned. Travis bumped my shoulder. "Dude, you okay? You look like you're about to pass out."

With a shake of my head, I looked at Travis. "Did he just give me this house? What about what happened, what I did to Brynlee?"

"Brody, I'm pretty sure you have proved not only to Brynlee, but to her family, how much you love her. Dude, you made a mistake, you've got to forgive yourself. Move on."

The door flew open as Brynlee walked into the room. "Brody!"

Melanie was right behind her with a grin as big as the state of Texas of her face. With a quick look over at Travis, she motioned for him to come outside.

"Brynlee, is everything okay? I thought y'all were at dinner."

Brynlee started laughing as she covered her mouth. Her eyes filled with tears as she laughed harder.

I quickly made my way over to her. "Sweetheart, are you okay?"

With a nod of her head, she went to talk and started laughing ... and then crying again.

"I'm so confused. Are you laughing or are you crying? Are you hurt?"

A shake of her head said she wasn't hurt.

"Did something happen while y'all were in town?"

Brynlee placed her hands on my chest and began taking in deep breaths. "That's it ... calm down and take deep breaths, sweetheart."

My stomach was churning as I tried to figure out what Brynlee was going to say. My hand went to the back of my neck where I rubbed it as I waited for her to talk.

Brynlee rolled her shoulders and slowly took in a deep breath and blew it out. "You were right."

With a tilt of my head and really confused look, I said, "I'm right about a lot of things, but you're going to have to be more specific."

Brynlee giggled as she threw her body into mine as I held her. "You were right about not hurting me, Brody."

She held onto me tighter as I tried to figure out what she was talking about. "Baby, you're talking in circles."

With a slight push away, she stood before me. Her eyes were searching my face as if she were trying to freeze this moment in time.

"You didn't sleep with Amy."

Just hearing the name caused nausea to rise up my chest as I pressed my lips together. *How in the hell did she know the girl's name?*

Brynlee's words slow sunk in. *You didn't sleep with Amy.*

"Wait. What did you say?"

Brynlee grinned as she wiped a tear away. "We ran into Amy tonight and when she heard my name she asked if I was your wife. She just launched into this whole one-sided conversation about how you were so drunk but talked nonstop about me. You got sick and she helped you to her bathroom. She said when she went to check on you, you had passed out on her bed. She covered you up and went and slept on the sofa. When she got home from work, she just assumed we had made up and you headed home." With a smile so big, she shook her head. "Brody, you didn't sleep with her."

My hands pushed through my hair as I tried to make sense of everything.

I knew it.

I'd always known deep in my heart I would never cheat on her.

"I knew it. I knew I would never do that to you," I said, as all the air in my lungs seemed to have vanished.

Twenty-Five

Brynlee

B rody stood before me, speechless. Words couldn't even describe how amazing I felt knowing that Brody hadn't slept with Amy. I'd moved on and forgiven him, but knowing the truth meant that Brody could move on as well. I could see the guilt in his eyes last night each time he made love to me.

"Babe, are you okay?"

Brody's mouth opened as he struggled to find the words to speak. Pulling me into his arms, Brody's mouth came down on mine and we lost ourselves quickly. Unlike last night, this kiss was desperate, passionate beyond belief as Brody's hands moved up my back. "I want to make love to you in our house, baby."

We had decided to sell our house shortly after Brody came back from Texas. It seemed silly to have it when I had moved back in with my parents and Brody was living in the main house.

"We sold the house," I giggled against his lips.

Brody pulled his head back and flashed me those dimples that I loved so much. "Oh my gosh. You don't know yet."

"I don't know what yet?" I asked with a confused expression.

Brody took a step back and let out a small laugh. "Your father … he gave us this house."

"Wait." I shook my head as if I heard Brody wrong. "What do you mean he gave us this house?" Pointing to the ground in front of me, I asked, "This house? This. House."

Tossing his head back, Brody laughed. "Yes! I was just as stunned and was still trying to process it when you came in and told me your news."

My head was spinning around as I pinched my eyebrows together and stared at Brody. "I thought you were remodeling it so Dad could turn it into a bed and breakfast."

"I thought so as well," Brody said with a shrug of his shoulders. "I think it was all part of his plan to begin with. I'm not so sure he ever had any intention of making this into a bed and breakfast, Brynlee."

My hands came up and covered my mouth as I laughed. I'd never felt so happy and so complete in my entire life. "This is our house? This is really ours?"

Taking my hand in his, Brody winked and said, "The perfect house to make *memorias bonitas* in."

With a nod of my head, I whispered, "Beautiful memories."

"**How** is she feeling?" I heard Melanie asking Brody.

"Tired. She's been sleeping for about four hours."

Melanie sighed. "I'm so glad the treatments are over."

My eyes felt like lead as I lay on the sofa. I wanted to open them, but I also wanted to just rest. I'd been more tired with the radi-

ation treatment than I had been with the chemo treatments. At least I wasn't sick to my stomach.

Melanie cleared her throat as I felt the sofa bounce a little. She must have sat down on the other end. "So, Crystal is coming to visit, huh?"

Brody let out a little moan of frustration. "Stop it," I whispered.

My eyes opened to see Brody sitting across from me and Melanie at the end of the sofa.

"Sorry, sweetheart, but she broke my best friend's heart."

I slowly sat up as Melanie jumped up. "What do you need?"

With a quick glance up to her, I gave her a shy smile and said, "Ice water and maybe an apple?"

Lifting her hand to her forehead, Melanie gave me a salute. "I'm on it!"

My body felt cold as I wrapped my arms around myself and rubbed my hands on my skin to warm myself up.

"You cold, sweetheart?"

"A little. Is Travis okay with Crystal coming?"

Brody shrugged. "I'm not sure. You know Travis. He makes a joke out of everything. He flirted endlessly with the manager at the bank. I was almost positive she was going to ask us to leave."

Melanie walked back into the living room with a small tray. Setting it down on the table, it contained a glass of water, an apple and a mug of hot chocolate. "Greatest invention ever was the Keurig!"

My hands wrapped around the mug as I took in a deep breath and let the warmth of the hot chocolate invade my body. "That's nice."

A knock at the door had Brody getting up to answer it. "Hey buddy."

Travis walked into the house with a huge smile on his face. "You're looking beautiful, Brynlee."

Feeling my face flush, I smiled. I had gotten used to not wearing the wig all the time and actually liked the fact that I didn't have to

mess with my hair. Melanie made me all these bows and scarfs to wear to make it more fun. "Thank you, Travis."

Glancing to his right, Travis frowned when he saw Melanie. "Mel, how are you?"

Melanie pulled her legs up and sat with them crossed in the chair as she tilted her head and glared at Travis. "I'm fantastic."

Travis narrowed his eyes as he stared at her. "Must be that little fuck fest you had earlier this morning."

Melanie moved about in her seat as she shot Travis daggers. "Fuck you, Travis. You're just jealous I'm seeing action and your little dick hasn't seen any in months."

Travis laughed as he plopped down on the love seat. Pointing to me, Travis said, "Thanks to your sister here, I've taken up a fitness class at the gym. Trust me, my dick as seen plenty of action with the hot little exercise instructor." Smiling, Travis looked at Brody. "Let me tell you, she's flexible as hell."

"Gross," Melanie and I both said at once.

"I'm glad you're going though, Travis. Once I get back to myself, I plan on teaching classes again. You can be in the front row of my first BodyPump class."

Travis' smile dropped as he shook his head like he had just been told something horrid. "To hell with that. It took me weeks to recover from that damn class. You lost a point just now, Brynlee."

"You can't take points away from my wife."

Travis jumped up and pointed at Brody. "I can! I still have nightmares about that whole experience." His body shook as he closed his eyes. "Oh God. Just the memory of it all."

Melanie laughed. "Pussy."

Travis' eyes snapped open. "What did you call me?"

Melanie tilted her head and flashed Travis an innocent smile. "When do you figure you'll actually grow up and act like a man, Travis?"

"W-what? Oh, I'm a man."

Snarling her lip up, Melanie roamed her eyes over Travis' body and then busted out laughing.

Letting out a frustrated sigh, I shook my head. "Ugh, will the two of you stop? One minute you're friends and the next you act like you hate each other."

The door busted open as Jacob came running into the house. "Travis!" he yelled as he ran right into the open arms of a smiling Travis.

I stole a peek over to Melanie as she watched the whole thing play out. She was biting on her lip, trying to act like it didn't affect her how Jacob had fallen totally in love with Travis.

"I have something for you buddy," Travis said as he walked over to his gym bag. He pulled out two shirts. Slipping one over Jacob, he then put the other one on.

It didn't take long for Brody and I to bust out laughing while Melanie stood up and gasped, "You did not!"

Jacob turned around and smiled as he looked down at his new T-shirt from Travis.

My pee-pee has a bone in it.

Pressing my lips together to keep from laughing, I looked over at Brody as he tried to catch his breath from laughing so hard.

This. This was what I loved. My family surrounding me with laughter filling the room. These were the moments I would hold close to me.

Twenty-Six

Brody

Travis came barreling into the tasting room and came to a stop right in front of Melanie and me.

"Hey there, Travis. What's wrong with you?"

Travis turned and looked directly at Melanie. "Can I talk to you?"

Melanie tilted her head as she chewed nervously on the corner of her mouth. "Start talking."

Travis looked up at me and then back to Melanie. With a quick glance over her shoulder, he spied the two employees who worked in the tasting room full time.

"Alone, Mel."

Melanie waved Travis off. "Oh sorry. I don't talk to douchebags alone. It's gotten me into trouble before."

Narrowing my eyes, I looked between the two of them. What in the hell was going on with them?

"Is something going on between you guys?"

Melanie and Travis both snapped their heads over with a look of revulsion etched on their faces. "No!"

Holding my hands up, I took a step back. "Okay."

"Melanie, that guy Brett? You need to stay away from him."

I don't think I'd ever seen Melanie stunned into silence. Her jaw dropped practically to the ground as she slowly shook her head in disbelief.

"Excuse me?"

"He's not good enough for you."

Hands to her hips, I knew what was coming. It wasn't lost on me that the moment I sat down to watch the show about to take place, so did Joe and Linda, the tasting room employees. We were digging in for a good showdown.

"He's not good enough for me? And how exactly are you qualified to know this? Last I heard you had already slept with half the town."

Travis jerked his head back as if he was mortally wounded. "No, I haven't. I've only slept with you and Jane."

Melanie balled her fists up. "Ugh. Jane! That reminds me—I need to kick her ass."

Travis attempted to not smile and failed miserably. Holy shit. He'd fallen for Melanie.

Clearing my throat, I asked, "Um, exactly how many times have the two of you hooked up?"

Linda rested her chin on her hands and wiggled her eyebrows. "Yeah, this is getting good," she said, as Joe nodded his head.

"Twice." Travis said as he puffed his chest up.

"Damn," Linda said as Melanie turned to look at her.

Pointing her finger at the other woman, she said, "You, hush up."

Whipping back around to look at Travis, Melanie stomped up to him and began jabbing her finger into his chest. "And as far as you

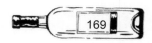

are concerned, that was twice too many times."

Travis scrunched his eyebrows together. "Huh? That didn't make any sense, Mel."

Shaking her head, Melanie waved her hands like a crazy person. "It made sense to me. Forget about what happened between us. It didn't mean anything."

Travis' breath caught and he was visibly bothered by Melanie's comment.

Swallowing hard, Melanie dropped her hands to her sides. "Brett cares about me and Jacob."

I'd never seen Travis look this angry. His eyes were practically on fire. "Is that so? When was the last time he took Jacob fishing?"

Melanie stood there in silence.

"How about just hanging out with Jacob? Does he know that he likes his peanut butter and jelly cut into four pieces and the crust has to be cut off? Does he know fresh squeezed orange juice is like crack for that kid and he would drink it until he floated away? What about his love of soccer? Has Brett played with him at all? Been to one of his games?"

Melanie stood in silence as her body began to tremble.

Travis was clearly pissed off. "No!" Travis shouted it so loud, we all jumped. "I'll tell you what he's been doing though, Melanie. Screwing the new waitress down at Huckabee's. Why don't you ask him about it, since he was bragging at poker last night to everyone about how good of fuck she was? While you're at it, ask Jacob what he thinks about Brett."

Melanie's hands covered her mouth as she cried. I'd never seen my sister-in-law cry like she was. A part of me knew it had nothing to do with Brett fucking around on her and everything to do with her realizing how much she cared about Travis and how much he cared about her and Jacob.

"My advice to you, sweetheart? Next time you want a guy to play stepdad to your son, try not to fuck another guy in the process."

Travis spun on his heels and headed out of the room as Melanie dropped her hands and screamed, "Fuck you, Travis!"

"Dude, maybe you should take it slow."

Travis knocked back another bottle of beer as he sat on my back porch and stared out over the vineyards as the sunset. "Do you know why I moved to California?"

I flashed Travis a *duh* look. "You missed me."

The bottle of beer came up and rested on Travis' lips as he laughed. "Yeah. That's it, bro. I missed you so much I left my family and moved thousands of miles away."

Shrugging, I said, "Well, I know you didn't quit your job, move away from your family, and settle thousands of miles away from your grandmother's pecan pie for some girl."

Travis glared at me. "No, you're right. I didn't. I came to start a new life and that's what I'm going to do. Fuck all these women. All they do is mess with your goddamn head."

"Melanie messed with your head?"

Travis looked at me like I had just grown two heads. "Yes! She did. Ever since we first hooked up, I haven't been the same. The first time Jacob smiled at me and told me he wanted me as a ... as a ..."

I couldn't believe what I was seeing. My best friend had tears pooling in his eyes. "You love Jacob, don't you?"

Travis shook his head and looked away. "He may have gotten under my skin some."

With a smile, I gave him a light punch on the arm. "Travis, why don't you just be honest with Melanie about your feelings. She obviously feels something for you if y'all hooked up a few times."

Travis sniffled hard and quick and stood up as he finished his beer. "Nah. There's no reason to talk to her. Melanie made it perfect-

ly clear she was only in it for a fuck. I'm heading out. I'll talk to you tomorrow."

I stood and reached my hand out to Travis. "Dude, I don't think that she was only in it for that."

Travis let out a gruff laugh. "Well, she sure moved onto this Brett guy pretty fast." Lifting his hands before letting them fall to his sides, he shrugged with defeat. "It doesn't matter anymore, I wish her all the best. I'll call ya tomorrow."

"Want me to walk you out?"

With a slap and squeeze of my arm, Travis smiled. "Nah, talk to you later."

After Travis left, I sat back down and stared out into the darkening sky. I couldn't worry about Travis and Melanie's problems. Tomorrow we found out if the chemo and radiation had worked. Then it was the next hard part. The mastectomy.

Closing my eyes, I got lost in the peacefulness of the evening sky as I prayed hard for my wife's future.

Twenty-Seven

Brynlee

Brody squeezed my hand as he whispered, "It's going to be okay, sweetheart."

With a forced a smile, I nodded as I wrung my hands together. My eyes scanned the walls of Dr. Malick's office as I tried to busy my brain.

"Did you send the flyers to the printer?" I asked as I looked at Brody.

With a wink and a smile, he said, "Yes. I also made sure Melanie added it to the events page of the website.

I nodded. "Good. We want to make sure we get the word out since this will be our first year doing the grape stomp."

Slowly I let a deep breath out as I tried to calm my beating heart.

"Look into my eyes, sweetheart." Doing as he asked, I was captivated by the love in his as he gazed back at me. "Take a deep

breath in and slowly let it out."

Brody's voice was calming. It moved through my body, and instantly, I relaxed.

"Close your eyes and tell me what you see."

My eyes closed as I took in a deep calming breath as I let myself go. "We're walking along a beach. A beautiful beach." Smiling, I shook my head. "We're holding hands and you stop to face me."

"What do I say to you?"

"Nothing. You're looking at me though, and I can feel how much you love me. You look so handsome."

I could feel Brody's stare as my body trembled with the slight chill that moved over me.

"I just told you something, and I don't know what I said, but you're smiling so big." A small chuckle escaped from my mouth. "Your dimples are out in full force."

Brody laughed as he held onto my hand. "It must have been something good then."

Nodding, I whispered, "Must have been."

"Hold onto that, Brynlee. That's our future."

The door opened and my breath hitched as I slowly opened my eyes and let reality settle back in.

Dr. Malick sat down and opened my chart. "How are you feeling, Brynlee?"

I fidgeted in my seat nervously. "Good. Not nearly as tired as I was during the treatments."

Peeking up at me, Dr. Malick smiled. "I'm glad. You're a fighter, Brynlee, and it paid off. According to your blood work and the body scan, the tumor is completely gone. You're cancer free."

My body fell forward as I buried my face in my hand and cried. Brody grabbed my shoulders and pulled me up into a standing position as he wrapped me in his arms.

"I love you. I love you so much, sweetheart."

The tumor is gone. You're cancer free.

After allowing myself a few minutes to break down, I leaned back as Brody wiped my tears away. "I love you too."

Turning back to Dr. Malick, I grinned. "I'm so sorry. I guess I needed that cry."

"You have every right. Brynlee, I need to let you know this isn't over. You've won a huge battle, and I need you to stay positive."

Brody held my hand as we both sat back down. "I know."

"Every three months you'll come back for blood work and a scan will be done once a year. After that you'll get blood work every six months. After five years of remission, you will be considered fully cancer free."

I nodded my head as I let his words sink in. The only thing I could say was, "Okay."

"The surgery is next week. We talked about everything that goes along with that and preparing your body for the implants. Do you have any questions?"

"No, I can't think of any right now." I turned to Brody. "Do you have any?"

Brody shook his head. I could see the relief on his face as his thumb rubbed across my hand over and over.

"You have my cell phone number and you know I'm here anytime you need to talk about anything or have any questions. How are you feeling about next week, Brynlee?"

"Honestly, I'm okay with it. I'm ready to do this."

Dr. Malick looked over to Brody. "What about you, Brody?"

With a quick squeeze of my hand, Brody took in a deep breath and blew it out slowly. "I'd much rather be sitting on a porch sixty years from now with the love of my life. I don't love Brynlee because of her breasts. I love her because of so much more."

With a smile, Dr. Malick nodded. "Brynlee, I know in your mind right now you're prepared. It's a tough thing psychologically. No matter how strong you think you are, you're going to struggle. Please make sure you talk to someone."

With a nod of my head, I smiled the best I could. "I promise I will."

Dr. Malick stood. "Dr. Morris is a wonderful surgeon and Dr. Walters is an amazing plastic surgeon. I'll be sure to stop by after to see you."

Brody and I both stood as we took turns shaking hands with the older man. "Thank you, Dr. Malick, for everything."

Smiling like crazy fools, Brody and I looked at each other as we walked outside.

"So what do you want to do to celebrate?"

With a seductive look, I licked my lips. "I want to go home."

Brody grabbed my hand and pulled me toward the car. "That sounds like a damn good plan."

Giggling, I felt like a high school teenager as Brody and I spent the rest of the afternoon alone while he showered me with love and attention.

"There she is!" I said as I waved my hand to Crystal. The moment she saw me she broke down into tears.

I held my arms out as she walked into them. "I'm so sorry. I swore to myself I wasn't going to cry. I promised myself!"

Letting out a chuckle, I held her close. "It's okay, I told you my good news."

With a quick wipe with the back of her hand against her cheeks, Crystal flashed me a smile. "I've missed you so much."

Another quick hug and Brody walked up. "Hey, Crystal. Let me grab your bag."

"Thanks so much, Brody. How have you been?"

I could tell he was forcing himself to be nice. Crystal had pulled a total bitch move and broken up with Travis after meeting some su-

per rich guy from Boston. She, of course, regretted it almost immediately, and even tried to make amends with Travis, but he wouldn't even take her phone calls.

"Been good. How about you, Crystal? Still dating your rich boy toy?"

"Brody!" I reprimanded him with a stern glare.

Crystal held her hand up to let me know it was all right. "It's okay, I deserve that. And to answer your question, no, I broke up with him. He wasn't what I was looking for."

"Huh. Crazy."

Widening my eyes, I silently pleaded with Brody to stop. With a quick roll of his eyes, he walked ahead of us as Crystal wrapped her arm around mine. "So, how are you feeling?"

"Better now that the chemo and radiation are over. Next big step is the mastectomy. I've been talking with a few women who went through it and they've been so helpful. I hope you don't mind, but Melanie had planned a support group meeting for tonight. It was planned a few weeks back, before I knew you were coming to town. Brody's parents are here as well as his sister Katherine."

Crystal bumped my shoulder as we walked. "You know I don't care. I just want to spend some time with you."

"I haven't done one of these before so I'm sure it will probably turn a bit emotional."

"As long as you have tissues," Crystal said with a wink.

"Yes! We totally will have them."

When we got to the truck I gave Brody a warning look as he gave me an innocent smile. "Behave, Brody Miles."

With a quick kiss on the lips, he whispered, "Always."

Glancing across the room, Crystal and Melanie caught my eye. Melanie had been shooting daggers at Crystal all night. I was glad to see the support group was upbeat and happy. I wasn't sure what to expect, but I was hoping it wouldn't be a crying fest.

I learned so much from other women who had gone through the different stages of their fight with breast cancer. The one thing I was dreading was the drain tubes after the mastectomy. Of all the things I'd done so far, that scared the piss out of me and I had no clue why.

Brody's mother came up to me and kissed me on the cheek. "Have I told you how beautiful you look, darling?"

With a flush on my cheeks, I gave Lynn a warm smile. "Thank you, Lynn. It means so much to me to have you here."

Lynn rubbed my arm lightly and then headed over to my mom.

Crystal sat down next me and bumped my knee with her knee. "So, they're going to put a balloon type contraption across your chest? Why, again?"

"They're short-term expanders. It's to stretch the skin to prepare for the breast reconstruction."

Crystal looked away and I knew she was taking a moment to get her emotions in check. Turning back to me, she smiled slightly. "You're so strong, Brynlee. I don't know if I could do all of this and stay so positive and upbeat like you have."

With a grin, I took her hands in mine. "I have my moments, Crystal. Especially right after I found out all the stuff that was happening with Brody. I had a good few hours where I felt sorry for myself. I questioned why this was happening to me. It's human nature." With a shrug, I took a deep breath and slowly blew it out as I kept talking. "But then you kind of snap out of it and realize this is your fight and only you can decide how you're going to fight it. I truly believe in the power of positive thinking and prayer. Knowing that I wasn't the only person to go through this was huge. Being able to talk to other women who have fought much harder fights and won was empowering. Their strength is infectious, their courage inspiring."

A single tear slowly made a path down Crystal's cheek as she shook her head and looked down. "I know it's wrong, but I keep asking, 'Why you?'"

"Why anyone? Why the mother of five kids, or the little boy who just got on the football team? The grandmother holding her first grandchild she prayed so hard for? The husband who celebrated his fortieth wedding anniversary with his wife? Cancer is a dirty, dirty player. It doesn't care what your sex, race, age or religion is. It's a rotten bastard that needs to be taken down."

Crystal wiped her tears away as her eyes seemed to have filled with a knowledge she hadn't had before. "Then I plan on being one of the people helping to take it down."

With a giggle, I wrapped my arm around her and said, "Hell yeah!"

Crystal stood and kissed me on the forehead. "We need a glass of wine."

I slapped my legs and stood. "Yes, we do!"

Crystal and I headed across the room, walking arm in arm. "By the way, I have the feeling your sister doesn't like me."

A quick glance over my shoulder showed Melanie watching Crystal and me. "That's just my sister. Once she gets to know you, she'll love you."

The doorbell rang as Crystal lifted her eyebrows and gave me a knowing look. "Um, I think there is something deeper there." Turning back to look into the living room, Crystal called out to my mother. "I'll get it, Mrs. Santos."

My mother grinned and sat back down. "Oh thank you, sweetheart."

Crystal practically skipped to the front door and pulled it open with an over-exaggerated hello.

"Why hellooo there!"

179

Travis stood on the front porch with a stunned look on his face as Crystal's whole body went stiff.

"Crystal. What … what are you doing here?"

Shit. Brody didn't tell Travis about Crystal coming to visit.

"Oh fuck," Brody mumbled from behind me.

Spinning around, I gave Brody a *what-in-the-hell* look. "You didn't tell him?"

Brody's eyes were wide as he looked between Travis and me. "I figured I didn't have to tell him. She was only here for a few days and Travis wouldn't even know."

My hands went to my hips as I shook my head.

Men.

Travis repeated himself. "Crystal, what are you doing here?"

The smile that spread over her face was unmistakable. She was beyond happy to see him. "I came to visit Brynlee. What about you?"

Travis snapped his eyes over to Brody and then me, before he looked back at Crystal. "I, um … I moved here a few months back."

"You moved here?"

Finally snapping out of my stupor, I walked over to the door. "Travis, why don't you come on in?"

"Oh yeah, thanks. I knew you had your support group tonight so I was going to see if Brody wanted to grab something to eat."

Brody walked up and reached out for Travis' hand as they shook. "Hey, dude. I've already eaten, but why don't you stay? I could use the company and there is plenty of food."

Travis smiled and walked in. "Sure, sounds good."

"I'll show you where the food is," Crystal said as she grabbed Travis' hand and lead him directly through the living room to the kitchen.

I wasn't sure what came over Crystal, but she stopped and got everyone's attention. "Ladies, this is Brody's best friend and a *very* dear friend of mine, Travis."

Travis blushed, Brody moaned and mumbled *"oh shit,"* and Melanie practically had steam coming from her ears.

The room went silent as six women stared at Travis. Of course his good looks seemed to have that effect on women.

To top off the whole evening, Jacob came running into the living. "Travis! Travis does your pee-pee have a bone in it right now? Mine does!"

Melanie swayed back and forth as she reached out and grabbed the back of the sofa. Of course, Travis looked around the room at all the women, and then stared at Melanie for a brief second. Turning back to Crystal, he flashed a panty-melting smile and said, "Yeah buddy, it's getting there."

"Travis!" Melanie and I both said at once as my sister pushed past everyone and picked up Jacob.

"What did we talk about, young man?"

Jacob laughed and looked at Travis. He loved the attention he got from Travis.

Melanie turned and looked at everyone. "I'm so sorry."

The entire room busted out into laughter as Jacob started laughing and Melanie moaned.

With a quick look in my direction, Melanie said, "I'm taking him back to my place."

Travis walked to Melanie and said, "I can take him."

Melanie snapped her head over and glared at Travis. "I don't need your help."

An angry looked passed over his face as Travis said, "Okay, you've made yourself perfectly clear."

Turning his back to Melanie, Travis smiled at Crystal. "You feel like catching up for a bit?"

Brody took a few steps toward Travis as I tried to figure what in the hell was happening.

"Travis."

Crystal didn't even give Brody a chance to talk. "Yes. I'd love to."

Before I even could utter a word, Travis was guiding Crystal back through the living room and out the front door.

Daring to take a peek at my sister, my breath caught in my chest as I watched tears pool in her eyes.

"Let me, um, find the babysitter. I'll be back in a few."

Turning on her heels, Melanie set off to find the young babysitter she had hired to watch Jacob tonight.

The room erupted into chatter again as everyone began talking. Brody walked up to me as he placed his finger on my chin, lifting my eyes to his.

"I'm sorry."

With a shrug, I smiled. "Doesn't matter. They're all adults, right?"

Those beautiful dimples popped out as Brody rubbed his lips across mine. "When are they leaving? I want to take you home."

Smiling against his lips, I said, "I'll work on clearing everyone out."

Brody wiggled his eyebrows and said, "I'm going to go get naked and crawl under our covers."

My mouth parted open slightly as I pictured my sexy husband naked and waiting for me. Pushing him out of the way, I walked to the middle of the room.

"If I could get everyone's attention. It was so amazing having everyone here tonight. Such an awesome support system we have with each other. Let's do this more often. Right now though, looks like it's time to wrap things up."

My mother stood slowly, giving me a stunned expression before shaking the dazed and confused look away and kicking her hostess status up another notch.

Twenty minutes later I said goodbye to the last person as I shut the door and turned to my mother. Kissing her on each cheek, I said, "We'll clean up tomorrow, Momma!"

I practically skipped all the way to what Brody and I now called our home, as dreams of what the night might hold danced in my head.

Twenty-Eight

Brody

My heart felt so heavy as I buried my fingers in my hair and paced the waiting room. Brynlee was in surgery and I had never felt so out of sorts before in my entire life.

"Brody, why don't you sit down?"

Glancing over to my sister, Katherine, I tried to smile. My parents had flown into town the day after we found out Brynlee was cancer free. Crystal left yesterday and I was feeling like Brynlee and I had no time alone really before the surgery.

With a poor attempt, I tried to smile. "I'm fine, Kat. Nervous energy and I can't sit down."

Angelo gave me a knowing look and stood. "Let's go get a coffee."

My eyes wandered over to Melanie, who was sitting next to her mother. With a nod, her eyes urged me to go.

With a struggled breath, I agreed.

Angelo and I walked in silence as we made our way down to the cafeteria.

"Do you remember last New Year's and the twelve grape tradition the Portuguese do?"

With a quick nod of my head, I said, "Yes, I remember." Brynlee had explained to me that at the first stroke of midnight, you ate twelve grapes before the clock brought in New Year's Day. Each grape represented a month and you were to make a wish with each one.

Angelo smiled. "Brynlee has always loved that tradition. When she was home for the holidays her senior year of college, she ate her twelve grapes and told us she made the same wish for each month."

With a lighthearted laugh, I shook my head. "I can see that. When she wants something bad enough, she goes all in."

Angelo's smile widened. "Yes, she does."

I paid the cashier as Angelo and I took our coffee and headed to the door that led outside to a sitting area.

"Of course, Catrina being who she is, she was dying to know what Brynlee had so desperately wished for. They went for a walk among the vines the next day and she asked Brynlee what she had wished for twelve times over."

My interest was piqued as I looked at Angelo, who wore the happiest expression I'd ever seen.

"Did she tell her?" I asked as we both sat down on a bench.

Angelo took a small sip of his coffee and nodded his head. "Yes, she shared it with her momma."

"Did Catrina tell you what the wish was?"

Angelo closed his eyes and pressed his lips together. "She did, and I remember such a fear creeping into my heart. Catrina told me I was being silly." Shaking his head, Angelo opened his eyes and stared at the water feature directly in front of us.

"Why did you have fear?"

Angelo turned and looked into my eyes. I was temporarily

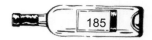

stunned when I saw tears spill from his eyes. "Someday, Brody, when your little girl wishes to find someone and fall in love, you will feel the same fear. The fear that some man, who you know will not be good enough for your little girl, will steal her heart from you. Her love will no longer be reserved for you, but shared with this man. That one day you're going to walk her down to this man and give her to him, and you pray so hard that he will treat her like the princess you know she deserves to be treated like."

My heartbeat pounded in my chest and I was positive Angelo could hear it. I concentrated on breathing as I thought about having a little girl someday with Brynlee.

"I knew the truth all along."

A look of confusion moved across my face. "What truth?"

The coffee cup came up to Angelo's lips again as he took another drink. "I knew you didn't sleep with that girl. If I even had the faintest thought you did, do you really think I'd have let you into my house like I did?"

Swallowing hard, I shook my head. "How … how did you know?"

Angelo turned and looked at me. "Did you know? That is what we should be asking."

The sound of the water caused me to look at it as I thought about his question. "I knew deep in my heart I could never hurt her like that. But I feared I had slept with Amy, thinking it was Brynlee. It drove the guilt which blocked the truth I knew in my very soul."

Angelo nodded. "You asked me how I knew the truth. Your eyes told me. One look into them and I knew."

I clamped down on my cheek to keep my emotions in check. The last thing I wanted to do was get upset while sitting next to my father-in-law.

"I need to ask you something, Brody, and I want you to be one hundred percent honest with me."

My head turned to look at him. "Of course, I'll always be honest

with you sir."

Angelo refused to look at me as he stared straight ahead. "How is she taking this? The mastectomy, I mean. She did so amazing with the loss of her hair, and I know you had a huge part of that. But this is a part of her and my very soul hurts just thinking about it."

My mind drifted back to the conversation Brynlee and I had once we got back together.

Sitting on the sofa, Brynlee was curled up into my side as my fingers moved lazily up and down her arm.

"When I have the mastectomy, will you look at me differently? Think of me differently?" A second didn't even pass by. "No. Brynlee, I'm not in love with you because of your breasts. Do I enjoy them when we're intimate? Of course I do. Here's the thing—I'd much rather have you for the rest of my life, and if that means your breasts go and you decide to never do reconstruction, I'll still love you with every ounce of my being."

Brynlee looked up at me and smiled. "I don't think I could love you more than I do right this moment."

Leaning down, I kissed her gently. "Good. Because I love you too."

"I think Brynlee has the same mindset I have when it comes to the mastectomy. I'd much rather have her for the rest of my life than her breasts. But that doesn't mean I don't think she is going to be affected by it, because I do. I think it's going to play with her head."

Angelo nodded. "She's strong, but be ready, *filho*. Our minds play tricks with our emotions. Be there for her, even if she tries to pretend she is okay."

"I will, sir. I promise you I won't let you or Brynlee down."

Almost a month had passed since Brynlee had her mastectomy and I couldn't believe how incredible she was doing. I'd never been so proud of her as I watched her toss her head back and laugh as two young girls giggled while they mushed grapes between their toes.

"I think they are enjoying themselves, don't you?" Melanie asked she stood next to me.

"She's amazing."

I could feel Melanie's stare. "Yes, she really is."

With a quick peek at my sister-in-law, I winked as she smiled. "So how are the tours going?"

With a clap of her hands, Melanie pushed out a deep breath. "I have to say, they are going good. And I'm even enjoying myself."

Lifting a brow, I asked, "And this surprises you?"

"Don't you know, Brody? I'm a cold-hearted bitch who has no feelings for anyone."

"That's not true. You have feelings for Jacob."

Melanie gave me a dirty look.

"So have you talked to Travis at all?"

With a quick snap of her eyes, Melanie looked away. "No. I've officially given up on all men, except Jacob and my father. Well, you too, but I have to include you because you're my sister's husband."

"Thank you for that."

"Don't read too much into it."

Chuckling, I nodded my head. "You'll find love when you least expect it, Mel."

Melanie wiped her nose and sniffled as she nodded. "Yeah, well, time is running out. I'm turning into an old person who stares at people. I caught myself staring at a couple the other day while they picked out a cucumber. Before, my mind would have thought *oh they're gonna have fun with that baby.* Now I just think about how I need vinegar because cucumbers soaked in vinegar sound really good."

I attempted to hide my chuckle but failed. "No, no, go ahead and laugh. Pretty soon you'll see me wearing the same green sweater with my white pants that are rolled up a few times so I don't trip on them."

That pushed me over the edge. Laughing, I shook my head and grabbed her as I pulled her into a hug. "Melanie, stop hiding your feelings. Just tell Travis how you feel."

"Psh, I'd rather not, thank you. Besides, he's probably back to talking to that little skank who came to visit. I'm sure she'll talk him into moving back to Texas, and then four months down the road when something better comes along, she'll drop his dick for a new, bigger-versioned dick. Although he's pretty well-endowed in that department." Melanie stared off into space as she smiled an evil smile as she licked her lips. "Big, thick, hard, well-endowed dick."

Covering my mouth to keep from throwing up, I pushed her. "Hey!"

"Jesus H. Christ. I don't need to hear that!" My body trembled as I tried like hell to erase the image from my brain. "God, you need to get laid."

With a chuckle, Melanie let out a breath and said, "Okay well, my work here is done. I guess I'll go see if Bryn needs any help."

With a shake of my head, I pulled out my phone.

Me: *Melanie was just talking about you.*

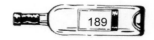

189

It wasn't even thirty seconds later.

Travis: *What did she say?*

Me: *Something about missing your… hold on while I try to swallow the puke in my mouth.*

With a chuckle, I decided to wait a few minutes before I gave him any more. When my phone rang, I had to laugh.

"Hey, what's up?"

"What's up? Really dude? You send me a text and tell me Melanie was talking about me, and then you leave me hanging."

Holding my laughter back, I waved to an older couple walking out of the tasting room. "Oh yeah, what was I saying? It's crazy here with the whole grape stomping party and all."

"Fuck the grapes! What did Melanie say about me?"

"Oh, something about you going back to Texas to be with Crystal."

"What?!"

Moving the phone from my ear, I laughed. I'd never heard Travis scream like a panicked little girl before.

"Why in the hell would she think that?"

"Oh hell, I don't know. Maybe because she saw you both leaving one night and she put two and two together. Not sure. There was something else though. Yeah, that's it, she broke up with Brett."

"What? And you're just now telling me this? What is wrong with you? Dude, I took a fitness class with you. We share a bond like no other. You have to tell me when the woman I love does something like this."

My eyes widened as my mouth dropped open. "What did you just say?"

Travis let out a frustrated moan. Brynlee was smiling as she walked up to me. Covering the phone, I said, "Travis just said he loved Melanie."

"Oh. My. Gawd! What?" Brynlee shouted as everyone turned to look at us.

"Is that Brynlee? What's wrong? Is she okay?" Travis asked.

"Um, yeah, she just stubbed her toe on a barrel."

"Ouch. That sucks."

I shook my head to clear my thoughts. "What did you say about Melanie?"

Silence.

Brynlee grinned from ear to ear. "Hey Travis, I hate to cut you off, but why don't you come over tonight for dinner? I'll tell you what Melanie said then. Gotta run!"

As I pulled the cell away from my ear, you could hear Travis yelling.

"That was so mean, Brody. Hey, did Melanie really say something about me?"

My body shivered again as Melanie's words invaded my brain. "Ugh ... yeah, but I'd rather just forget it." Draping my arm over her shoulders, I led Brynlee back to the tasting room and to her office.

"What are we doing?" she asked with a wicked smile.

"Operation Get Travis and Melanie Together."

With a little jump and a scrunched up nose, Brynlee grabbed a notepad and our evil plan began to take shape.

Twenty-Nine

Brynlee

I stood in the mirror and stared at myself. The worst part about the mastectomy had been the stupid drains. After my first visit, I had those removed and then it was the process of expanding and getting ready for the reconstruction.

My hand moved up to where my hair was slowly beginning to grow back.

"I don't even look like the same person," I whispered into the air.

"You look more beautiful than I've ever seen you."

I looked up to stare at my husband's reflection. I wasn't sure how he did it, but he always made me feel so adored and treasured. Even when I had days where I just wanted to feel like shit, he brought out the best in me.

His dimples practically took up his whole face as he smiled. *My goodness he is so handsome.* His t-shirt was soaking wet from his

run and it clung to his broad chest in the sexiest way. My breathing increased as I bit down on my lower lip while desire pooled in my stomach.

One woman in my support group, Shelly, said she and her husband hadn't had any type of sexual encounter since she was diagnosed. My heart broke for her as she told Melanie and me how much she missed contact with him. Melanie had gone out and bought her some sexy panties and a teddy and told her it was time to get her sexy on again.

Staring at my husband, I realized how often he had made me feel beautiful. From the first moment my hair began falling out, to when I woke up after a part of me was taken away. Each step of the way, he had made me feel wanted, loved, and desired. I prayed that Shelly followed through with Melanie's challenge to seduce her husband.

"You look handsome," I whispered as I continued to look at him through the mirror.

"You look fuckable."

My cheeks blushed as I took in my appearance. I was only wearing a pair of pink boy shorts and nothing else. I swallowed hard as I stared at the empty spot where my breasts once were.

Brody stood behind me and smiled as he placed his hands on my shoulders. My body trembled with anticipation. He had been so delicate with me every time we were together. This one time, I wanted him to treat me like he needed me desperately.

My head dropped to the side as Brody's lips grazed across my neck and up to my ear. Nibbling on my ear lobe, I moaned and pushed my ass into him.

"God, Brynlee, I want to bend you over and fuck the shit out of you."

My voice was breathy. "Please, Brody. Please take me."

"I don't want to hurt you."

My head shook frantically. "I need to feel how much you want

me."

Brody turned me around and backed me up until I hit the mirror. As he dropped to the ground, he took my panties with him. I stepped out of them as my hands went to his hair.

We hadn't had sex since the mastectomy, but Brody had brought me to release plenty of times with his hands and mouth. I knew he was giving my body time to heal, and I loved him for showing me attention and taking care of my needs.

My leg was soon over his shoulder as he spread my lips apart and buried his face. My head dropped back against the mirror as I sucked in a breath.

My hips soon began to pump as Brody slipped two fingers inside of me and licked my clit so fast. The room began to spin as I called out his name while my body trembled with the powerful orgasm.

With my eyes still shut, I attempted to drag in air. The loss of Brody's mouth on my body was noticed but my body was still feeling the aftershock of the intense orgasm.

I jumped and opened my eyes when his hand landed on my stomach. As I took in his perfect naked body, I couldn't help but smile.

"Turn around and put your hands on the mirror, Brynlee."

"W-what?" I asked as my voice trembled.

"I want you to see me fuck you. I want you to see the desire in my eyes as I pound into you so hard you'll feel it for days."

My stomach dropped and my heart began beating hard. It was one thing to lie in bed and let Brody take me away, but he wanted me to look at myself in the mirror. When I turned around, I took my body in again as my mouth dropped open. No matter how hard I tried to pretend like I was okay with everything, a part of me wasn't. A part of my body was gone and I was angry with that.

I wanted to protest, to tell Brody I couldn't, but my eyes caught his in the reflection and something passed between us.

"Brody," I whispered as I placed my hands on the mirror.

His dimples came out as he moved his hand lightly across my stomach and down between my legs. "Do you have any idea how much you turn me on?"

A sob escaped from my lips as I slowly shook my head. Reaching with his hands, Brody took his length in his hand and pushed against my body. "Do you feel that, baby? Do feel how much I want to bury myself inside of my wife and stay there forever? To be connected as one? Fuck, it's my favorite thing to do, Brynlee."

One tear and then two, followed by more, began rolling down my face as Brody pushed my legs apart and slowly eased inside of me. I gasped at the pain of him filling my body so full. I never once looked away from him.

"Look at yourself in the mirror, Brynlee."

I shook my head and closed my eyes. "I can't."

Brody pulled out and pushed back into me, harder, as I cried out with a mixture of pleasure and pain.

"I want you to see how fucking sexy you are when I'm buried so deep inside of you."

With another painfully slow retreat, Brody thrusted back into me hard again. My stomach clenched as I opened my eyes and looked at him.

"You're so beautiful, baby. I need you to see what I see every time I look at you."

Brody grabbed onto my hips and began driving faster. A growl from the back of his throat caused me to lick my lips as I felt another orgasm building.

"Baby, please."

With a deep breath, I tore my eyes from Brody's reflection and looked at myself in the mirror. A sheen of sweat was building on both of our bodies as Brody fucked me fast. Quickly glancing up to him, I saw him staring at me as he moved in and out of me.

My eyes went back to my body as I watched my husband take

what will always be his.

"Harder," I panted as his grip tightened and I began to meet him thrust for thrust as I watched him fuck me.

I was stunned by how much I liked watching him do this to me. His right hand moved around me as he began playing with my clit. "Yes," I hissed as I felt him hitting the magical spot.

"Baby, I'm not going to be able to hold out much longer. I want to pour myself inside of you now."

My eyes looked down at his hand working me up and I lost it. Screaming out his name, my legs began to shake as my orgasm started in my toes and rolled up my entire body and back down again.

Brody moaned as he called out my name. I could feel him tremble as he poured his cum into my body as I watched between my legs. When he finally stopped and pulled out, I saw his cum moving down my leg and I couldn't help but smile.

Hottest moment of my life.

Brody brought his fingers up to my mouth and ran his index finger along my lower lip as I opened my mouth and followed his finger with my tongue.

"God, I love you," he said as his eyes pierced mine.

In that moment, everything changed. Smiling, I turned and wrapped my arms around his neck.

"You make me feel so alive. I love you so much."

Brody's arms held me tightly as he pressed his lips against my neck. "I didn't hurt you, did I?"

"No. It felt amazing."

Pulling back, my eyes searched his face before I smiled and stared into those beautiful green eyes of his. "You brought me back when I didn't even realize I had left."

The back of his hand moved slowly down the side of my face as he shook his head. "My love will always hold onto you. I'll never let you go, sweetheart. Never."

Brody bent over and picked me up as he carried me over to our

bed. Gently laying me down, he kissed my lips and then crawled into bed next to me. We lay in bed and held each other as we talked about our future.

A future filled with love, hope, dreams, and lots of happy memories.

Thirty

Brody

Brynlee danced around the kitchen as she took the lasagna out of the oven and placed it on the wire cooling rack. As I leaned against the counter, I couldn't contain the love bubbling up inside of me as my beautiful wife sang terribly off-key. She had the cutest damn hat on that had a giant-ass pink bow.

She looked gorgeous and I loved the glow on her face.

When I walked back into the bedroom after our run, I was stopped dead in my tracks as I watched Brynlee staring at her body with a frown on her face. Everything about her was beautiful and I knew I needed to show her in the rawest way possible.

Brynlee cleared her throat, pulling me from my thoughts. "So, Operation Get Travis and Melanie Together. What's your plan?"

With a shrug, I said, "I don't really have a plan. I'm kind of winging it."

She stared at me with a disbelieving look. "You're winging it?"

I tossed a carrot into my mouth and winked. "True love always wins out. We just need to give them a little push."

Brynlee pulled out five plates and set them between the lasagna and salad. "You do realize this is my sister we're talking about. Hard headed. Loves sex. Swore she would never settle down again. The same girl who left to go on a date once and said the guy was gonna need Viagra just to keep up with her?"

With a shake of my head, I chuckled. "Melanie is for sure one of a kind, but I'm almost positive Travis has the energy to keep up with her … healthy sexual appetite."

"Gross."

I lifted my brow as I tilted my head. "You went there, sweetheart."

"Touché."

The doorbell rang and Brynlee and I both raced to answer it. Throwing the door open, my heart dropped.

"Oh no," she whispered.

Travis stood there smiling, with a girl standing next to him. "Hey y'all. I hope it's okay that I invited a friend to come along."

Brynlee shut the door in Travis' and his friend's face.

Turning to her, I gave her a puzzled look. "You just shut the door in their faces!"

Her hands came up over her mouth as her eyes widened. "He brought a girl! He. Brought. A. Girl! Who does that?"

"Um, single guys who are tired of being single?"

Brynlee held up her hands as if to make me stop talking. "No! You don't just invite someone over when you've been invited over to dinner with the idea that those people who invited you might not have made enough food for his *friend*!"

My lip snarled as I whispered, "Huh?"

"Crap!"

She turned back to the door and opened it as she plastered on a fake smile. Travis and the poor girl looked confused as hell.

199

"I told him to let you know I was coming. I'm so sorry to be an inconvenience."

"It's okay, my wife still has cancer-brain."

The girl's mouth fell open. "Oh my, I'm so sorry."

Brynlee let out a nervous laugh. "It's okay, I've been given the all clear. Oh, um, come on in."

Giving me a look that said *do something*, I shrugged and followed Travis and the girl into the living room.

"Brynlee, Brody, this is Amber. We work together."

With a smile, I reached my hand out for hers. "It's a pleasure to meet you, Amber."

Brynlee hit me on the arm and gave me a little push. Turning, I nodded and then looked back to Travis.

"Hey how about I get some drinks. Amber, what would you like?"

"I'm easy."

"I bet," Brynlee said under her breath as Travis gave her a stunned look.

"Travis, want to give me a hand?"

Pinching his brows together, Travis nodded. "Uh…okay."

The moment we got out of Amber's view, I grabbed Travis. "What are you doing with this girl?"

Travis looked at me with a stunned expression. "Hopefully getting into her pants later tonight?"

"No! You're fucking ruining this operation!"

Shaking his head, he asked, "What operation? Is Brynlee having another operation? Shit!"

"No, you fuckhead. Operation Get Travis and Melanie Together."

Closing his eyes, Travis held his hands out, trying to make sense of all of this. Snapping them back open, he gave me a blank expression. "What in the hell are you talking about, dude?"

I let out a frustrated sigh. "This dinner was supposed to be about

getting you and Melanie together. You know, a little push in the right direction."

Horror filled Travis' eyes. "Melanie's coming over for dinner?"

It was time to go in for the kill. "And Jacob. And I had that little bit of information to tell you what she said about you."

"Oh fuck," Travis said as his hands hit his face and scrubbed down it. "Damn it, Brody. How was I supposed to know you and Brynlee were up to no good tonight?"

My head jerked back. "No good? Dude, I'm thinking about little Travis here. His happiness."

Travis snarled his lip. "Dude, don't talk about my dick like that. It freaks me out."

"Sorry," I said with a nod of my head. "You're right—that was a little too much."

"A little?"

Waving my hands around to get the conversation back on track, I said, "Anywho, Melanie's going to be here any minute, and you've got some girl who most certainly thinks she is hooking up with you, standing in my living room."

"Fuck, what am I going to do?"

Looking up like I was coming up with some brilliant plan, I snapped my fingers and pointed at Travis. "Hey, how did you get here?"

"Amber drove. My truck's still in the shop."

Before I had a chance to tell him my idea, the doorbell rang.

"Shit!" We both called out as we tried to run into the living room together and hit head on.

"Son-of-a-bitch, watch it buttmunch!" Travis yelled out as he pushed me out of the way and ran up to Amber. "I need to talk to you. Alone."

"On the back deck," I said with a smile.

Travis pointed to me. "Yes!"

Poor Amber practically had her arm pulled from her socket as

Travis dragged her through the living room and out to the back deck.

Brynlee looked at me with a confused look. "What's going on?"

"I'm assuming Travis is about to give Amber the boot."

Melanie began banging on the door as Brynlee rolled her eyes. "Gosh, she is so impatient. Is Travis sure he wants to be with her?" Brynlee opened the door and smiled. "Hey big sis! Hey my little man!"

Jacob came running in. "I smell something good, Bryn-Bryn."

"Lasagna, buddy. Your mom's favorite dish."

Melanie pinched her eyebrows together. "No it's not. It's yours."

Brynlee smiled and shrugged. "Oh. That's right."

With a quick peek over my shoulder, I saw Travis guiding Amber down the back stairs.

Melanie turned and headed back for the door. "Oh crap, I forgot to grab my sweater out of my car. Let me go grab it."

Brynlee and I both ran to the door and blocked it as we shouted, "No!"

Melanie's eyes widened in surprise as she looked between both of us. "What the hell is wrong with you two?"

"Nothing. It's just … I, um … need some fresh air. I'm hot." I said as I waved my hand in front of me.

One eyebrow lifted as Melanie looked at me suspiciously. "You're hot? Why?"

My mouth blurted the first thing that came to mind. "Too much sex."

"What's sex?" Jacob asked.

All eyes landed on Jacob. "Something your mother loves very much and the reason you're here buddy," Brynlee said as she took Jacob by the hand and led him into the kitchen. "Let's go see if we can find any coloring pencils and books."

Jacob jumped and did a little fist pump. "Yeah!"

Melanie watched the two of them retreat into the kitchen before

she turned and gave me that look. The one that says she knows something's up but she could really give two fucks what it is.

With a quick smile, I said, "Is your car unlocked?"

Melanie stepped around me as she opened the door. "I've got it, Brody. Thanks."

Panic set in as I saw Travis talking to Amber at the back of her car.

"Really! I can get it, Melanie!" I shouted as Travis looked over and then quickly looked back at Amber.

And that's when he did it. He pushed her and Amber went down as I grabbed Melanie's arm. "Wait!"

"What's Travis doing here and whose car is that? Was that here when I pulled up?" How Melanie had missed the car I had no idea and I didn't care.

Looking at Amber's car and then back to Melanie, I let out a nervous chuckle. "No clue." Turning her body around, I pushed her back into the house. "Let me find out why Travis is here and then I'll grab your sweater."

Melanie rolled her eyes and mumbled. "Whatever."

Once the door shut, I glanced back over to Amber's car, where Travis was helping her back up.

"What in the hell? Why would you push me? Twice!"

Oh hell.

Travis looked at me and then back to Amber. "I'm married!"

Amber's eyes widened in shock. "Oh my Gawd! What?"

Damn. That was all he could come up with?

"Yeah, I'm sorry. I thought I could do it. You know, have an affair."

Amber shook her head, as if trying to understand what she was hearing. "An affair? Are you fucking kidding me?"

Before Travis could respond, he fell to his knees and cried out to the heavens. Amber took him down with one swift knee in the balls.

"You asshole! I feel sorry for your poor wife. I hope like hell

you don't have kids you son-of-a-bitch."

Amber quickly got in her car and took off like a bat out of hell down the driveway.

As I walked up to Travis, I couldn't help but laugh. "Well, that's one way of getting rid of her."

Travis slowly fell to his side and laid in a fetal position on the ground.

"Fuck. You," he managed to get out as he cradled his junk in his hands.

"I'll never … be able … to have kids! That bitch!"

Squatting down, I nodded my head. "You did admit to wanting to use her to cheat on your pretend wife. I'd have been pissed as well."

I was almost positive Travis was trying to conjure up daggers from his eyes.

"What in the hell are you two doing? Why are you on the ground, Travis?"

Turning, I looked up to see Melanie standing there with her arms crossed over her chest.

"Hey there, Melanie," Travis said, still cradling his junk.

Melanie tried to hide her smile. "Hey there, Travis. You having fun holding yourself?"

"Yep."

With a quick nod, Melanie glanced my way. "I'll get my own sweater while you two do whatever it is you're doing out here."

Melanie headed over to her car but stopped and looked back at us. "Who was the girl in the car that sped out of here?"

Travis jumped up as he sucked in a breath and cursed. "Co-worker dropping me off. Truck's in the shop."

This time, she did smile. "Cool."

I was internally fist pumping. Operation Get Travis and Melanie Together was off to a promising start.

Thirty-One

Brynlee

"What is this again, Bryn-Bryn?"

"Lasagna, buddy."

Jacob turned to Melanie. "Mommy, why don't you make this? It's yummy!"

My sister smiled at her son and then shot me a go-to-hell look. "'Cause Lasagna is Bryn-Bryn's specialty. Really it's the only thing she knows how to cook."

My mouth fell open. "That's not true. I'm a very good cook."

Melanie took a bite and winked. "Uh-huh."

"Brody, tell her how good of a cook I am."

"She's a great cook. What's your specialty, Mel?"

Giving Melanie a smirk I said, "Oh, Mel's specialty isn't with her hands, it's with her mouth."

Travis started choking as he quickly reached for his drink.

Jacob laughed and said, "Your mouth, Mommy? Is it singing?"

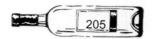

205

Melanie sat there stunned. A look of pure humiliation etched on-to her face. *So this is how this felt? I rather liked this.*

"It's more like humming, buddy. The vibration is the key. Isn't that right, Travis?" Brody asked as he winked at Travis.

Travis glared at Brody. "Dude, what are you doing? What did we talk about?"

"Mommy has a very purty voice. She hums all the time."

My fork came up to my mouth as I said, "Oh, you don't have to tell me, Jacob. She was known for that in high school."

"What?!" Melanie shouted as she slammed her hands on the ta-ble.

Travis leaned forward and smiled. "Really now?"

"Has Mommy ever singed for you, Travis?"

With an evil smile, Travis shook his head. "No buddy, she sure hasn't."

"Do you want her to?"

Melanie was white as a ghost as her eyes moved back and forth from Jacob to Travis. You could tell she didn't know who to talk to first.

"More than anything, buddy."

Melanie's face blushed as she looked down at her food. "I think we should change the subject."

"Mommy, sing for Travis now! He will be so happy."

Travis wiggled his eyebrows as he pushed his chair back and motioned for Melanie to come over.

Narrowing her eyes, Melanie pointed to Travis. "Stop it! This isn't funny."

Brody laughed. "I'm enjoying this. Brynlee?"

Nodding with enthusiasm, I said, "Yep."

Jacob laughed as he looked around the table. "Travis, do you love my mommy? Do you want to be my daddy?"

The room fell silent as Melanie sat back in her chair as she stared at Travis. Travis grinned from ear to ear.

"I love your mommy and you more than anything, buddy. It would be an honor to be your daddy."

Jacob smiled. "Yay! We can go fishing all the time."

Tears built in my eyes as I stared at my sister. A single tear rolled down her cheek as Travis pushed his chair out and stood. Melanie slowly followed his lead, never taking her eyes off of Travis. Jacob took that as a sign we were all supposed to stand as he climbed up in the chair. "Bryn-Bryn, Brody, stand up!"

Brody and I both stood as I looked between Melanie and Travis.

"I love you, Melanie. I think I've loved you ever since you argued with me about who got to give the toast first."

Melanie covered her mouth as she tried to hold back her sobs. "W-what are you saying?"

Travis walked around the table, stopping to pick up Jacob and throw him over his shoulder as Jacob started laughing. He walked up to Melanie and held out his hand as she placed her hand in his. "If you'll have me as your husband, I promise to love you and Jacob until I take my last breath."

Tears now spilled over onto my sister's cheeks as she nodded her head and said, "Yes! Oh my gosh yes!"

Melanie stood up on her toes as Travis brought her lips to his. I couldn't help but start crying as Brody wrapped his arm around my waist.

"Operation Get Travis and Melanie Together was a success."

With a slight nod, I wiped my tears away. "It was the lasagna."

Three Months Later...

"I cannot believe how fast your hair is growing, Bryn."

Running my hand over my hair, I smiled. "I know! Did you

know Stacy's hair didn't even fall out during chemo?"

"Crazy. I bet in another three months yours will be mid-cheek!"

I nodded and said, "It's so dark, too! Before I know it, I'll have long hair again."

"Hell yeah, you will, Bryn."

"Mommy! Did Santa get my letter?"

Melanie wrapped Jacob up in her arms and kissed him as a sinking feeling hit my chest while I watched my sister with her son. I plastered on a fake smile and went back to cutting out sugar cookies.

"Yes! Of course he did. Hey, why don't you go see if Travis and Brody need help putting up the tree in the living room?"

"Okay! Is Daddy gonna put up a tree in our living room too?"

My head snapped up as I looked at Jacob and then Melanie. Her eyes pooled with tears as she cleared her throat and blinked a few times. "Jacob, do you want to start calling Travis *Daddy*?"

With the sweetest smile I'd ever seen, Jacob nodded. "Well, he is my daddy, silly Mommy!"

Travis walked into the kitchen and looked at Melanie. "Baby, what's wrong?"

Her hand went to her mouth as she began crying. "I think Mommy is happy crying again, Daddy!"

Travis started toward Melanie and then stopped. His eyes widened and he looked down at Jacob. "Hey, Daddy! Mommy said we get our tree next!" Jacob began jumping as he grabbed Travis' hand and then Melanie's.

I couldn't help feel a tinge of jealousy race though my body. I was so happy for my sister, but at the same time, I wanted desperately to have what she had.

Travis picked up Jacob and hugged him tightly as he whispered, "You just made me the happiest man in the world, buddy."

Goosebumps formed on my body as Brody wrapped his arms around me. "We're gonna be next, sweetheart."

Doubt filled my mind as I tried desperately to push it aside. I

pressed my lips together and nodded. Brody spun me around and cupped my face in his hands.

"Look at me," he whispered as my eyes captured his. "It's going to happen."

"How do you know?"

Brody's eyes looked over my shoulder as he smiled. "I just know."

"Bryn-Bryn, are you crying happy tears too?"

I glanced over my shoulder and nodded. "I sure am, buddy. I sure am."

Travis set Jacob down as he skipped out of the kitchen, but not before saying, "I sure hope Santa brings me a little brother like I asked for."

My mood changed instantly. Trying to keep from laughing, I looked at Travis and Melanie's faces as a look of fear passed over them.

"Shit," they both said at once.

Brody laughed and clapped his hands together. "Oh man. I'm so glad we actually mailed that letter!"

Travis rolled his eyes. "Oh yeah, 'cause *Santa* is gonna make that happen." Travis made air quotes as he said *Santa*.

Brody gasped. "Dude, you don't believe in the Christmas magic? Don't you know if you mail your letter to Santa at least one wish will come true on it? The wish you want the most."

Melanie hit Travis on the stomach. "We need to send out a counter letter stat!"

As everyone started laughing, I smiled and made a mental note to myself to send out a letter to Santa. Stat.

Thirty-Two

Brody

I quietly slipped out of bed and headed to the living room where I had stashed a pair of jogging pants, a t-shirt, and sneakers.

Quickly getting dressed, I headed into the kitchen and pulled the quiche Brynlee's mom made and put it in the oven as I turned it on to 350 degrees, per Catrina's instructions.

I sent off a quick text to Brynlee's father letting him know I was on my way up to the house. One peek in our bedroom showed Brynlee was fast asleep still. I'd kept her up most of the night making love to her until she collapsed with exhaustion.

Jumping into my truck, I headed toward Brynlee's parents' house. Angelo was standing in the yard as a little yellow Lab jumped up at him.

Parking, I got out of the truck and whistled, causing the little bugger to stop jumping and turn to look at me. Bending down on a knee, I called him, "Hey, little buddy!"

Floppy yellow ears took off running toward me as a smile spread across my face.

Little puppy breath hit my face as I picked the little guy up and let him give me kisses.

"He's cute … but boy oh boy, is he a handful," Angelo said with a roll of his eyes.

"Ah man, Brynlee is going to go insane when she sees him," I said as I chucked and held the eight-week-old yellow lab up.

The front screen door opened as I glanced up and saw Catrina walking out. "He is a handful, Brody. Poops everywhere!"

"You're going to be just what the doctor ordered, little fella." Scrunching up my nose, I held him in front of me. His sweet brown eyes grabbed a hold of my heart.

Catrina walked up to me and gave the puppy a kiss. "Brody, is she doing okay? Melanie mentioned that Brynlee seemed rather down."

I gave Catrina a reassuring smile. "She has her moments when she lets herself think too much." I said with a reassuring smile. "Seeing how happy Travis, Melanie and Jacob are I think threw her into a funk."

Catrina looked surprised. "She's not happy for her sister?"

"Oh yeah, she is very happy for Melanie. She's been talking an awful lot about babies. Us having a baby. When her mind starts drifting, she starts worrying."

Angelo walked up and put his arm around Catrina. "The good Lord wouldn't put her through all of that for nothing."

"She froze a few eggs as well. She needs to stop worrying."

Letting myself laugh, I shook my head. "This is Brynlee we're talking about." I pushed out a breath and shook my head. "It's going to be okay. This little guy is going to keep her busy the next few months."

Angelo moaned as he shook his head. *"Esse cão é uma ameaça!"*

"I have no idea what you just said, Angelo." Portuguese was the next thing on my list to learn.

Catrina laughed and lightly hit her husband's stomach. "Stop it. He is not a menace. He is precious and just needs some training."

With a roll of his eyes, Angelo tossed his hands up in the air and began speaking in Portuguese as he walked back into the house.

"Don't pay attention to him. He's just grumpy because Santa didn't leave him a puppy." Catrina leaned in closer and whispered, "He snuggled with him all night last night."

My eyes widened. "Angelo snuggled with the puppy?"

Catrina pointed her finger to me. "If you tell him I told, I will deny it!"

Laughing, I kissed my mother-in-law on the cheek. "I better get back before sleeping beauty wakes up. We'll be by around one, right?"

"Yes! See you then. Kiss my daughter for me."

Holding the puppy up, I called out, "I will!"

Fifteen minutes later I was hiding the puppy in the laundry room and tossing him at least ten different toys. A little bit of puppy food in the bowl and I was sure I bought myself at least an hour. He'd eat, play and then fall asleep.

Shutting the door, I turned and yelled out like a little girl.

"Holy shit!" I shouted as Brynlee jumped and called out as well.

"What? Oh my gosh! You scared the crap out of me, Brody!"

My chest was heaving as I tried to control my breathing. Shit, that was close.

"Why are you sneaking out of the laundry room?"

My hand pushed through my hair as I looked back at the door and shrugged. "Oh, I was just putting a load of laundry in and didn't want to wake you up."

The sound of a squeaky toy went off as she pinched her eyebrows together and tilted her head. "What was that?"

"The washing machine. I need to, uh, take a look at it. It's been

making some weird noises."

Another squeak and I started pretend coughing. "Shit, something went down wrong."

"You're not eating anything."

"Spit. Swallowed my own spit wrong."

Brynlee gave me a look of disbelief as she shook her head and turned. She grabbed her coffee mug and began making her morning hot tea.

"Merry Christmas, by the way," she said with a sexy smile on her face.

As I walked up to her, I wrapped my arms around her and pulled her to me. "Merry Christmas, sweetheart."

Squeak.

"Do you want to open your presents now?" I blurted out in an attempt to cover up the noise the puppy was making.

Squeak! Squeak!

Brynlee glanced over toward the door. "Brody, that sounds more like a toy squeaking than the washing machine."

"Nope. It's the washing machine." Taking her by the hand, I led her out into the living room and pushed her down onto the sofa. "Here, why don't you relax? I'll make your tea and the breakfast quiche your mom prepared is heating up."

Brynlee gave me the sweetest smile. "I could get used to this kind of treatment."

A loud bang came from the laundry and Brynlee quickly jumped up just as quickly as I pushed her back down. "I'll see what that was. I think I left something on top of the washing machine."

Squeak! Squeak! Squeak! Bang!

I turned the TV onto HGTV and turned it up louder than it needed to be while I let out a nervous chuckle. "Damn washing machine."

Brynlee's face looked unconvincing. "Uh-huh."

With a wink, I pointed to the presents. "Why don't you play

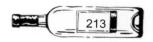

Santa and start dividing out the gifts? Travis, Mel and Jacob will be here soon."

With bright eyes, Brynlee jumped up and said, "Okay! Melanie said Jacob had them up at six this morning wanting to open presents."

I reached down and hit the up button on the volume and headed into the kitchen. Finally, she was distracted and not focused on the laundry room. I stopped in the middle of the kitchen and listened.

Silence.

With a grin, I took the quiche out of the oven then got plates down. "Damn, this quiche smells amazing!"

Brynlee turned the TV down and called out, "I know! I've never tasted any better. Oh, it smells heavenly."

Motioning with my hands to bring the heavenly scent in toward my nose, I licked my lips and got ready to dish it out.

Then it happened.

The puppy barked.

I quickly coughed to cover the sound, although, my cough sounded nothing like the little bark coming from the laundry room.

"What was that?"

I glanced casually over to Brynlee and made a what-are-you-talking-about face. "What was what?"

She tilted her head and looked up as she thought about what she just heard. "Brody, that sounded like a dog."

A nervous laugh escaped from my lips as I jerked my head back. "What? A dog? It was probably something on the TV you heard."

My phone beeped as I pulled it out of my pocket. It was from Travis.

Travis: *On our way up to your place in about an hour. Did she love the pup?*

Me: *I haven't given it to her yet.*

Travis: *Why not?*

Me: *I have a plan dude!*
Travis: *Damn, haven't you figured out your plans never work?*

Pulling up his number, I glanced into the living room to see Brynlee back to piling up the presents into different piles. We were having our own Christmas morning alone together, then Travis, Melanie and Jacob were coming over, and then it was up to Angelo and Catrina's for a traditional Portuguese dinner.

"Wow. Did you miss my voice?"

I let out a grumbly growl as I moved across the kitchen, through the dining room and out onto the deck. "What do you mean my plans never work? All my plans work, dickhead."

"The turtle?"

I rolled my eyes. "Jesus H. Christ. Are you ever going to let that go?"

"No! That damn thing almost bit my fucking dick off!"

"It's a turtle. It couldn't possibly bite your dick off."

Travis laughed. "Dude, I know you have cock-envy, but that little turtle had a wide mouth-span. He could have bitten it off."

"Cock-envy? Are you seriously for real right now? You think I have cock-envy?"

"If the jockstrap fits…"

I let out a few quick laughs as I shook my head. "Dude, my cock is way bigger than your cock."

"Yeah, I don't think so, Brody. We measured our cocks that one night." Melanie began talking in the background as Travis said, "No, Mel, we were all drunk and looking through *Playboy* magazines. We were like twenty at the time." I rolled my eyes as I peeked into the house. Brynlee was standing there glued to some show on HGTV.

I let out a frustrated sigh. "Dude! I won! My cock was the biggest of them all!"

"Brody, you don't have to get Little Cock Syndrome. We all know who is the bigger man."

"Ugh! Fuck you, Travis!"

"Oh! My! Gawd! AH!"

My eyes widened in horror. "Oh shit! Code red!"

"What the hell is code red?" Travis asked in a panicked voice.

"Brody! It's a puppy!"

"Fuck! She found the puppy because you were distracting me with your big cock talk."

"Ah, so you admit my cock is bigger than yours."

Tearing the phone away from my ear, I shot it the finger. "I hate you right now you asshole!"

"Merry Christmas, dude. See ya soon."

The line went dead as I rushed back into the house. Skidding around the corner, I came to a dead stop when I saw Brynlee holding the puppy in her arms. He was licking her face as she laughed.

With a smile that spread from ear to ear, Brynlee began crying. "You got me a puppy!"

Even though I had a huge pink bow and a giant pink basket to put the new puppy in, this was by far the best way for Brynlee to find him.

"He was barking and I knew there was no way in hell that was you coughing on the back porch."

I set my phone down on the island and headed toward her. "I wanted to put a big pink bow on him and have him poke his head out of a basket. You ruined my plan, little buddy."

Brynlee giggled as she placed her hand behind my neck and pulled me in for a kiss. When our lips parted, she smiled. "This was perfect."

My chest felt light as my stomach dropped. There was so much happiness in her eyes. I knew what she really wanted was a baby, but this little guy would be our first baby.

"He doesn't have a name yet."

Brynlee bit down on her lip as she lifted him up and stared into his eyes. My heart began to beat harder as I watched her. It was the

first time in weeks I saw true happiness in those eyes.

"Trigger."

I lifted my eyebrows and repeated, "Trigger?"

"Yep. Because the moment I saw him, he triggered a memory."

She dropped down to the floor and let Trigger climb all over her.

I quickly sat down next to them and laughed when Trigger began pouncing over to me. "What was the memory?"

"The first time I ever saw you."

With a frown, I let out a gruff laugh and said, "I don't know whether that's a good thing or a bad thing."

Brynlee smiled and shook her head. "It's a very good thing. The moment your eyes met mine, something in me changed. It was like a feeling I had never experienced before came to life. My life has never been the same since." She picked up Trigger and kissed him on the nose as he barked and tried licking her face. "And the moment this little guy looked up at me with my brand new scarf wrapped all around his body, something inside of me came alive. A sense of hope."

With a grin, I motioned to Trigger. "He is cute, isn't he?"

"Cute? He is the most handsome boy ever!"

"Hey!" I protested as I bumped her arm.

"That doesn't include human boys. You're still top dog in that department."

A feeling of love swept over my body as I watched Brynlee play with Trigger. An overwhelming sense of desire had me standing and pulling her up with me as Trigger spread out on the floor and almost instantly fell asleep. I unbuttoned my jeans and pushed them down, exposing my dick to her.

Brynlee licked her lips as she looked at my hard length. I quickly pushed her cotton shorts and panties down as I pushed two fingers inside of her to get her ready for my dick. Picking her up, I slowly lowered her onto me as we both moaned.

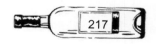

"Feels so warm," I whispered.

Brynlee began moving as my dick hardened even more. "Yeah, baby. That feels so good."

I sat down in the chair as Brynlee fucked me. My head dropped back as I felt her squeeze around me. "Baby, I'm so close. Brynlee, you need to come."

"It feels so good, I don't want it to end," she said as she rode me.

"Faster," I panted out as Brynlee gave me her all.

She buried her face into my neck and called out my name as she came. It didn't take me long to explode; I came hard.

"That was amazing."

I ran my hands over her back as I sighed in contentment. "Hell yeah, it was."

"Don't pull out of me yet."

With a smile, I stood up and was going to walk us into the living room when I took one step and slipped. I dropped straight to the floor, making sure I kept Brynlee safe as she landed on top of me.

"Holy fuck! Are you okay?"

"Yeah, I hit my knees but I'm okay. What in the hell did you slip—"

Brynlee's mouth dropped open as she slowly looked back at me as she pressed her lips together. A sick, sinking feeling moved over me as I thought about the warm mushy stuff I stepped in.

"It's dog shit, isn't it?"

Biting down on her lip, Brynlee nodded her head as she tried not to laugh. Then she said, "Welcome to puppy parenthood."

Thirty-Three

Brynlee

Three Months Later...

A s I sat on the examination table, I rubbed my hands down my pants, trying to calm my nerves. I couldn't help but notice the empty feeling in the pit of my stomach as I waited for Dr. Malick to come into the room.

Brody paced in front of the window as he read something on his phone. "Did you get the job?" I asked, trying to busy my mind. Brody glanced up and flashed me those dimples.

"We did. I'm not gonna lie and say I'm not terrified to be re-modeling someone else's kitchen, but she liked the work Travis and I have done."

My heart about burst from my chest I was so proud of Brody and Travis. They both found something they loved doing.

The door to the office opened and Dr. Malick shook Brody's hand and then quickly patted me on the shoulder. "Great news, blood

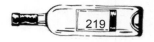

work and scan all came back negative."

I breathed a sigh of relief, as did Brody.

"How are you feeling?"

"Amazing!" And it was the truth. The last three months I had finally felt like myself. The reconstruction surgery was done, my hair finally had a cute short bob thing going on, Trigger finally stopped going potty in the house, Brody was beyond happy working alongside me at the vineyard, and then starting up a new business with Travis. Life was amazing.

"Good, I'm glad to hear that. You look happy and relaxed. I like that."

Brody took my hand and kissed the back of it. "Dr. Malick, are we in the clear for trying to have a baby now?" he asked.

I held my breath as I waited for his reply. "I think you are more than in the clear. It's been beyond the six months and you're feeling good. I don't see why you can't start trying."

Brody and I jumped up as he pulled me into his arms. My tears feel freely as the idea of us starting a family swept over me.

"Trigger is going to be so happy!" Brody said as I laughed and buried my face into his chest.

Life was indeed amazing.

Walking along the trail, I let out a sigh as I dropped my head back and felt the light rain gently hit my face. Ever since I was a little girl, I loved to walk around in the rain. It was calming and so peaceful to listen to the rain gently watering the earth.

Trigger ran ahead of me and barked at a bird that had landed on the ground to take in the rain as well.

"Bad puppy! Leave her be, boy!"

He watched the bird fly off before he pounced back over to me.

220

I couldn't believe how big he had gotten. Dropping down, I hugged his neck. "My big baby boy. Today's your five-month birthday. What shall we do to celebrate?"

Trigger barked and kissed me quickly as I chuckled. Standing, I patted my leg for him to follow me back to the house. As I made my way back toward the house, I mentally checked off the things I had to do on my to-do list. Melanie and Travis were getting married in less than a month and the wedding was going to be here at the winery. Something else I'd wanted to do for some time. I was hoping with Melanie's wedding, my father would see how amazing of an opportunity it would be to open up the winery and vineyards for weddings.

Lost in thought, I wandered back toward the house as the rain gently fell. Trigger started barking and took off ahead of me, even though I called him back, he was gone.

"Damn dog," I mumbled.

As I came around the corner my heart stopped and my breath hitched.

Amy.

Trigger was trying to jump up on her as Brody grabbed him and brought him into the house.

My heart began to pound in my chest as I slowly made my way toward the house. My feet felt like they were walking through a mud pit as I forced myself to pick them up and walk.

Why was I so freaked out? I knew they hadn't slept together. My head began racing as thoughts began to flood my mind. Maybe she liked Brody. What if she was trying to take him from me?

As I approached, I noticed her hands on her very swollen stomach. I stopped dead in my tracks.

She was pregnant.

Air. I can't breathe in any air.

Brody was laughing at something Amy had said has he tossed his head back. Finally he glanced over to me and his smile faded. It

was then I saw another man walk up and wrap his arms around Amy and rest them on her stomach.

With a forced smile, I started walking again. I could see it in Brody's eyes; he was worried about my initial reaction.

"There she is," Brody said as he flashed me those dimples.

Amy turned and smiled warmly at me. "Brynlee! It's so good to see you again. Brody was just filling us in on the good news."

I looked Brody's way as I asked, "Good news?"

Brody's smile faded some. "You beat-cancer-head-on-and-won good news."

My face blushed. *What is wrong with me today?*

With a bigger smile, I nodded and said, "Oh yes! Duh! That news!" I pointed to Amy's belly and said, "It looks like you've got some good news to share also."

Her face glowed and a tinge of jealousy raced through my veins. I wanted that glow.

"I'm so sorry, where are my manners? Brynlee, this is my husband, Rick."

Rick extended his hand to mine as he gently shook it. "It's a pleasure to meet you, Brynlee."

With a quick nod, I said, "The pleasure is all mine."

I looked between Amy and Brody, waiting for someone to explain to me why she was here … at our house.

Amy let out a nervous chuckle. "I'm sure you're wondering why I'm here."

With a casual shrug, I said, "Maybe just a little."

Rick wrapped his arm around his wife as Amy gazed up at him with nothing but love in her eyes. I needed to stop behaving like a scorned woman. Amy never did anything to me.

"We were cleaning out Amy's room where she had been living with Jane, and we came across a watch."

Brody held up the watch his parents had bought for him when he graduated from UT. His name was carved on the back of it. "I

222

must have taken it off in my drunken state and tossed it on the floor."

He would take it off every night and set it on the end table before getting into bed. With a small laugh, I shook my head as relief instantly relaxed my overly tense body. "He normally took it off and set it on the side table. He must have just dropped it on the floor."

Amy laughed. "Well, when I saw the engraving we knew we needed to bring it back before we headed out to Arizona."

My eyebrows lifted. "You're moving to Arizona?"

Rick rubbed Amy's stomach as they both grinned from ear to ear. "Yes, Rick has been offered a promotion at work, and Arizona is where he needs to be."

"Well if you ever feel like coming for a visit, you know you're welcome here for a glass of wine or two." I said with a genuine smile. I was happy for Amy. After knowing her husband cheated on her and she moved to Napa Valley to start a new life, I was glad she met a good guy.

"If you don't mind me asking, when are you due?"

Amy's hands glided over her stomach as she said, "June 27."

"Boy or girl?"

Rick chuckled. "We're not finding out. We want it to be a surprise."

Brody wrapped his arm around my waist and pulled me closer to him. I was positive he knew how I was feeling. It wasn't like I wasn't happy for Amy and Rick, I truly was. My heart was just sad as I wondered if that would ever be me.

"I would want to be surprised too," I said with a wink.

"Listen, we'd better take off. We're driving, and I'm sure Amy is going to have to stop every hour to pee."

Everyone laughed as Brody and I walked them back to their car. After saying goodbye and wishing them both the best, Rick drove off down the driveway.

Brody turned me to face him. He cupped my face within his

hands and gently brushed his lips across mine. A single tear rolled down my cheek as he used his thumb to wipe it away. "What if God doesn't want me to get pregnant because the cancer's going to—"

Brody placed his finger over my lips to keep me from talking. He slowly shook his head and stared into my eyes. "Brynlee, listen to yourself. That is not the woman who fought for her own life only to give up so easily. Sweetheart, it's only been a month since we started trying. Stop worrying about it. Let's just focus on us, your sister's wedding, the amazing cruise I'm taking you on in a couple of months. We've got this. It will happen when it's supposed to happen."

Sniffling, I nodded my head. "I know. I'm not sure why I'm so emotional about this. I know I need to just breathe."

Brody brought my lips to his as he gently kissed me. We were lost in our kiss as it deepened and became more passionate. Soon I was in his arms as Brody carried me into our bedroom. The whole world slipped away as Brody made slow sweet love to me.

The moment we both came and softly called out each other's names, if felt as if life had begun all over again. Our love couldn't have been any stronger in that moment. Brody whispered how much he loved me against my lips as I wrapped my arms around him. Something magical happened between us and I couldn't help but feel the love deep within my soul.

Looking deep into his beautiful hazel eyes, I smiled and finally let go of that young girl who thought she had her whole life planned out. That wasn't me anymore. My husband wasn't the same man I met that day when he flashed me that panty-melting smile.

We were different. In a way, the cancer made me a better person. I just needed to finally learn to let the past go and embrace the future.

Thirty-Four

Brody

With a deep inhale, I slowly pushed it out and smiled. "What a beautiful June morning."

"I'm going to forget my vows. I just know it."

With a quick peek over to Travis, I tried not to laugh as he paced back and forth on the deck.

After another invigorating breath, I sighed with satisfaction. "Man, you can smell the fresh air. Such a beautiful morning."

"Melanie will act like it's okay if I forget them, but then when we're alone, she'll kill me!"

"I think we should do some yoga stretches."

Travis stopped pacing and glared at me. "What?"

"Yoga. Come on," I said as I dropped to the wood deck and got into a downward dog. Trigger came running over and did the same damn thing. I swear Brynlee had been teaching him yoga. "Look! Even Trigger is getting into it."

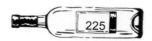

225

Travis' eyes widened in shock as he looked between me and Trigger. "I'm not doing your pansy-ass yoga!"

"Why? Because you're too manly to do yoga? *Please.*"

I moved into another position and took in a deep breath.

"Fuck," Travis, said as he dropped down next to me and Trigger barked. "Yeah, fuck you too, you little bastard."

"Hey! Don't talk to my dog like that, buttmunch."

Travis' body slumped as he looked at me. "What are we, in middle school?"

Grunting, I got into position. "Let's start off with a seated head to knee."

Travis moved awkwardly into position. After a few minutes, we switched sides.

"All right, let's get into a cobra position."

Travis followed my lead as I got on my stomach and pushed up with my arms. Travis grunted as he said, "Feels like my back is going to break, dude. Shit!"

With a chuckle, I got into another position. "Side plank it! Keep your palm facing out and balance."

Travis fell over on each side. "Move it along, dude."

Grinning like a fool, I decided it was time to have fun. "Next we're gonna do an eagle."

"Sounds cool," Travis said as he clapped his hands together. It had taken me months to get this damn move down. I wrapped my right leg around my left as I intertwined my arms together and balanced on my one leg.

"Are you fucking kidding me right now? I'd like to be able to use my dick tonight, Brody. You look like you're squeezing the hell out of the poor fellow."

"Nah, if I can do it you can. We both know my dick's bigger."

Travis pushed me, causing me to lose my balance. Letting out a laugh, I motioned for him to get into position. "Come on, just try it."

Travis's face turned serious as he started to get into position. A

few times he lost his balance, but he finally had it down.

"Deep breath in and slowly let it out."

Travis did what I said as he closed his eyes. Melanie came walking up the stairs with a look of pure horror on her face.

"Now softly hum."

"Hum?"

"Yeah dude, it will totally get you refocused on your vows."

Pressing her lips together and covering her mouth, Melanie
stood there and watched Travis.

"Humm … hum …"

"Dude! Don't say the word. Do it. Om … Om …"

Travis lost his balance and got back into position. "Om … om
… om …"

Melanie's shoulders were shaking as I forced myself not to
laugh. "That's it, dude. Get in touch with your inner self."

Travis' leg began shaking as he continued to repeat *om* over and
over. By now I had my phone out and was recording him. Trigger sat
in front of him and watched intently.

"I'm not feeling relaxed, Brody. My fucking hamstring is about
to cramp!"

"Don't stop the pose! It will pass."

"It's not going to pass. Cramp! Cramp!"

Travis' eyes popped open as he fell to the floor and cried out in
pain. "Oh my God! Worst cramp of my life!"

"Pull your foot back."

Travis glared at me. "That's for your calf, you stupid idiot!"

With a shrug, I glanced over to Melanie. "Any suggestions?"

Travis twisted around on the floor and saw Melanie staring
down at him. He quickly jumped up, only to fall right back down.
Melanie looked at me and said, "Don't turn my future husband into a
yoga-loving, pansy-ass like you, dickhead."

Travis pointed to me and shouted, "See! I hate you right now!"

Throwing my head back, I laughed my ass off. "My work here

227

is done!"

I headed into the house with Melanie right behind me as Travis continued to moan about his hamstring.

"Just write them down, babe, and then read them."

"What? I can do that?" Travis called out as we both headed into the house.

"What do you mean she's sick?"

Catrina looked around as she called out instructions for last-minute details. The wedding was starting in less than an hour and guests were already showing up.

"Melanie and Brynlee both ate the crab dip. Melanie just feels queasy, but Brynlee is throwing up."

"Shit."

I headed into the house, taking the stairs two at a time. I rushed into her old room and to the bathroom. Brynlee was sitting on the floor with her head in her hands, moaning.

I dropped to my knees and took her by the shoulders. "Sweet-heart, are you okay?"

She dropped her hands as she looked at me with a ghostly ex-pression. "Food poisoning is worse than the chemo! I feel like I'm going to throw up my right lung."

"Not the left?" I said, trying to joke.

Brynlee narrowed her eyes at me and said, "Not a time for fun-ny, Brody. My sister is getting married in less than an hour, and I'm puking my guts up."

"It's okay, let's get it all out of your system. Let me go grab something for your stomach."

Brynlee waved her hands around. "Don't bother. Mom already gave me some stuff. I haven't thrown it up … yet. Maybe that's a

good sign."

My fingers pushed a piece of her hair behind her ear as I gave her a smile. It had grown so fast in the last few months and was now halfway to her shoulders. The rich brown wavy hair felt good against my fingers as I moved my hand through her hair.

"I love you."

Her eyes met mine as she smiled. "You're really saying that to me when I'm on the floor puking?"

"I am. I came so close to losing you that I don't take a single moment for granted."

Tears began to pool in Brynlee's eyes as she got up and wrapped her arms around my neck. "I love you too. So very much."

A light knock on the door had me getting up to open it. Melanie stood on the other side of the door looking white as a ghost.

"You okay, Mel?"

She slowly shook her head. "I'm scared." Brynlee jumped up and took her sister in her arms.

"No! Melanie, you're just nervous. It's going to be okay, sweetie. Travis loves you and Jacob so much."

When Brynlee pulled back, Melanie wiped her tears away. "No ... no, that's not what I'm scared of."

Brynlee looked into her sister's eyes and asked, "Well, then what, honey?"

Melanie swallowed hard as she said, "I'm scared you're going to throw up during the ceremony."

Brynlee dropped her hands to her side and shook her head. "You're such a bitch."

Melanie wiped her snotty nose and exclaimed, "What?! You'd be worried about the same thing and don't deny it."

Brynlee lifted her hand and began pointing to Melanie. "Okay, you listen here—"

I stepped between both of them and turned to Brynlee. "All right, that's enough. Brynlee, go rinse your mouth out with some-

thing strong." With a spin on my heels, I faced Melanie. "Go get your makeup fixed and I'll make sure Brynlee does as well. We've got a wedding we need to get ready for, ladies."

Melanie leaned in closer to me and whispered. "I don't think it's the crab dip." With a wink and wipe of another tear, Melanie took off and headed back to her parents' room where she was getting ready.

My heart slammed against my chest as I turned back and looked at my wife. She had her head back as she gargled mouthwash. She spit it out and turned to face me. Her face had the most beautiful glow to it and I wondered how I hadn't noticed it before.

"What? Is there puke on me anywhere?"

The only thing I could do was shake my head. Words were lost as I took in her appearance. "No, you look beautiful."

Grinning like an innocent little girl, I fought to hold back the urge to take her home and make love to her.

"Thank you. I should go get my makeup fixed."

"How's your stomach?"

"It's weird, it just went away. Must be the stuff mom gave me. It was probably some secret Portuguese concoction."

I placed my hand on the side of her face as she leaned into it. "Yeah, probably. I'll see ya downstairs in a bit."

Brynlee placed her hand over mine. Nothing but love swam in her beautiful green eyes. "Okay, see you in a bit."

A quick kiss on her lips and I watched her walk away. I leaned up against the door jam and tried to catch my breath.

Brynlee's pregnant.

Thirty-Five

Brynlee

My heart soared as I watched my sister head out hand-in-hand with Travis to her honeymoon. Covering my mouth, I silently cried as my parents each gave her a kiss and spoke to her in Portuguese as Travis looked on.

"I love you, *Papai* and Momma," Melanie said as she hugged them both. Turning to face me, our eyes met and I could see just how happy she was. I lifted my hand and mouthed, *"I love you,"* as Melanie pursed her lips together and nodded.

Jacob was on Brody's shoulders as he gave both Melanie and Travis high fives. My sister slipped into the limo and then she was gone.

A hand softly squeezed my shoulder as I turned to see my father standing there. "Walk with me, *meu amor.*"

"Of course, *Papai.*"

With his arm extended out, I wrapped my arm in his as we be-

gan walking down toward the vineyards.

"Are you okay?" I asked as I watched his expression.

"I am, but a bit sad as well."

I tilted my head as I watched him. "Why are you sad?"

He shrugged and said, "Both my *meninas* are married and moved on."

My head dropped to his shoulder as we slowly walked. "But you haven't lost us. How many parents can say both their kids live within minutes of them?"

With a nod, he sighed. "I know. I know. But that doesn't make it any easier. I remember walking with you like this not too long ago and you had little pigtails in your hair. The only concern you had was if Momma was going to make dessert or not."

With a giggle, I let the memory in. "I remember that day. I had won some award at home and begged her to make my favorite dessert."

We stopped walking as my father closed his eyes and let the silence surround him. I knew where I got my desire to do this—from my father.

"Love has a strong hold on this family."

"Yes, it does."

"I often walk among these vines and wonder what I ever did to receive the blessings in my life. Your mother being at the top of that list."

With a smile, I let out a soft chuckle. "Something happened to me when you first got diagnosed with cancer."

My head dropped to the side as I asked, "What happened?"

His eyes closed as he said, "I got angry with God. So very angry."

Tears began to build in my eyes as I tried to blink them away. "You were my little girl, and how dare he try and take you away before you got to really live your life."

"*Papai.*"

"Your mother took my hand one day and we went for a walk. All I could picture was you running up and down these vines." A small laugh passed through his lips as I smiled.

"Every dream I ever dreamed for you flashed before my eyes when you told us about the cancer and then what you thought had happened with Brody. You were hurting so much during all of that and I stood back and watched how you handled it."

My father turned to me as a tear rolled down his cheek. "Love had a hold on you, Brynlee. It was more than just our love for you, or Brody's love for you. It was something so much bigger than us. That day with your mother I realized that and I asked for forgiveness."

I walked up to my father as he held his arms out. Burying my face into his chest, I breathed in my father's cologne.

"*Papai*, we're both so very happy."

He wrapped me up tighter in his arms as he kissed the top of my head. "I know, *meu amor*. I know."

My father and I walked for a bit longer before heading back up to the reception that was still going strong. Brody was teaching Jacob how to play horseshoes as my mother moved from person to person, making sure everyone was happy.

Feeling the happiness bubbling up inside of me, I took it all in.

Closing my eyes, I thanked God for the beautiful gift he had given me.

Life.

Three days after the wedding, Brody and I headed to Seattle to board the cruise ship to Alaska. I couldn't wait and had been making plans for each of the seven days. Brody finally took me by the arms and looked at me with a serious look in his eyes. "*Sweetheart, we don't*

have to plan every second of every day. Let's just enjoy this. "

I was practically jumping up and down as we waited to board the plane. "How are you feeling?"

With a quizzical look, I shrugged. "Fine. Why?"

"Just curious is all. You excited?"

"Yes!" I grabbed Brody's arm and squeezed it as I did a little jump. "Oh Brody, do you think we'll see a moose? I just really want to see a moose!"

Brody chuckled and said, "Maybe."

"Ugh," I said as I rolled my eyes. "I just want to see one. It doesn't even need to be up close. Just one! Preferably a boy."

"A bull."

Pinching my eyebrows together, I stared at Brody. "No, a moose. I don't want to see a male cow."

With a quick laugh, Brody pulled me to him and kissed me quickly on the lips. "God, I love you."

Smiling, I did a little excited jump as I squealed with delight. "This is going to be the best trip ever!"

Three days later Brody and I had flown back to Seattle and were now checking into The Woodmark Hotel in Kirkland. Turned out boats and me didn't get along together.

Brody opened the door to the room and I gasped. The first thing I saw was a giant window and beyond that the lake. "There's a private balcony also."

"It's beautiful," I whispered as I made my way across the room. As I pushed the doors to the balcony open, a cool breeze hit my face, causing me to close my eyes and smile. I took in a deep breath and slowly blew it out. This felt amazing and a far cry from me hanging over the balcony on the ship with my face green the whole time.

Heat radiated through my body as Brody wrapped his arms around me. "Is this better, sweetheart?"

With a giggle, I nodded. "Yes. I'm so sorry I ruined our cruise."

Soft lips moved across my neck, and I tilted it, allowing Brody better access. His hand moved down my stomach where he paused for a second and moaned. My knees felt weak as my head dropped back to him. Brody moved his hand and began lifting my skirt as my breathing increased.

"I want to fuck you right here on the balcony with you holding onto the rails."

I bit down on my lip and quickly glanced around. No one from another room could see our balcony. Trees and foliage were abundant. My heart felt as if it dropped to my tummy as I pushed my ass into his growing dick.

His lips grazed across my neck and over to my ear. "Is that a dare?"

I couldn't help the smile that spread across my face. "Do you want it to be?"

Brody dropped down and slipped his hands under my skirt as he pulled my panties off. Lifting each leg, I tried to calm my beating heart. Were we really going to do this?

Covering my mouth to keep my giggles at bay, Brody used his foot to spread my legs apart as he slipped his fingers inside of me.

"Damn, baby. You're so wet."

With a glance over my shoulder, I gave him a sexy smile. "I want you."

Moving quickly, Brody has his hard length out as he slowly moved his hand up and down his shaft as I moaned. "Brody, now."

With a wink, he moved closer to me and lined himself up with me. One push in and we were moaning. "Hold onto the rail, baby."

I gripped it and got ready. "Brody, I don't want sweet and slow."

My body jumped as his lips gently kissed my neck again as he

pulled out and then pushed back in quickly.

"Yes," I hissed. "Harder."

Brody dug his fingers into my hips as he gave me what I asked for. "Fucking hell, you're squeezing the fuck out of my dick, baby. I'm not going to last long."

The door to the balcony above us opened and a couple started talking as Brody slowed his pace down. Grabbing on to the rail, I pushed back into him, causing him to moan. The couple above stopped talking. "Harder, go faster!" I cried as Brody came to a stop. I looked over my shoulder and giggled; he had a horrified look on his face and pointed up.

I decided life was too short not to be naughty once in awhile. "Fuck me harder!"

Brody smiled a wicked smile as he pulled out and slammed back into me. It was raw, passionate and hot-as-flipping-hell. "Oh God!" I panted out as Brody gave me everything.

"That's it, oh God. Ah ... feels ... so ... good!"

Brody moaned as he slowed down just a bit, and I knew he was trying to hold off until I came. I whimpered as Brody hit the spot over and over. "Yes! Right there, harder."

"Fucking hell, baby. You need to come."

I knew the couple was still outside on their balcony as they listened to the private show they were getting. There was something naughty about what we were doing. Then it hit me. "Brody! I'm coming!"

Brody pumped faster and harder as he let out a grunt and came. "Ahh ... fuuuck ... baby, I'm coming so fucking hard."

Our breathing was so labored, and Brody slowed down to a stop but stayed buried inside of me. It was then we heard the faint sounds of two bodies slapping together and a soft moan.

I covered my mouth and peeked over my shoulder at Brody as he pulled out of me and zipped up his pants. Spinning around, I stared at him as we listened to the couple above us having sex.

"Oh yeah, oh yeah, baby, that's it," the girl said in a hushed whisper that was still loud enough for us to hear. Brody made a funny face as if he was impressed about what was happening above us.

I placed my hands on his chest as we moved closer to each other. "Yes! Yes! Oh God."

I lifted my eyebrow as I tilted my head. My lower stomach pulled as I realized I was getting turned on again by listening to the couple above us. Brody smiled and his dimples popped out as he licked his lips.

Soft moans from above began to push me over the edge as I slipped my hand under my skirt. Brody's eyes lit up with excitement as he watched me touch myself.

His lips pressed against mine as he whispered, "Does hearing them turn you on, baby?"

"Yes," I whispered back.

The sounds of their bodies slapping together had Brody pulling back and getting undressed as I pulled my hand out from under my skirt and did the same.

I was shocked to see Brody's dick getting hard again as he watched me rub my clit.

The girl above us was coming as she tried to keep her moans of pleasure covered.

"Brody," I said as he grabbed my hands and pulled me back into the room and over to the bed where I quickly crawled on and laid down.

Two seconds later, Brody was moving in and out of me. The door to our balcony was still open as we heard the guy upstairs call out in pleasure as he came. He wasn't nearly as discreet as she was.

"Fucking hell," Brody said as sweat began to bead on his forehead as he continued to fuck me hard and fast.

I covered my mouth as one of the most intense orgasms I'd ever experienced raced through my body. Brody reached up and moved my hands as I cried out in pleasure when I felt his dick swell and he

called out my name. We both came together hard for the second time in less than ten minutes.

Brody pulled out of me and fell to the side of the bed as we both dragged in air as our chests heaved.

"Being naughty … is so much … fun." I said with a giggle as Brody laughed and pulled me back on top of him.

"My dick is exhausted and trying to figure out what in the hell just happened."

I sat up and rubbed against his now soft dick. I teasingly slapped his chest and laughed. "That was naughty."

Brody wiggled his eyebrows. "That was fun."

My finger went into my mouth and I bit down on it. "Very fun."

With a few circles of my hips, I was stunned to see I was getting turned on again. Brody grabbed onto my hips and said, "Baby, I appreciate your appetite, but I'm spent. There is no way he's coming back up any time soon."

Jutting my lower lip out, I sighed. "But I'm horny again."

Brody's eyes widened. "How? I just fucked the hell out of you twice!"

With a laugh, I shrugged my shoulders. "I just am—it's weird. It feels like I can't get enough of you."

Brody quickly rolled me over as he kissed my lips. "Let's go eat first. Then I promise, I will take care of you when we get back to the room."

That's when it hit me. I was starving. "Yes!" I said as I popped up out of bed. "I'm so hungry. Let's go eat."

I was up and getting dressed before Brody could even figure out what had happened.

With a chuckle, he headed out to the balcony to retrieve his jeans.

We were about to head out of the hotel room when we heard banging. Brody and I stopped and looked at each other. "No way."

Running back to the bed, we both jumped up and placed our

ears to the wall.

"They're fucking again." Brody said with a disgusted look on his face. I couldn't help but giggle.

"We did too."

We could hear both of them moaning and calling out as the bed hit over and over against the wall.

Brody jerked his head back and dropped his mouth open. "They're competing with us, those assholes!"

With a slight shake of my head, I frowned and said, "No. Do you think so?"

"Yes, baby, fuck me harder!"

We both jumped off the bed and looked up.

"Damn the walls here are pretty thin," Brody said.

I placed my hands on my hips. "Oh no, if she thinks she's gonna try to outdo me with sex, she has another thing coming."

"Someone's coming, that's for sure."

The banging increased as we both jumped back onto the bed and put our ears to the wall. The guy grunted as the girl cried out and the banging began to slowly come to a stop.

Silence.

"Oh. Oh," I said as I waved my finger in front of me in contempt. "Hell no. It's so on."

Brody gave me a serious look. "We need to get a game plan down. Come on, let's re-fuel."

Thirty-Six

Brody

"We need to start with oral sex. I have the best orgasms with it. I mean, like mind-blowing orgasms."

I nodded as I took a bite of steak. "Right."

"Then, I'm thinking we try a little backdoor action."

Choking on my piece of steak, I looked at Brynlee. "W-what?"

"Yeah, like push a finger inside as I come. We missed that on our one year anniversary, so we need to start making up for that."

I swallowed hard as I reached down and adjusted my growing dick. We needed to get up to our room, stat.

"Then I think you need to take me from behind. That should make the bed rock good."

My head was starting to spin as I began feeling light. I wanted to feel Brynlee's pulsing clit up against my tongue this very second.

"Again, when you take me from behind ... do the finger." She held her index finger up and raised her eyebrows as I moaned.

240

"Brody, get your head in the game!"

"Oh, it's in," I replied as I moved about in my seat. "He's all in. Let's leave. Now."

A young couple walked into the restaurant as Brynlee and I both looked at them. "Do you think that's them?" I asked as we watched the hostess bring them to a corner table."

"Hmm … could be. Everyone else that's come in has been old. Too old to keep up with us like they did."

The waitress walked over and asked if we'd like to look at the dessert menu. Brynlee wasn't really one for dessert, so I said no.

"No wait, do you have chocolate mousse?"

I laughed as I shook my head and looked back over to the couple. *Oh no, they are not.*

My mouth fell open as I watched the guy clearly getting the girl off under the table.

When her eyes looked up and met mine, she smiled. There was something extremely awkward about this.

Darting my eyes away, I kicked Brynlee. "Ouch!"

"We have to go."

"No, I want my dessert. I'm craving it bad."

"No, seriously get it to go."

"I don't want it to go, Brody. I want to eat it here."

I stole a glance back over to the table where the girl was still staring at me as she licked her lips and bit down.

Oh fuck. I'm totally getting creeped out here.

"Um, sweetheart, I really think we should go have dessert upstairs." I glanced back over to the couple.

Brynlee glared at me. "Brody, I don't want dessert in the room, and what are you looking at?" Brynlee must have followed my eyes because she gasped. "Is he?"

"Yes."

"Is she seriously eye-fucking you right now?"

"Yes. I'm extremely uncomfortable. Plus she made me lose my

hard-on."

"She's getting turned on by you watching. That bitch."

I pulled my eyes away and could feel the sweat building on my brow. "Okay, well let's go."

"What? No way, finger me under the table."

My head snapped over to Brynlee as my mouth hit the floor. "Come again?"

"Do it. I'm not wearing any panties."

My heart started beating faster in my chest as I leaned in closer to her. "You're not wearing any panties?"

With a naughty smile, she shook her head. "Nope. And I'm very, *very* wet right now."

With a dazed and confused look on my face, my eyes stared into hers. "Where is my wife? What have you done with her?"

Brynlee smiled. "Come on, Brody. Let's have some fun."

"No, let's not get kicked out of the restaurant and possibly the hotel."

Brynlee sucked in a breath of air. "She's coming! Look at her."

"I'd rather not."

"Oh wow. That's hot as hell."

Damn it. I turned and saw the guy kissing on her neck as her body jerked ever so slightly with her orgasm. When her eyes opened she looked straight at me. I quickly looked away. "Let's get out of here, please."

"Um, yeah maybe we should, 'cause now she's getting him off and he's staring at me."

"What?" I said as I looked back over there. Sure enough he was giving my wife a come-fuck-me look.

"We're out of here," I said as I stood up and took Brynlee by the hand. Tossing a hundred onto the table, I asked the waitress to send the dessert up to our room.

I practically pulled Brynlee's arm out of her socket as I dragged her to the elevator. All I could think about was how she had been

talking to me ... fingers ... ass ... no panties. As soon as the door shut, I hit the stop button, unzipped my jeans, and fucked my wife fast and hard.

When we were finished and I slowly pulled out of her, Brynlee gave me a concerned look. "Just please tell me it wasn't her looking at you that turned you on."

The fear in her eyes gutted me. "Fuck no. It was you telling me you didn't have any panties on and fucking you from behind, fingers in your ass, and all that talk."

With a slight smile, she bit down on her lip. "Good."

The next two days were spent exploring the Kirkland area. At night we fucked like rabbits as we tried to outperform the couple above. Each morning Brynlee woke up feeling sick. As the days went on, the more I had to fight to keep my thoughts to myself. The last thing I wanted to do was get her hopes up.

I was sitting out on the balcony reading while I waited for Brynlee to come back from the corner store. She wanted to go for a run and then pick up some stuff we needed. We only had two more days here and then it was back to Napa Valley.

The door to our hotel room shut as I sat up and looked behind me. Brynlee was setting two bags down on the desk. She glanced outside and smiled when she saw me looking. Then her smile faltered and my stomach dropped. Something happened.

Quickly standing, I made my way to her. "Hey, what's with the worried look on your face?"

Tears were beginning to build as she squeezed her eyes shut. "I ... I wasn't wanting to get my hopes up, but all signs point to it."

With her face now cupped in my hands, I leaned down and looked into her eyes. "What, sweetheart? All signs point to what?"

She began chewing the corner of her lip as she reached into the bag and pulled out a pregnancy test.

My whole body tingled as my face upturned into a wide-ass grin. "Baby, I've been wanting so badly to ask you if you thought

you might be pregnant."

Her eyes lit up. "Really? Why?"

I kissed her as her arms wrapped around my neck. Her hands pushed through my hair as she grabbed a handful and pulled slightly as I moaned into her mouth.

"Tell me why?" she spoke against my lips.

"For one, you're horny as hell."

Brynlee giggled.

"You look different. There's a glow about you that I can't really explain. Have you missed your period?"

"I haven't had one in two months. I've just been so afraid to even think it, let alone find out, that I kind of just pushed the idea to the side."

"The sickness?"

She scrunched her nose up in the most adorable way as she said, "Yeah, I can't talk myself out of that one."

I took her hand in mine. "So, let's find out."

Expelling a quick breath, Brynlee said, "Okay. Let's do this."

I opened the box and took out the test as we walked into the bathroom. Brynlee held her hand out as I gave her the test.

"One thing, no matter what it says, we're going to make love to one another. As much as I want to prove to the couple upstairs we're the ultimate in fucking, I want you to make love to me."

My lips brushed over hers as I said, "I love that idea."

Brynlee peed on the stick and then set it on the counter as we both stared at it. "What will it do?"

"There will be two lines if it's positive."

My hand reached down for hers as I forced myself to breathe. I knew Brynlee was holding her breath as well, because when I said, "Breathe, baby," she took in a deep breath.

We both sucked in a breath as I stared down at the stick and said, "There are two lines."

"I've got another one. Hold on!"

244

Brynlee raced out of the room and came back in with four more tests. "Jesus, how many did you buy?"

"Six," she said as she began opening them. "Help me open them and hand them to me."

"Wait!" I said as I grabbed a towel and set it on the counter. "Sorry, but something about pee-soaked sticks on the counter grosses me out."

Brynlee rolled her eyes as she took one of the tests and sat down. She started peeing and we formed a little work line. She'd pee on one and then force herself to stop, then pee on another and another, until I had five more tests lined up.

As we waited, I bumped her shoulder. "I'm super impressed you were able to stop and go like that with your pee."

Her face blushed as she waved me of with her hand. "Melanie and I used to see who could stop and go the most. I guess I built up the muscles for it."

I couldn't help but laugh as I reached down and kissed her. When we looked back down, tears began to build in my eyes. Two more tests showed the double line. One test had a plus sign, and said *yes,* another said *pregnant,* and the last one showed a plus sign. Brynlee and I turned to each other as I reached up and wiped her tears away.

"We're pregnant," she barely spoke as her voice cracked.

"Happy Mother's Day, sweetheart."

Brynlee threw herself into my arms as we both broke down crying and laughing at the same time. We spent the rest of the afternoon in bed. We made love and then talked about our future. Brynlee was of course worried about Trigger and how he would react. She was concerned about if there was still anything from her cancer treatments still in her body. After reassuring her all was okay, we drifted off to sleep in each other's arms.

I'd forever hold this day close to my heart.

"**I** cannot believe this is our last night here. I've had so much fun here."

I wrapped my arms around Brynlee as I gently kissed her neck. "I have too. And this place will always be special to us because we found out we were having a baby here."

Brynlee spun around and draped her arms over my shoulders. "Super special. Shall we head out to dinner?"

"Let's," I said as I gave her a quick peck on the lips. Brynlee grabbed her sweater as we headed to the door. Opening it, we stopped dead in our tracks as the couple from upstairs stood before us.

They both smiled big as Brynlee took my hand in hers and squeezed it. "It's been so quiet down here, we thought you had left," the girl said with a wink.

"Um, well, I guess we, um … decided to give you guys a break," Brynlee said with a nervous chuckle.

The guy eye-fucked the hell out of Brynlee as he smiled bigger. I wanted to pound his face in for the way he was looking at her. My eyes wandered over to the girl, who was doing her own fair share of eye fucking as she licked her lips and looked between Brynlee and me.

"Listen, I'm tired of being turned on beyond belief listening to the two of you fucking. We'd like to join you this evening."

Oh. Holy. Fucknuts.

"For dinner?" Brynlee asked as I closed my eyes and barely shook my head. Damn, I loved how innocent my wife was.

"No baby, for dessert," the girl said as her husband nodded.

"Oh well, I'm not sure if we're going to be—"

I placed my finger over Brynlee's mouth as I said, "Brynlee, they want to have a foursome."

Her mouth dropped open behind my finger as she sucked in a breath of air.

"I'd love to feel your husband's dick buried inside of me while my husband fucks you from behind."

"Um …" Brynlee and I both said at once.

I let out a curt laugh as I held my hands up. "Listen, as much as we uh … appreciate the offer, there is no way in hell that's ever going to happen."

The guy nodded. "I get where you're coming from. Can we watch the two of you fuck then, and then you watch us?"

"No!" Brynlee shouted out. "No, no, no. Okay, listen it was fun to do something naughty because we're on vacation and all, but yeah, this ends here. You two seem like you have a very active sex life, but we are very happy with just the twosome thing with no other eyes watching. Listening was different." Brynlee held her two fingers up to her eyes and then pointed to the couple. "No watching. Just listening. No wait. No more listening. I'm actually pregnant … just found out, so yeah, naughty time is over for us," Brynlee said with an awkward laugh.

The girl jutted her lip out and pouted. "I bet you taste like sweet vanilla."

Brynlee's eyes widened in horror. "I think we're done talking now." Brynlee took a step back into our hotel room as she pulled me along with her. "Bye-bye."

The door shut and we both stood there stunned.

With my mouth still hanging open, I looked at Brynlee. "Did that just really happen? 'Cause shit like that doesn't happen to people like us. Travis and Melanie maybe, but not us."

Brynlee busted out laughing and I quickly followed. Soon, we were both holding our stomachs as tears streamed down our faces.

"Oh my gosh. I can't wait to tell Melanie!" Brynlee said as she finally got her laughter under control.

Blowing out a deep breath, I cracked my neck a couple times.

"Whew. Man, I needed that laugh. I haven't laughed like that in a long time."

"Me too," Brynlee said as she fixed her makeup in the bathroom mirror. Stepping back into the room, she flashed me a sexy grin and asked, "Ready for dinner?"

"So ready."

As I headed to the door, Brynlee grabbed my arm and stopped me. "Was there at any moment during that conversation where you thought maybe you might have been interested in their offer?"

My lip snarled and I said, "Fuck no."

Brynlee breathed a sigh of relief as she covered her heart with her hand. "Oh thank God. I mean, I'd be all down for watching porn with two couples, but I don't want to ever do anything like that."

My eyebrows rose up. "My sweet little Brynlee would watch porn?"

Chewing on her lip, Brynlee nodded her head. "Why not? It might be kind of fun."

My eyes closed and I shook my head slightly. "I'm going to have hard-on all throughout dinner."

With a giggle, Brynlee gave me a quick kiss as we headed out for our last night in Kirkland.

Thirty-Seven

Brynlee

One Month Later...

"Wow, it's so hot outside," Melanie said as she fanned herself on the back porch of our parent's house.

I peeked over to the thermometer and it read eighty-nine. "It's only eighty-nine out."

"In case you didn't realize, Bryn, that's hot."

With a shrug of my shoulders, I took a sip of my ice water and looked out over the vineyards. "I had a dream last night."

"Oh yeah? A naughty dream?"

I glanced over to Melanie and smiled as she rested her head against the back of the chair with her eyes closed. She was using a magazine to fan herself off.

"No, unlike you, my thoughts aren't consumed by sex."

My statement was untrue. I'd never been so horny in my life as I had been the last few months. It was the pregnancy—I was sure of it.

Melanie sighed. "I can't help it if I have a very healthy sex life. Or the fact that my husband keeps me very, *very* happy."

"Gross."

"Jealous much, Bryn?"

"Ha! Please. Our sex life is so good we got approached by a hot couple wanting to ... um ... what's that called? Pitch it with us?"

Melanie sat up and turned to face me. "What?"

With a smirk, I nodded and said, "Uh-huh. That's right."

With a quick shake of her head, she squeezed her eyes shut and then looked back at me. "Don't you mean ... swing?"

I pinched my eyebrows together and thought for a second. "Oh that's right. It's called swingers or swinging or something like that."

Melanie's jaw dropped open as she held up her hands. "Whoa. Hold the fucking fort here." With a laugh, she tried to focus on what she was saying. "You mean to tell me, a couple approached you and Brody—" Melanie pointed to me, as she continued talking. "You two, they asked the two of you to swap?"

"By swap, do you mean switch up couples and have sex?"

Throwing her hands up and shaking her head, "Yes, Brynlee! That's what I mean!"

With a tilt of my head, I gave my sister a satisfied grin and nodded. "Yes. They asked us to play naughty with them."

Melanie fell back in her chair and started laughing hysterically as my smiled faded into a frown. "Um, excuse me. Why is that so funny?"

Her arms wrapped around her stomach as she laughed so hard tears streamed down her face.

"It's not that funny, Melanie," I said as I stood and placed my hands on my hips.

"What's going on?" Brody asked as he and Travis walked up the stairs and onto the deck. Travis and Brody started laughing just by watching Melanie laugh.

"Oh ... I ... can't ... breathe!" Melanie called out.

Travis turned to me and said, "What has her so tickled?"

"Oh, she thinks it's funny that some couple asked Brody and I to bat with them."

"What?"

Melanie busted out laughing again.

"Sweetheart, they were swingers. It's called swinging."

That's when Travis lost it. "Holy shit. No way. They asked you two?" He began pointing between me and Brody."

"Yes! Why is that so funny?"

Melanie was now on the floor as Travis buckled over in his own laughing fit.

I rolled my eyes and looked at Brody who was attempting not to laugh. "Don't you dare laugh, Brody Gregory Miles."

"I'm trying, baby, but it is kind of funny."

With a shake of my head, I kissed my husband and winked. "Pregnancy has made me soft."

Melanie stopped laughing as she jumped up and said, "What?" Travis stood up and Melanie immediately pushed him out of the way, causing him to tumble over the chair and do a pretty impressive flip in the air before landing on his feet.

"Dude! That was amazing!" Brody called out as he walked over and high-fived Travis.

Travis puffed his chest out and said, "I'm Super Dad."

"Did you say you're pregnant?"

My eyes widened as I realized I had slipped. Brody and I were going to tell everyone at Sunday dinner since I was now past the first trimester. My parents had started up an old family tradition of Sunday supper at their house. Since Brody, Melanie, Travis and I all lived on the vineyard, my parents thought it would the perfect way to end out the week.

I smiled and shook my head. "We were planning on telling everyone at dinner Sunday."

Melanie covered her mouth as tears formed in her eyes. I was

stunned by her reaction. She was not one to ever react with tears.

"Mel, are you okay?"

Travis walked up to her and pulled her to his body as her head fell against his chest. My eyes darted up to Travis' as he tried to hide his watery eyes.

"Well gosh, had I known everyone would be so emotional, I would have given you some kind of warning."

Melanie quickly whipped her tears away. "How far along are you?"

My stomach fluttered as I said, "A little over thirteen weeks."

Melanie's hand went to her mouth again as she spun around and jumped into Travis' arms.

Brody looked just as confused as I was. Sheesh, did my family really not have any faith that I would get pregnant?

When Melanie pulled back, Travis kissed her gently on the lips. She turned and faced me with the goofiest smile on her face as her eyes sparkled. "Oh, Bryn. I'm almost twelve weeks pregnant and we were going to tell you guys at dinner on Sunday."

A wide grin moved across my face as tears quickly formed and fell down my cheeks.

"We're pregnant together?"

With a quick nod of her head, Melanie and I embraced each other and cried even harder.

"Dad's gonna have a heart attack knowing his little girl had sex!"

I couldn't help but laugh harder. Somehow I just knew Sunday dinners would never be the same again.

Thirty-Eight

Brody

Six Months Later...

"Merry Christmas!" Brynlee called out as we walked into her parent's house. Catrina was walking out with a plate full of cookies and brownies as I dropped all the presents and grabbed a few of each.

"Oh, Mom, this looks great." Catrina had insisted that Travis and I start calling them Mom and Dad shortly after the announcement of the upcoming new grandbabies.

"I made your favorite dessert, Brody," Catrina said with a wink.

My mouth instantly drooled. "*Coscorões?*"

"Yep!"

Brynlee giggled. "Momma, you're going to spoil him if you keep making him and Travis all these goodies."

"They're my boys. It's my duty to spoil them so they in turn spoil you."

I kissed Brynlee quickly on the lips. "And do I have plans to spoil you later."

A smack on the back of my head caused me to holler out. "Ouch!"

With a quick glance over my head, I felt my entire body go stiff. Angelo was standing there glaring at me. "I heard that. You keep your filthy hands off my little girl."

Brynlee waved her father off as she put her hands on her swollen belly. "Considering I'm due in a week to have his baby, I think you're a little late, *Papai.*"

Angelo narrowed one eye at me as he snarled his lip. "You're lucky I love you so."

With a smile, I held out my arms. "Ah … Dad!"

Trying to hug my father-in-law, he pushed me away. "Go help the women, you fool."

Glancing into the living room, I saw Travis sitting on the couch watching football. "How come he gets to sit and watch TV?"

Angelo turned and glared at me. "Because he didn't talk dirty to my daughter in my own home."

I lifted my brow and nodded. "Point taken." I headed off into the kitchen as Travis shouted, "Dude, can you grab me a beer?"

I choose to ignore Travis as I walked into the kitchen and smiled at the sight before my eyes.

Two very pregnant women were sticking their fingers into the bowl of frosting. My eyes roamed over Brynlee's body as I fought to keep my emotions in check. She was in such a different place last year at this time. Her smile said it all. She was happy.

When her hands rested on her tummy, my heart dropped to my stomach. God, how I loved her.

"So, any contractions, girls?" Catrina asked as she pulled the ham from the oven.

"I wish," Melanie said with a sigh.

"Every now and then I'll feel some, but the doctor said I'll know

when it's the real deal."

"At least you only have one more week. I've still got almost two. Blah."

I quickly walked up to Catrina and took the pot of potatoes from her. "I'll mash them," I said with a smile. The women continued to talk as if I wasn't even in the room.

Brynlee sighed as she said, "Ugh, if I have this baby on January first, I swear I'll cry."

Catrina stopped what she was doing as I dumped some milk and butter into the pan that held the potatoes. Brynlee walked up and poured black pepper and a pinch of salt in them as she turned and headed back over to the table.

"Why do you say that, Brynlee?"

With a shrug, Brynlee said, "I don't know, Momma. I just don't want the baby having to have a birthday on a holiday."

"We could win some money if we have him on News Year's Day."

All three women turned and stared at me. With a shrug, I said, "What? We could. Don't couples who have a baby on New Year's Day get entered in to win something?"

Melanie shook her head. "Seriously? You're really going to be *that* guy?"

"What guy?"

Brynlee laughed as she shook her head. I went back to mashing the potatoes as Melanie started in about how she had tried to bribe her doctor into inducing her.

With a quick glance over to Brynlee, I stopped what I was doing as I looked at her. She was standing there staring down at the ground.

"Brynlee, sweetheart what's wrong?"

Her head snapped up as her eyes caught mine. All I saw was fear as I dropped what I was doing and walked over to her. Placing my hands on her shoulders, I lifted her eyes to meet mine. Pressing

her lips together, she lifted her eyebrows as her chin trembled.

"My water just broke."

It took a few moments for her words to sink in when I jumped back and looked her up and down.

"What?" Melanie and I both said at once.

I quickly turned to face Melanie. We both nodded and shouted out, "The bag!"

"The carseat! Did you get the carseat checked like I said?" Catrina called out.

Travis came walking into the kitchen with a smile that vanished the moment I pelted my truck keys in his face.

"Get the bag!"

Travis froze as he looked between Brynlee and Melanie.

"Dude! Code blue or pink! We need the bag!" I shouted as I wrapped my arm around Brynlee.

"Who's in labor?" Travis shouted.

"Brynlee!" I yelled out as I pushed him out of the way. "We need the bag."

"Okay um … bag … right." Travis took off running and then skid to a stop. Running back, he handed me my keys. "You just take Brynlee to the hospital and I'll meet you there with the bag."

Damn, why hadn't I thought of that? How did I plan on getting her to the hospital?

Travis gave me a wink. "It's okay, dude. I know what you're thinking right now." Leaning in so only Brynlee and I could hear him, Travis whispered, "Bigger dick, bigger brain."

"You do not have a—"

Brynlee hit me in the stomach as she gave me an imploring look. "Right, sorry." Pointing to a retreating Travis, I shouted, "This is not over!"

I sat in the chair as my knee bounced up and down. Brynlee was hooked up to some contraption that monitored the contractions and every time I saw one building, I would jump up and stand next to her.

"Here comes one!" I shouted excitedly as I got up and took her hand.

Brynlee's eyes were closed as she pursed her lips and slowly said, "Yes, I know. I can feel it."

"Oh man ... this one looks big."

Brynlee squeezed the hell out of my hand as I darted my eyes back and forth between the monitor and Brynlee. "Breathe through it, sweetheart. That's it." I pulled a deep breath in through my nose and slowly pushed it out through my mouth. "That's it, let all that air out and breathe through the contraction."

Brynlee's eyes snapped open.

"Shut. Up."

I couldn't help but smile. "Damn, you're beautiful when you're mad."

"No, I'm being serious. If you don't shut up, I'm going to have the nurse kick you out of the room."

I laughed and then stopped the moment she glared at me. Swallowing hard, I took a step back and sat down as I held up my hands in defeat. The magazine next to me caught my eye so I picked it up, and quickly began reading about how to exfoliate your skin using all natural organic products.

Every now and then I'd peek up at the monitor or glance over to Brynlee.

When Brynlee started panting hard, I checked out the monitor. Jumping to my feet, she pointed to me. "Stop! Do not utter a word. Give me your hand."

Sticking my hand out, Brynlee grabbed it. Her contraction had passed so I wasn't sure why she wanted my hand. "Oh holy shit!" I shouted when she squeezed and another contraction hit

I dropped down as I held onto the side of the bed with my other hand. Whispering out a call for help. "Help … man … down!"

"Your wife kicked cancer in the ass. Did you really think she wouldn't have a strong grip?"

Looking up at Melanie, I mouthed, *help me.* With a grin from ear to ear, she shook her head and mouthed back, *no.*

When the contraction was finally over, Brynlee dropped my hand and I quickly ran to the other side of the room to the safe zone. Melanie took my place next to Brynlee as I looked at her with a look of horror. "I wouldn't do that if I were you. She'll squeeze your child right out of you."

Melanie shot me a dirty look as she rolled her eyes and looked down at Brynlee, who was currently possessed by some unbelievably strong spirit.

"Hey, Bryn. How are you feeling?" Melanie reached up and pushed a piece of Brynlee's hair back as I sucked in a breath of air and waited for the beast to strike.

"I'm doing good. They're getting stronger, but I'm good."
Huh? Wait. What?

"Good sweetie. You just keep focusing on your breathing through each contraction."

Brynlee nodded and gave her sister a sweet smile.

My eyes widened. "She's faking!" I cried as I pointed to Brynlee. When Melanie turned to look at me, Brynlee shot me an evil eye.

The door to the room opened and Travis walked in. "Thank God!" I said as I ran and wrapped my arms around my best friend.

Travis awkwardly patted me on the back as he said, "Um … there, there, Brody."

"Here comes one, Bryn." Melanie said in an all-too-chipper mood. Pulling back from Travis, I motioned with my head for him to leave. "Save yourself before it's too late."

Travis pulled his head back and looked at me before leaning in

closer. "Dude, have you been drinking?"

"No!"

"Brody! Oh God, this one hurts," Brynlee called out as I turned and Travis pushed me toward my wife.

"Brody, get over there."

My body trembled as I walked over to the side of the bed. Slowly putting my hand out, Brynlee grabbed it and I saw my life flash before my eyes. Travis was in the room though, so I had to suck it up.

Brynlee began panting as I reached up and pushed her hair away from her forehead. "I'm sorry I yelled at you."

I couldn't help but smile as I leaned over and kissed her forehead.

"All right. Let's see what's happening shall we?" The doctor said as he walked in. Melanie and Travis stepped over to the side of the room.

"Wow." The doctor looked up and smiled. "No time for an epidural."

"What?!" Brynlee and I both shouted.

"The head is crowning."

The nurse that was standing behind the doctor quickly began moving around and doing things as Brynlee squeezed my hand. Looking down at her, I saw excitement and fear both dancing in her eyes.

Flashing her the smile I knew she loved, the ones with the full-force dimples, I leaned in closer as I brushed my lips across hers. "I love you, sweetheart."

A tear rolled down her cheek as she smiled. "I love you too. This is it."

With another kiss, I whispered against her lips. "This is it."

"Nurse, please can we clear the room," the doctor said.

It was then I decided I needed to see exactly what it looked like when the head was crowning. One look and the room started spin-

ning.

"Oh. My. God."

The next thing I heard was Melanie yelling for Travis to catch me.

Thirty-Nine

Brynlee

Brody peeked to see the baby's head crowning and I knew the moment I saw his face, he was gone.

"Oh no," I whispered.

"Travis! Oh my gosh, grab him before he hits the floor," Melanie shouted.

The nurse and Travis both caught Brody before he hit.

"He's safe!" Travis said with a laugh as everyone looked at him. "Um … I'll just bring him over here to the little sofa not big enough for any normal size human being to lay on."

Melanie shook her head and said, "Travis, just get him out of the way."

Stepping up next to me, Melanie smiled and lifted her shoulders as she said, "Looks like you're stuck with me until your pansy-ass husband wakes up."

I didn't want to laugh, but I couldn't help myself.

"You've got this, baby sister."

I pressed my lips together and fought to control my emotions. "He's going to miss it."

"No, he'll be there for the most important part. I promise."

With a quick nod, I bit down on my lip. "She's coming."

"Or he!"

Laughing, I sucked in a deep breath as another contraction swept over my body.

"All right, Brynlee. Give me a good push."

My body was quickly becoming exhausted as I pushed over and over again. Then he touched me and I felt a renewed energy. Melanie kissed Brody on the cheek and moved aside.

"I'm here, sweetheart. I'm so sorry."

"S'okay," I panted out as the doctor looked up.

"One more, Brynlee that's all I need."

Brody took my hand and kissed the back of it. "One more."

Sitting up, I pushed with all my might. Instant relief, followed by the cries of our baby.

I wasn't sure if I was laughing or crying. Maybe it was a mixture of both, but the doctor had Brody cut the umbilical cord and then next thing I knew, a beautiful little boy was held up.

"Say hello to your son."

The doctor placed our son on my stomach as Brody and I both started crying.

"Hello, my beautiful baby boy."

He had a head full of dark brown hair and the most beautiful blue eyes I'd ever seen.

Brody reached over and kissed him as he whispered, "Hello there, Benjamin Angelo Miles. We've waited forever for you."

Brody turned as our eyes met. "Thank you for making me the happiest man in the world. Thank you for our son."

The nurse picked up our son and smiled. "Let's get him all checked out, and then I'll bring him back over for you to feed him."

I watched her walk to the small room as she began taking care of my son. Tears rolled down my face as I thought about our little miracle.

Turning back to Brody, I smiled. "Every cloud brings a silver lining."

Brody pressed his lips against mine. "God, I love you so damn much."

My hand went around Brody's neck as I pulled him to deepen the kiss.

Brody stood by my side as the doctor finished with me. He stood and took Ben in his arms as he smiled down at him. Walking over to us, he placed him in my arms. "Mr. and Mrs. Mile, here is your son, Benjamin Angelo."

As I held my son in my arms, I got lost in his eyes. I'd never imagined I could ever love someone as much as I loved this little guy.

Brody ran his finger lightly across Ben's cheek. "He looks like you."

With a giggle, I shook my head. "I think he looks like you."

"A hundred bucks Travis says he looks like him."

We both started laughing as the nurse and doctor left the three of us alone to bond. This was by far the most amazing moment of my life.

Three weeks later I walked across the waiting room holding a sleeping Ben in my arms. "So do you think Travis will pass out?" Brody asked my father.

"Nah, he's a tough cookie."

Brody's eyes widened. "I'm tough."

With a light pat on the arm, my father said, "Of course you are,

Brody. Of course you are."

With a snarled lip, Brody looked at me as I smiled and winked.

"Let me hold my grandson. Your pacing is making me nervous," my mother said as she stood and walked toward me. I handed her Ben, as I rolled my stiff neck. Brody's parents and his sister had come to visit for a week after Ben was born. Needless to say, neither one of us had gotten much sleep.

Brody stood and walked over toward me. "Do you want to go get a tea?"

"That sounds good." Glancing over my shoulder, I looked at my mother and father doting on our son. "Mom, *Papai*? Do you want something?"

My father didn't even bother to look at us as he lifted his hand and dismissed us. "Go. Take your time, we've got this."

Brody and I headed to the elevator when Travis came running around the corner. He must have pulled something because he made a horrible face as he went down.

"Oh my gosh, Travis!" I said as I rushed over to him. Grabbing his hamstring, he slowly stood up. "I'm okay!"

"Are you sure? Did you pull anything?"

I looked over my shoulder to see my parents walking up. "Oh Travis darling, are you okay?"

"Yeah, Mom. I'm good. I was just excited."

"See, if you did yoga that wouldn't have happened."

Travis shot Brody a dirty look as Brody lifted his hands. "I'm just sayin'."

Travis shook his head and turned to us. "It's a girl! We had a girl!"

"Oh Travis!" I shouted excitedly as I wrapped my arms around him. Brody slapped him on the back and gave him a big ole grin.

"Congratulations, Travis. I'm really happy for you," Brody said.

Travis wiped a tear away and nodded. "Thanks."

After my mother and father congratulated him, Travis asked

who wanted to go in first. I took Ben from my mother's arms and told them to go first.

As Brody and I sat down, he started laughing. "What's so funny?"

Brody let out a long sigh. "Oh man, I just really want to be around when it really hits Travis. He had a girl, and boys just like him are going to want to date his daughter."

With a chuckle, I shook my head. "Yeah, or when Melanie realizes she had a girl who will most likely be exactly how she was. A rebel."

Brody and I both let out a contented sigh.

"Life is good, isn't it?"

With a chuckle, I smiled. "Very good."

Forty

Brody

Nine Months Later...

"I t's time for the grape stomp!" Brynlee called out as she held Ben up and he laughed. "You ready to see your cousins, Jacob and Renee?" Ben blew bubbles with his mouth as he smiled bigger and tried to talk to Brynlee.

"I can't wait for him to get older and learn everything there is to learn about the vineyard," Brynlee said with a smile.

With a chuckle, I shook my head as I packed up Ben's diaper bag. "According to your father, Ben already knows his grapes."

Ben looked up at me and grinned as Brynlee put him in his stroller. "If it were up to my father, Ben would already know the difference between Cabernet Sauvignon and a Shiraz."

"The cabernet ... black currant with a touch of cedar. Then you have my favorite, the Shiraz, with its black pepper and dark choco-

late. Damn, where have you been all my life, wine?"

Brynlee laughed as she sauntered up to me. "My father said you have the gift. He said wine makes you happy, he sees it in your eyes."

With a shake of my head, I whispered, "No. You make me happy. Discovering something that you're passionate about made me passionate about it. The true gift is being able to work by your side every day."

"It has been amazing. And watching Ben and Renee grow up together. How lucky are we?"

I nodded and smiled. "Very lucky indeed."

Brynlee's eyes lit up. "We could put Ben in his playpen. We have a few extra minutes."

Looking over her shoulder, I smiled. "No need for the playpen. He's out."

Brynlee spun around. "Oh my gosh, hurry!"

I'd never undressed so fast in my entire life. I picked Brynlee up and walked over to the one wall that was bare and pushed her against it. "So tell me, Mrs. Miles. Is being fucked against a wall everything you ever thought it would be?"

I pushed into her as she gasped and clenched down on my dick. "Oh Mr. Miles, it's everything and then some. If only my husband would talk less and move more."

Lifting an eyebrow, I pulled almost all the way out and then pushed into her again ... harder and faster.

"Oh God."

"You want more?"

Brynlee grabbed onto my shoulders and squeezed her legs around me as she began moving herself. "I need more. Brody, please."

And just like that, Brynlee and I were one as I moved in and out of her body in fast fluid motions. She dropped her head back and tried like hell to keep her moans inside as she whimpered. I buried

my face into her neck and came, spilling every single ounce of cum into her body as I slowed down. I'd never get tired of this.

"Don't move, Brody. I just want to stay like this. It's my favorite place in the world to be."

My lips grazed across her neck as I spoke softly. "It's my favorite place too."

After a while, I carried her over to the sofa where I sat down. I slowly pulled out of her, her warm lips cradling my softening dick.

Pure fucking heaven.

"Thank you," I whispered.

"Thank you!"

I shook my head. "No, thank you for not giving up on us."

Brynlee bit down on her lip and smiled slightly. "I can say the same thing. You never gave up on us either."

"Do you even remember who that young couple was anymore? Before that night, or your cancer? Do you even remember who we were?"

Brynlee shook her head. "No, do you?"

My hands cupped her face as my eyes took in every single inch of her. "No. But I do remember a young couple so madly in love we jumped in feet first, and everything happened after that first night shaped us into who we are now. Every path we took led us to this exact moment."

Brynlee leaned forward and softly kissed my lips. "Do you know what this moment needs?"

"What?"

Moving her lips to my neck, she gently placed kisses until she reached my ear, where she whispered, "A glass of Shiraz."

Three and a Half Years Later…

Brynlee's thumb moved across my index finger as she chewed on her other thumbnail. "Sweetheart, stop chewing on your thumbnail."

Dropping her hand to her lap, Brynlee closed her eyes and swallowed hard. "Take a deep breath in and blow it out."

Doing as I said, Brynlee took a deep breath through her nose and slowly blew it out. My phone beeped as I pulled it out and smiled. I faced my phone to her and Brynlee let out a giggle.

"What are they doing?"

I turned the phone and glanced back down at my four-year-old son and our niece Renee. "I think they're helping your mom make grape jam."

Brynlee let out a soft chuckle. "Renee is just like Melanie though, I swear. Look, she's reaching up to put jam in Ben's hair." With a sigh, Brynlee shook her head. "He loves helping Mom in the kitchen."

"Tell me about it. He threw a fit the other night when I told him he couldn't help Grammy make cookies because it was three in the morning."

Brynlee smiled bigger and was about to say something when there was a quick knock on the door and it opened.

Dr. Malick came walking and sat down at his desk as he looked between Brynlee and me. "I'm sure you want me to just cut to the chase. The blood test and the scan all confirm that you are indeed cancer free, Brynlee. Congratulations."

We both stood up and embraced, as I held onto my wife as tight as I could. I never had any doubt, but something about hitting that five-year mark lifted a weight off my shoulders, and I was sure it did for Brynlee as well.

"Brynlee, that other test you requested—"

Brynlee pulled back and looked at the doctor. "Yes?"

Dr. Malick smiled and nodded as Brynlee let out a disbelieving

laugh. Turning back to me, she placed her hands on the sides of my face as I watched tears pool in her eyes. "Happy Father's Day."

My stomach flipped and my heart slammed against my chest. "You're pregnant?"

Chewing on her lip, she whispered, "Yes." Our lips immediately crashed together as we quickly got lost in our kiss. It didn't matter that the doctor was sitting there. Nothing else in this entire world mattered except for the fact that God had answered my prayers … again.

When we finally pulled apart, I winked and said, "This calls for a glass of wine."

Brynlee lifted a brow. "I think I'll stick with grape juice for the next eight months."

The End

A Note to the Reader

I 've been trying to write this book for over a year now and something always seemed to get in the way. I'm not really sure why I was so hell bent on writing a book about breast cancer, but I was. I had the story running in my head for so many months and there were so many times I wanted to stop my current work in progress and just start on Brynlee and Brody's story. I never did though.

Then finally this past September, I started writing their story. I submerged my world into research and talked to a few different people who have had cancer touch their lives one way or another. My heart broke, yet at the same time these women who fought with everything in them to beat this beast amazed me. My friend Karen Bell (who fought and won her fight against ovarian cancer) was a HUGE help and helped me so much with this book and for that I will be forever grateful to her.

In the middle of writing the book, my sister Mary was diagnosed with breast cancer. I'll never forget the moment she told me. It felt like I was dreaming and I wasn't really hearing the words she was saying. In my mind I kept thinking there was no way I was writing a book about breast cancer and my sister had breast cancer. What

were the odds of that? In some small way, I feel like God had a hand in keeping me away from this book until I needed to start writing it. Every doctor appointment I took my sister to, I understood so much of what they were saying while my poor sister sat there trying to process the enormous information being thrown her way. I'm so glad I was able to be there for my sister. She had a bilateral mastectomy, and does not have to have any radiation or chemotherapy, and her prognosis is very good! For that I give all thanks to God!

My sister was fifty-one when she had her first mammogram, even with being hounding for years to get one she still put it off. BUT when she did finally get one, the mammogram caught her stage 1 breast cancer. Early detection is key y'all! Get your screening mammogram as soon as you turn forty! Unfortunately some insurance companies will not pay for early screening which is something I hope we can get changed.

Starting at age forty-five, get your mammogram every year! Until then, do your monthly self breast exams. Cancer does not care what age you are, what color your skin is or if you are female or male.

I can't say it enough ... early detection can save your life.

1 in 8 women will develop breast cancer over the course of her lifetime.

Acknowledgements

I want to thank Karen Bell for her invaluable input when it came to writing this book. Thank you, Karen, for not only answering all the questions I had, but for reading over the story for me as well. You are an amazing women and a true fighter and you do it all with a positive attitude and a smile on your face.

Thank you to my beta readers, Kristine Mayer, Laura Hansen, Karen Bell, Elizabeth Thiele, and my post edit beta reader, Nikki Sievert.

A HUGE thank you to my editor, Tiffany Hamburger. You make it so easy to work with you! THANK YOU from the bottom of my heart!

Thank you to Erin Noelle for proofing *Who We Were* and being the last set of eyes on it! You are amazing and I look forward to working more with you on future books! Thank you for making this book even better with your input!

Thank you to Julie Titus. You always take the words and make something beautiful with your formatting. Thank you so much! I always wait anxiously to see what you come up with each time!

To the readers: Thank you for taking a chance on this book. I

273

hope it touches your heart while reading it like it touched my heart while writing it.

Playlist

"The Day We Meet"
Ben Rue
Brody and Brynlee meet for the first time

"You're Beautiful"
James Blunt
Brody and Brynlee at The Oasis for dinner

"Your Everything"
Keith Urban
Brody and Brynlee making love for the first time

"Home Ain't Where His Heart Is"
Shania Twain
Brody loses it and tells Brynlee he is unhappy with his life in California

"While You Loved Me"
Rascal Flatts
Brody after Brynlee tells him to leave

"One Day You Will"
Lady Antebellum
Brynlee and Melanie up at the windmill

"Amnesia"
Josh Abbott Band
Brody on the plane with Travis heading back to Brynlee

"(Everything I Do) I Do It For You"
Bryan Adams
Brody telling Brynlee he would always be there for her after she told him about having breast cancer

"Shake"
Victoria Justice
After Brynlee gets her hair shaved

"Can't Take My Eyes Off You"
Lady Antebellum
Brody and Brynlee dancing at the benefit dinner at her parent's vineyard

"It's Not Just Me"
Rascal Flatts
Brynlee and Brody after making love the night of the benefit dinner

"Love Has A Hold On Me"
Amy Grant
Brody and Brynlee together after her mastectomy

"When You Kiss Me"
Shania Twain
Brody making love to Brynlee after telling her they'll get pregnant soon

"How Can We See That Far"
Amy Grant
The birth of Benjamin Angelo

WANTED SERIES

Wanted
Saved
Faithful
Believe
Cherished
A Forever Love
The Wanted Short Stories

BROKEN SERIES

Broken
Broken Dreams
Broken Promises

JOURNEY OF LOVE SERIES

Unconditional Love
Undeniable Love
Unforgettable Love

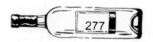

KELLY ELLIOTT

LOVE WANTED IN TEXAS SERIES

Without You
Saving You
Holding You
Finding You

STANDALONE

The Journey Home
Predestined Hearts
Searching for Harmony

For upcoming books and more information about Kelly Elliott, please visit her website.

www.kellyelliottauthor.com

For exclusive releases and giveaways signup for Kelly's newsletter at

http://eepurl.com/JoKyL

Printed in Great Britain
by Amazon